Cloudless

Cloudless

RUPERT DASTUR

FIG TREE
an imprint of
PENGUIN BOOKS

FIG TREE

UK | USA | Canada | Ireland | Australia
India | New Zealand | South Africa

Fig Tree is part of the Penguin Random House group of companies
whose addresses can be found at global.penguinrandomhouse.com

Penguin Random House UK,
One Embassy Gardens, 8 Viaduct Gardens, London SW11 7BW

penguin.co.uk
global.penguinrandomhouse.com

First published 2025
001

Typeset by Falcon Oast Graphic Art Ltd
Printed and bound in Great Britain by Clays Ltd, Elcograf S.p.A.

The authorized representative in the EEA is Penguin Random House Ireland,
Morrison Chambers, 32 Nassau Street, Dublin D02 YH68

A CIP catalogue record for this book is available from the British Library

ISBN: 978–0–241–65470–5

www.greenpenguin.co.uk

MIX
Paper from
responsible sources
FSC   FSC® C018179
www.fsc.org

Penguin Random House is committed to a
sustainable future for our business, our readers
and our planet. This book is made from Forest
Stewardship Council® certified paper.

For my parents,
Bill and Elisabeth

The Welsh Hill Country

Too far for you to see
The fluke and the foot-rot and the fat maggot
Gnawing the skin from the small bones,
The sheep are grazing at Bwlch-y-Fedwen,
Arranged romantically in the usual manner
On a bleak background of bald stone.

Too far for you to see
The moss and the mould on the cold chimneys,
The nettles growing through the cracked doors,
The houses stand empty at Nant-yr-Eira,
There are holes in the roofs that are thatched with sunlight,
And the fields are reverting to the bare moor.

Too far, too far to see
The set of his eyes and the slow phthisis
Wasting his frame under the ripped coat,
There's a man still farming at Ty'n-y-Fawnog,
Contributing grimly to the accepted pattern,
The embryo music dead in his throat.

– R. S. Thomas, An Acre of Land, 1952

2004

November

Iraq Body Count: 1,676[*]

---

[*] The public database of violent civilian deaths in the invasion of Iraq, 2003 onwards.

315. [. . .] the media reported that Mr Annan was urging caution.* In a letter to leaders of the US, UK and Iraq he warned of the potential impact of major military offensives on Iraq's political process and warned: 'The threat or actual use of force not only risks deepening the sense of alienation of certain communities, but would also reinforce perceptions among the Iraqi population of a continued military Occupation.'

– *The Report of the Iraq Inquiry*, Volume VII, Section 9.3
(John Chilcot, 2016)

* BBC News, 6 November 2004, 'Kofi Annan's Letter Criticizing the Imminent Assault on Falluja'.

I

One of the hens isn't laying but Catrin hasn't told John yet, knowing he'd wring its neck that same day. She doesn't want to think about dead things. Today. Tomorrow. Not until Harri is home from the war.

The eggs are pleasurably warm in her icy fingers as she retrieves them from their straw nests. Her breath clouds as she stretches into the huts. The flies dance about in the cold air and feathers stick to the smooth shells. The hens cluck and bob. She counts the eggs, counts the birds, shakes her head. There'd be a reckoning soon. But not today.

Checking her watch, Catrin hopes Rhys has pulled himself from bed. He's already missed the school bus once this week and she doesn't have time to drive him in, but with his GCSEs next summer she'll be damned if she lets him skive again. John has a different opinion – says there's no need for periodic tables or Shakespeare on a farm – but the boy's got to have choices, doesn't he? She's always said that about her sons. They deserve options; can't have the farm hanging round their neck, heavy as an albatross.

The November air is frosty and despite the many layers she's wearing Catrin is cold beneath her skin. The sky is paper-white with a smudge of grey. John is already worrying about the winter, saying the berries are on the bushes early, that he can taste snow in the air, that his leg is playing up, which is always a sign. He still talks about the snowfall of '63, back when he was a lad, just as his father had talked of '47. They'd spend days and nights digging dead ewes out of the snow. Whole flocks gone in a flurry of white. The weather, the sheep, the horses. That's all he ever talks about, when he talks at all.

Catrin licks her cracked lips as she reties the wool scarf tight around her neck – folds it in half, pulls the ends through the loop – and picks up the carton of eggs before returning to the yard. A breeze funnels between the kennel and stable blocks, towards the large stone farmhouse that lies opposite. The building is a mottled grey, built from mountain rock, the same heft and colour as the stone used for the miles of winding dry walls that separate fields and boundaries; walls that rise into the hills and stretch up around the peaks, rolling all the way down to the valleys and towns below. The sky is dark and wide, and down here, where there's often the bustle of men and beasts, the air carries the smell of livestock, turned earth and manure; but higher up, where the land is steeper and the sole company to be had is a peppering of ewes, there's a freshness unlike anything else – a freedom she'd fallen in love with all those years ago when she'd first met John, before they were married, before the boys.

She shivers, thinking of the Christmas lights and decorations that will be going up soon in the shops down in Llandudno Town. John will complain it's too early, like he does every year. It's not even December, he'll say, his eyebrows heavy. He's become so morose of late and it's beginning to rust her mood; something will snap soon, she knows it. There's only so much weathering a person can take.

Walking back home, she visualizes her day ahead. She's read all about the potential benefits: picture your future and it'll come to pass. She imagines herself in a steaming bath, scented candles, a book. Fat chance. The magazines at the hairdresser's were all about pampering yourself, putting yourself first, but if she did that there'd be nothing to eat and they'd all be wearing the same clothes each week. Besides, she likes the quiet when she can fold clothes, listen to Melvyn Bragg's *In Our Time*. She likes his voice and the things he knows. She can forget about Harri all the way out there, Rhys and his studies, their lack of money, which is grinding them all down like baked earth beneath a boot. Things are so tight she's been speaking to John about letting the farmhands go; not something either of them had ever imagined doing.

Entering the farmhouse, Catrin's slapped by the sound of the telly blaring from the living room. She slugs off her boots and then pauses by her piano. Its solid presence fills the hall. For now, it stands silent and waiting, ready for her touch. A wedding gift from her parents, her piano is her peace, her past, her independence – the one thing in this old house that is hers alone.

The telly thunders out an American accent and Catrin enters the living room, eggs in hand. She finds John there, dressed in jeans and a thick fleece. He's perched on the edge of the sofa, arms crossed.

George Bush is on the screen, standing in front of a lectern.

'You should be out with the ewes,' says Catrin. 'The lads will be waiting.'

'The bastard's been elected again,' replies John. His voice slices through the air, the sound of a saw through wood.

'Turn it off, won't you?' says Catrin. She's tried to avoid the news these last few weeks.

'You know what this means, don't you?' says John, at last craning round to look at her. 'Listen to the bastard. Cut his teeth in his first term and now says he's ready to make a *big difference*. A fucking difference? Can you believe this man?'

'I've got to make breakfast,' says Catrin. 'Is Rhys up?'

'Listen to this, Catrin. Just listen.'

On the TV, the newly elected George W. Bush commits to sending 125,000 troops to the front lines of Iraq by January next year. He says that with God's help they'll bring down strongholds in the cities and in Fallujah –

'Is Rhys up?' Catrin repeats. Her voice comes out louder than she intended, interrupting the President with his expansive, winner's smile.

'Did you hear that? Fallujah. That's where our Harri's been sent.'

'He'll be back soon enough.'

'Six months.' John shakes his head.

'R&R in three,' she says.

'And anything could happen,' says John, his eyes storm-dark. 'Anything.'

'Don't say that,' says Catrin. 'Don't you say that.' She is trembling. The eggs feel heavy in her hands.

'I never wanted him to join,' says John. 'I said it back then and I'll say it now. But you pushed and pushed.'

'He wanted it, John. You remember how it was: he came home all fired up, saying how they'd pay for university; how they'd take him around the world kayaking and mountaineering and the like. And all they'd want in return, once he'd graduated, was a few years of service.'

'He was only sixteen.'

'I didn't know this would happen.' And she hadn't. So much had changed.

'You had us sign the papers,' says John. 'If we'd waited, at least until he'd been to Bangor, he might have changed his mind.'

'It was his choice, John. And he got himself that scholarship, didn't he? You were proud enough then. Neither of us knew this was –'

'It's the Army, Catrin. What did you expect? That he'd be playing toy soldiers?' With that, John returns his attention to the TV, reaches for the remote and turns up the volume.

Catrin retreats to the kitchen, her hands tightly balled, thoughts like shattered glass.

An Aga hums at the far end of the room, its heat offering some respite in the late-autumn weather. A wooden table stands in the middle, one leg thinner than the others, splintered down by the claws of an old moggy. There's a heap of unopened letters and a stack of *Racing Posts* on the worktop. Catrin takes in the smell of dog and cat and the hint of last night's dinner: corned beef with new potatoes. Beneath one of the ceiling lights, she sees a spider dancing a delicate web, its long legs connecting thread. Flint, her old dog, is under the table, his tail beating up and down as he regards her with a single open eye. She dumps the eggs on the table and kneels down on the floor to rest a palm on his warm, black fur. His legs are going, poor old boy. But he eats well enough.

Catrin closes her eyes and breathes in and out, slowly, counting out the seconds, just like she'd taught Harri when he was a little boy and he'd come in, upset at someone or something, nose running. She'd held his heaving shoulders, her voice calm and comforting, until his lower lip stopped its trembling. She wonders what has happened to the last twenty-plus years. The thought of decades slipping through her fingers like dry soil gives her pause. In some ways, John's right. How could she have let her baby go like that? But Harri had been so certain it's what he wanted and there'd been no hint of war back then.

'Mam?' Catrin looks up and sees Rhys staring at her. Her little boy, sixteen going on seventeen. How the years amass, one after the other.

'You're up.'

'Miss Marple strikes again,' he says.

She smiles. 'The cheek.'

'He's getting old,' says Rhys, nodding at Flint.

'Don't remind me,' replies Catrin. She looks him over: his short brown hair is still damp from the shower. There are freckles over his nose. He's broad-shouldered like Harri – both boys take after their father. Rhys's socks are odd, but that's a battle she gave up long ago. He was old enough to dress himself.

'You've only got time for toast. Bus'll be off in twenty. Now make us a quick tea, won't you? Your da is still here so make it three. Use the flask.'

'He's here?'

'Watching the news. Bush has been re-elected.'

'Bastard.'

'None of that, Rhys.'

'It's what Da thinks.'

'Can you just get on with the tea, please?'

'I'm getting, see.' Rhys gives a wolfish smile and Catrin has the sudden urge to put him on her knee, bounce him up and down, never let him go, tell him she'll always keep him safe no matter what. But he's old enough not to need his mother and it'd be a lie, wouldn't it? She can't always be there. Harri was proof enough of that.

The phone rings and Catrin looks at it. She's already come to hate the way it sounds like an alarm. Always she wonders: could it be her Harri in trouble?

Or perhaps it's Matthew Edevane? Ever since she'd heard he was back in town, Catrin had been expecting a call. Hoping for it, even.

She picks up the receiver, feels both relief and disappointment at the voice she recognizes. It's their neighbour – John's old friend Tim Evans, his voice croaking like he's sucked the soot from a chimney. Catrin listens while watching Rhys spread marmalade over buttered toast.

'We're doing okay,' says Catrin. 'Yes, I'll tell him. And to you. Take care now.' She puts the receiver down, walks over to the window, picks a Vaseline from the collection of bottles and tubes on the ledge and applies some to her hardened, winter-wrecked lips. She misses the spring hyacinths and summer dahlias, the way the world is all softness and scent.

'The gathering's been pushed back to next Monday,' she explains.

'So I'll have the weekend off?' asks Rhys.

'Maybe,' says Catrin.

'What about Monday? Da said he wanted me working one of the dogs.'

'You can't miss school. Not with your exams this year.'

'Next year,' counters Rhys.

'School year. This school year.'

'Da says –'

She holds up a hand. 'Please, Rhys.'

'Have you heard from Harri?' he asks, changing tune.

The sudden shift of conversation takes her off-balance. 'It's only been three days,' she replies.

'It's bullshit, you know.'

'Let's not do this now.'

'Well,' he says, getting through the last of his toast, 'time for me to go.' He pulls his black polyester tie from his jacket pocket.

'Be good –'

'Work hard –'

'And stay out of trouble,' concludes Catrin.

'Every damn day. I know, I've got it,' says Rhys. He pauses at the door. 'Hwyl am rwan.'

Bye for now. It's what Harri would say.

Catrin watches as her boy goes out of the door, sees him pause in the yard, hunching his shoulders against the cold, before striding off down the road; after a fifteen-minute march along winding lanes he'll reach the bus stop. And that's it, she thinks. She'd be alone if it weren't for John next door, eyes burning a hole through the TV.

She'd have liked more children, a whole brood to look after and love.

And lose.

That voice, that ever-present voice, so quick to invade.

~

Catrin advances beyond the protective warmth of her home. Flint, her trusty black Lab, is with her. The two of them step into the morning, greeting it for the second time with another shiver. Her breath fills the air as she zips up her coat and makes her way towards the kennel, where the sheepdogs will be alert to her approach. Behind the farmhouse and outbuildings, the hills rise up and out, bathed in the last of the dawn's light and a lingering mist. The ewes will be huddled together, keeping warm beneath their thick coats, while their feet press against the frost-hard grass.

Opening the door to the kennel, Catrin is met by an acrid, canine smell – thick fur, saliva, flatulence. The kennel is home to four working dogs that clamour at her approach, stretching out and clambering against the metal bars of the enclosure, rising up on their hind legs, front paws against the gate.

'Sit,' says Catrin. The four settle down.

She slides the bar to the left and opens the metal gate and tells the dogs to get on. They rush forward, muzzles sniffing at her trousers, tongues reaching towards Flint, who accepts their greeting with an old authority. They scramble along the corridor, paws scratching against the grey linoleum. Catrin follows, Flint at her side.

The dogs gambol along the path that leads beyond the farmhouse. They pass the lake and run towards Coed Ty-mawr, a large wood that John and Catrin significantly added to more than twenty years ago – the legacy of an old government conservation initiative that still brought in close to five hundred pounds in revenue each year. It was the perfect place to be alone, to find solitude and peace among the trees, the birches, beeches and maples. The boys used to enjoy coming here, too. Deep into the woods there is, somewhere, an old treehouse they'd played in.

Noses following fresh animal prints across the leafy floor, the dogs chase after scents left by the small, nocturnal creatures of the undergrowth. Catrin stalks a trail between wooden spines and roots, a gloved hand reaching out to grip the bark. She loves this wood, loves the way it has flourished, loves its feel of permanence, the steady, certain advance of branch and leaf, the sense of seasonal change it brings, the promise of renewal after winter. She used to come here more often, usually to get away from the noise of the house or to marinate half-formed harmonies, compositions in their genesis. There is one there now, gathering at the back of her thoughts, coalescing like the sudden chirping of birds about to take flight. Her fingers twitch, pressing ghostly keys. Later, she will go back to the piano, solidify the sounds with each testing touch.

Once the dogs have stretched and done the morning business, Catrin leads the four of them back into their kennel. Flint watches, panting.

She lifts the lid of the large chest freezer by the rear wall, peers at the small frozen bodies wrapped in old shopping bags and does a quick count. They're running low – John will have to go out with quad and rifle again soon. She pulls out two of the rabbits, removes each one from the plastic and places them on the large wooden board. She feels the bodies of the small animals, stiff with ice. Catrin picks up the hand-axe from the shelf above, her fingers tight around the weapon.

She thinks about the long six months, waiting for Harri. If

only she could close her eyes and fast-forward, skip straight to the end.

But Harri is out there and she is here, home at the farm, and time will pass as it has always done: season by season, month by month, day by day. There is no going forward or back, there are just moments following on from moments. There is the soil and the sky, the animals in the hills, the rising and setting of the sun and the small necessities in between.

Catrin lifts her arm and brings the sharp blade of the axe swinging down into the centre of the first rabbit, cutting through fur and flesh. She works the tool free and then repeats the action until the animal is split in two. Flint licks at the bits of bloody ice that fall to the floor. By the time the second rabbit is halved, her breath is heavy, steaming in the grey light that filters through the high windows above the breeze-block walls. Filling the stainless-steel bowls, Catrin turns to the four dogs. They watch, eyes bright, wet noses poking through the metal bars. She tells them to sit, opens the gate, then slides the bowls along the concrete floor. The dogs pounce on the food, pink tongues licking at the frozen meat.

Biting her lips at the cold, Catrin washes her hands in the sink before wiping them dry on the rag hanging on a nail above. She touches the copper pipes and shakes her head, wondering when John will get round to insulating them. She's already bought the lagging, tape and clips; all he has to do is to put the sleeves on. But wasn't that always the case with John? Last year the pipes had frozen and they'd had to lug buckets over from the farm-house, the horses and dogs watching them slosh water about as they filled dog bowls and horse troughs.

She looks back at the dogs gnawing on frozen fur and meat. It can't taste of much, dished out like that, but John has always insisted, said it slowed them down and reduced the risks of a twisted gut. God knows they didn't need an episode like the

Turners'd had a few years back: their old sheepdog Penny arching her spine, retching, mouth foaming. Dead within a few hours and the vet, Cai Bracken, shaking his head, saying there was nothing he could do, though he'd tried all he could and there was the bill to prove it, over a thousand pounds in all, and later the insurance company sliding this way and that, snake-like, saying the operation should have been confirmed by them first, and Lisa Turner demanding to know how exactly they were supposed to do that on a Sunday past ten at night, their dog at death's door and to hell with their terms and conditions, hadn't they paid their pound of flesh each month and wasn't that what the damn insurance was for, emergencies like that, wasn't it to help people like them and the animals they cared for and loved?

Catrin thinks again of Harri and John's words come back to her, bone-deep: *Anything could happen.*

$\sim$

When she leaves the kennel, Catrin's surprised to find Simon lurking in the yard, looking up at the house, hands in his pockets. He's typical of the farmhands who work the hills, with his wide shoulders, hair the colour of faded straw and a smattering of red in his two-day stubble. The lad's worked on the farm since he was thirteen, supporting his own parents, who'd had troubles enough. John used to have him walking the dogs and helping with the horses but for several years now he's been working the sheep. He's the same age as Harri and Catrin feels a keen affection for the young man.

'Simon. Everything okay? You look lost.'

He gives a warm smile and shakes his head as if he's dispelling a dream. 'John said to come see you about the wages for last week,' he says, his dark-brown eyes round and serious.

Catrin pictures John making his excuses and feels her lips thinning into a tight grimace. But it isn't the lad's fault so she holds her tongue.

'Come inside, won't you? We'll sort things out now.'

'That would be grand, thank you.'

There's an old-fashioned way to Simon that Catrin finds endearing and it cools the heat in her. He follows her into the warmth of the house and in the kitchen she pulls out some bread and jam, has him sit at the table, puts the kettle on to boil.

'Now what was it John said to you?'

Simon pulls out a piece of lined paper from his pocket, the rows of numbers in two columns written in pencil. He hands it over to Catrin.

'My hours are on the left,' he says.

'And he told you to come here and ask, is that right?'

'That's right.'

Catrin can feel her insides twisting and tightening. With her back to Simon, she pours boiling water, adds some milk, stirs.

'Has he paid the other lads?' she asks, not turning around, not able to, not right now. The teaspoon clatters around the side of the mug.

'I couldn't say, I'm afraid.'

'I see,' says Catrin. She composes herself, turns to face him and offers the steaming brew.

'I think he might not have got round to it, though.' He was always a tactful boy.

'I see,' repeats Catrin. 'Would you mind waiting here a moment? I'll be back in two ticks.'

She heads up the stairs and stops in front of the bookshelves on the landing, pulling out an old, hollowed copy of *Miller's Antiques* from the top shelf. Inside there's a sizeable roll of notes – money she's earnt from her weekly piano lessons. Fifteen pounds an hour. She begins counting out the fives, tens and twenties, watching them pile up. Safe from the taxman and, more importantly, safe from John. Or so she's always thought. They had an unspoken agreement when it came to her lessons: her work, her money, her spends. It tore something in her, to be doing this, for John to be betraying her like this.

Back in the kitchen, Simon has finished up and is stroking Flint, who stares unwaveringly at the side plate littered with crumbs, drool gathering at the edges of his lips.

'Here we are, then,' says Catrin, handing over the wages, carefully collected with a rubber band. 'I'm sorry about that. John did mention he'd not had time to go to the bank this week.' The lie sits uncomfortable with her, but it's better than people talking, whispering that the Williams family don't pay their workers.

'That's grand, thank you,' he says, rising to his feet. 'There was one other thing.'

'What's that?'

'Harri's there now, isn't he?'

'That's right. They flew out last week.'

'Could I have his address, do you think? You know, where to send airmail and that. If it's not too much trouble?'

Such a sweet young man, thinks Catrin. John would say he was a little limp-wristed but what of it? She reaches for a note-pad and pen on the kitchen table and scribbles down the details. She knows them by heart, has repeated them over and over again like a chorus. 'It's kind of you,' she says with a smile. 'He'll appreciate that. I know he will.'

'Thanks,' says Simon, folding the paper, slipping it into the back pocket of his jeans before heading for the door. 'And thanks for the cash.'

Once he's left, Catrin sinks into the chair. The farm is in trouble and one day there'll be the men in their suits saying they're ever so sorry, Mrs Williams, ever so sorry. Meek and mild they'll be, while they explain that debt isn't something you can magic away, that no amount of smiling and keeping on and carrying on negates the neat stack of red zeroes.

She has tried to talk to John. Something needed to change if they were to keep the roof over their heads. But John would just shrug her off again and say it was no concern of hers. But how could it not be? And, behind it all, Catrin can hear her mother saying, 'I told you he was no good. I warned you, didn't I? Said it wouldn't be the life you expected.' Her mother was right in that last respect, at least. The farm, when you had to work it, was a far cry from watching fat cows in butter fields.

She goes back upstairs and opens the book containing her hard-earnt cash. It isn't much but it allows her the occasional pleasure: a haircut, a manicure, a new book; something that reminds her there's a life beyond the farm, that reminds her that even now she is smart and can scrub up well; that she deserves to be loved.

Catrin scans her books, which are scattered among Harri's own second-hand copies. She'd been so proud when he'd gone off to Bangor University, following in her own footsteps. She remembers packing up the car with all the things he'd need for his time away: his own bedsheets, suitcases filled with clothing, toiletries, kettle, toastie-maker. She'd helped Harri get settled, sorting out his desk, bed and cupboards; all the while, memories of her own start at university had filtered over the present and she'd felt the heavy press of time.

Catrin had made it on to the motorway before the tears had fallen. *My boy*, she'd thought. *My Harri*. When she'd got back to the farm, the house had been emptier and quieter. John had been in the kitchen after a day's work with the sheep. 'Well,' he'd said. 'That's that.'

Catrin pulls a book of R. S. Thomas's poetry from the shelf, scans the contents and finds the poem about the old farmer working his fallow fields. Her hand traces the lines until she comes to the right bit. There it is, the farmer in the field: alive but rotting nonetheless.

~

Catrin's stomach growls as she pushes against the old church door. She's missed lunch and is already running behind schedule. There had been a problem with one of the stock orders for feed and she'd been on the phone for almost an hour. The horses will also need seeing to when she gets back.

Catrin's ambivalent when it comes to God but she likes the way the Church brings people together. And she enjoys playing the organ, with its bellowing pipes. Their new vicar, Susan, was refreshing after the dour old Gerald, who was High Church and too liberal with the incense but too conservative with the wine. And his sermons! Dull enough to send even the most devout to sleep.

She takes a deep breath of the holy air and tries to think holier thoughts. She enjoys the smell of old polished wood and centuries of candle smoke that have seeped their way into the ancient brick of St Mary's. The cavernous space is empty and her feet clip-clop on the stone flags like horse's hooves. Two of the windows have new flower arrangements ready for Remembrance Sunday, the work of Betty Jones, a widow who's been doing the church flowers for several decades. Every year the results are more chaotic, with hacked bits of foliage bundled together, but no one likes to say anything. Catrin walks over to check the floral block has been watered. It's as dry as the nose of a sick dog.

After rescuing the bedraggled arrangement, she heads over to the organ and settles herself on the saggy seat. This is what she's been waiting for. She presses her two hands on the keys like someone unschooled, feet on the pedals, releasing a tuneless, furious roar of noise into the church, all her frustrations of the morning and beyond. As the thunder turns into a wheeze, she releases the pressure on the keys and pedals and then, from the chaos of sound, she begins to arrange her hands, flexing her fingers, and with barely a pause she dives into the opening of Bach's Tocatta and Fugue in D minor, the single-voice flourish spiralling down, thrumming through the ear and sending the heart beating wildly. She repeats the whole piece twice, indulging in the music in the same way she will sometimes escape to town for a manicure or a sugary cupcake. Because even dependable Catrin, who's always ready with a smile and who keeps going no matter what, deserves the occasional moment of joy. *Yes*, she thinks, fingers pressing down. *Yes, I do.*

When at last the music stops, Catrin licks her cracked lips, immediately regretting it; she knows it only exacerbates the problem but she can't seem to break the habit. Checking her watch, she releases a sigh, not wanting to move just yet. The sudden stillness and silence of the church fills her with the sense of things on hold. She could fall asleep here, content to let the world outside spin without her. But, no, she must get on.

She wonders what Harri will be doing and pictures him sitting in the heat of that dust-filled land, taking apart his gun, cleaning it, putting it back together again. That was something he'd learnt to do on the farm, breaking it down to stock, action and barrel; sitting at the kitchen table with cleaning rods, bronze brush, chamber brush and even a toothbrush for those tricky bits; applying some oil to the action but not so much it clogs up the inertia mechanism. He learnt other things, too: how to hold a gun, keep it safe, keep it close, keep it ready. He learnt how to kill. She wonders what this would do to her boy, going as he was from pointing a gun at an animal to pointing it at a man, a woman. Even a child. Would he have to do that?

She'd read about it. The way insurgents would strap explosives to a young boy or girl and push them out in front of allied vehicles.

The groaning of the church door and swash of cool air announces the arrival of the vicar, her cheeks flushed, eyes sparkling behind gold-framed spectacles that have turned steamy. She spies Catrin by the organ.

'Hello, there,' Susan calls, wiping the lenses on her cassock.

'Afternoon,' says Catrin. 'I'm just collecting the music for Sunday.'

'Cold out there,' says the vicar.

'It'll get colder yet.'

'I hope not! And how's the family?'

'They're keeping well, thank you. Same old.'

'And Harri?'

'He's fine,' says Catrin. 'Doing his bit.' What else is she supposed to say?

'You've heard from him, then?'

'Not yet but you know how it is. They deployed only a few days ago so he'll be settling, establishing patrol routes and all that.'

'Yes, of course,' says Susan, cheeks returning to a lighter shade of pink.

'It's not like he's working at the Tesco down the road,' adds Catrin. She starts sifting through sheets of music and makes a move to stand.

'No, no, of course not,' replies Susan. 'But everything is all right, is it, Catrin?'

'Everything's fine, yes. Fine. Why wouldn't it be?'

'That's good. That's very good. Well, my door's always open if there *is* anything you want to talk about.'

Catrin notes the crow's feet at the corners of the other woman's eyes. It's hard to tell how old she is. When Susan first arrived in the parish, she caused quite a stir. A female vicar, short hair, never married. People talked.

'Thank you,' says Catrin. And she means it, even though part of her wishes Susan would mind her own business and not go about scrambling a person's thoughts. Asking someone if they were *all right* was kind but it also made you wonder at it. Worry at it. And talking didn't bring Harri back; it didn't balance the books or change the past. Far better to get on.

Shaking her head, she shuts the lid of the organ with a thud, gathers up her music, smiles and heads for the exit.

Outside, Catrin steps between the graves of the dead, her greying hair blowing in the wind. She looks above the dates, the names, the ages on the tombstones. She will not think about it. She cannot think about it. Her son is serving his country. He'll return a hero. That is all there is to say.

∼

In the dead of night, Catrin wakes up to the gentle snoring of John, his bulk hidden beneath the thick duvet. They had argued again and she had gone to bed early, leaving him to nurse a whisky.

It wasn't a war on terror, he'd said. It was a war *of* terror and their son was caught right in the middle of it.

Dreamy-eyed, sleep-distilled thoughts drifting in and out of focus, Catrin slips from the sheets, steps along the cold wooden floor and listens to the creak of boards that murmur early-hour greetings. Home. This place, with blood and bone, life and death, old and new histories running through the fabric of the building. She pauses by Rhys's door, listens. It wasn't so long ago that she might have quietly turned the handle, put her head through the gap, checked he was sleeping safe and sound. But these last few years have quaked that easy relationship and now he wants his space, his privacy, his independence. He doesn't need or want his mam worrying over where he is or what he's doing. She's had to learn to knock.

Feeling the tight twist of time, Catrin enters Harri's room with its empty bed. She whispers his name as if he might be there, repeats it again as if she might summon him, an apparition, spirit. She touches his bedsheets, looks at the posters, the books, files of old university work.

She leaves on tiptoe and shuts the door with the slightest of sounds, before heading down the stairs, guided by the moon's light. Flint wanders through from the kitchen and follows her into the living room, where she switches on the TV, mutes the volume. She can't avoid the news, no matter how much she might wish to.

Catrin takes a seat on the sofa, wrapping her dressing gown tightly around her body. The television shows a British journalist in khaki clothing, helmet and body armour. The man's face is red and sweaty. Catrin leans forward, her eyes reflecting the images in miniature. The pictures flash, illuminating the room, casting shadows against her face, which is beginning to gather the full flavour of her forty-six years. She keeps her eyes on the young men behind the reporter, rifles in their hands, smiling at the camera. They occupy a land of rubble, buildings unbricked, dust and danger beneath their feet. Catrin had said she wouldn't do this, had promised herself she wouldn't obsess over headlines, but here she is, already drawn to the faces that play on repeat, wondering if one morning she will come down to find Harri's caught on film, his image transmitted through space and time, beamed through millions of TVs across the world.

Flint, who can sense that there is something amiss, suddenly rises up on to his four legs, slowly staggers over to Catrin and rests his head upon her lap, and, as she feels the weight of his jaw upon her knee, they hear the litany of rain coming down upon the mountains, swelling the streams and rivers, soddening the earth.

'Oh, cariad, love,' she says, her eyes beginning to fill.

And, because she is alone, and because no one can see her, and because John is right that anything could happen, and because he's wrong in so many other ways, she lets them fall, silent and shining as they catch the light of the moon.

349. Lt Gen Kiszely had reported significant structural damage in Fallujah and that the city was 'littered' with IEDs which would need to be located and made safe before reconstruction could begin in earnest.

– *The Report of the Iraq Inquiry*, Volume VII, Section 9.3

2

John purses his lips around the whistle and blows, giving the 'Come by' command, the high-low-high sound sending the sheepdog Lola pivoting. He watches as she turns with extraordinary agility and arcs around the left flank of the sheep, her black nose splitting the air. Her open mouth reveals rows of sharp, pearly teeth and red tongue. Her ears are alert, eyes keen. Up here, the wind is strong and the greys and whites of her coat stream back. The sheep pitter and patter back and forth, bunching up, bleating, moving steadily forward. John can see a favourite sheep of his up ahead, leading the flock, although these older ewes are generally more sure-footed, knowing what's what. He'll have to replace them in a year, but that's not something he needs to worry about now. He whistles again and his dog darts back. One of the ladies has bolted out to the right.

There's almost no protection high up here in the fells and the wind whips up a chill. The land around him is hard and unforgiving; the soil is frozen. What grass remains is crisp with frost, offering little for the ewes to put their teeth to. John leans on his staff and scans the hillsides, looking for the other shepherds and their farmhands. It's a good clear day, perfect for the gathering. In the distance, coming down the valley to the left of the copse, he can see a flock being driven down and elsewhere he knows others will be watching to make sure the ewes end up in the right areas. He casts an eye behind him, checking the rolling terrain to see if a speck of white appears – the inevitable stragglers, those that have got themselves lost. He'll come up later, on the quad bike, with one of the other dogs, let them work their muscles, get the heart pumping.

He turns, coughs, spits green phlegm. Last week, Rhys had come back from school with the lurgy and this morning John felt the itch at the back of his throat. The boy should be here, but it's Monday and Catrin won't have it. He's got to pass his exams, she says, keep the doors open. Algebra and Pythagoras, countries and capitals.

John shakes his head. A few years ago and he would have struggled to point to Iraq on a map. Now he can draw its borders with Saudi Arabia, Jordan, Iran, Syria and Turkey. He can reel off a list of regions, cities and towns in that faraway country as if it were his own. He coughs again. Spits. He takes a step forward, winces at the ache pulsing in his left leg.

As they make their way down towards the lower ground, he spots a dark bird circling in the sky. A bad sign. Sure enough, one of his sheep lies on the ground, its body – or what remains of it – spread out, a patch of fleece and bone. That was more money in the bellies of the birds and beasts that skulked at the edges of his vision. He'd like to send the fuckers to hell but there was no stopping them.

A long, single-sound whistle puts Lola on hold. She'll wait there, keep one eye on the ewes while John makes his way towards the carcass, his staff tapping on the ground before him. By the look of things, it's been dead two or three days. Eyes plucked from the skull by the black-winged bastards. The ravens can be the worst, harrying at the soft bellies of the lambs. One sits perched on top of the nearby drystone wall, its shining eyes regarding him warily. John leans down, picks up a small stone, flings it. The corvid caws, dances a step or two to the right, then hops back again, laughing. It knows he'll move on soon enough and then it can get back to feasting. A few years back he'd had a trap. Caught the fuckers and later got his revenge with the barrel of a gun.

The ewe's ribs show, red and raw and bloody. A fox, maybe two or three joining the scene, after the first'd had its fill. And to think that in a fortnight they'd be voting on the Hunting Act. As if foxes were soft toys you'd tuck up with your child. Fucking townies. What did they know?

Sometimes he'd get a call from one of the schools asking if they could bring some kids up to look at the animals. Sure, he'd say. Sure. But it would be Catrin giving them the tour, because John wasn't good at that sort of thing. He thought they should see the blood and spit and shit, but no, no, it was the softness of things, the lamb wool and whatnot that brought in the money. And they needed money, didn't they? He needed money. So let the kids read their books about fantastic foxes. What did it matter? Money was money.

He looks down at the carcass and heaves a sigh. He'll have to clear up the mess later. More work, more paperwork. He coughs, spits, walks on. He whistles again and the dog springs up, resuming her stride. She's a good worker, she is.

John walks down the mountain with his flock, the animals bleating as they go, their black faces and thick coats shuffling forward against the greens, browns and greys of the Welsh winter hills. A few break off, pause, dip their heads to the sparse grass, nibble slowly and stupidly, but there's too little to be had up here. After he's brought them down to the gathering point, where they'll be counted, he'll take them to the lower fells surrounding the scattered farm buildings. His ladies will be well-nourished with additional feed, and morning, afternoon and night he'll keep his eyes on them, until they're tupped and he has a whole brood of lambs in the field, gambolling about on their fresh young legs.

As they work their way down, John spies Tim's Land Rover snorting its way along the narrow path towards the cattle gate. It splashes through large puddles, jerking left and right as the land dips and rises.

Some of the ewes make a dash forward and the others follow, the one with the dark smudge on its face still at the front, her feet stepping lightly on the ground. The land becomes steeper and John walks with care, watching the placement of his own feet, making sure they are steady, legs balanced. An ankle sprain can bring a farm to a standstill and, with the ground as wet as it is, it would be easy for the rubber soles to go sliding. He'd have liked to have brought the quad bike here but the gradient is too steep and, besides, he has only to recall his da, poor bugger, to know the dangers of mishandling machinery.

John's hands are ice; his leg aches; and the back of his throat feels like raw meat. He coughs and spits. How much of his life has this land soaked up? It'll have all of him by the end and he's okay with that, let it have him, body and soul, it's what he was born for and it's good enough for him, even if it wasn't good enough for Harri. Christ, enough of that. Just keep walking, you old sod. Get the job done.

He whistles: two short, sharp sounds that get Lola running on, pushing the sheep forward. He marvels at her speed, her intelligence. A good sheepdog. Good enough for trials, he'd say, but he's not sure he has it in him for that any more. Too many damn things to think about, too little money, too many debts, too little patience with the bureaucracy and politics of the competition and its officials. Still, nice to see the potential, to know it's there. He remembers buying her as a pup off Jones Senior, seeing she had some spirit in her, the first of the litter that staggered up to him, curious, interested to see what he was about. He liked a dog with gumption, though the head-strong ones were always harder to train, needed a firmer hand, more patience when they acted mule-like. He ought to be getting Rhys a pup of his own soon; the lad ought to be bonding with his own dog if he was to be of real help in the years to come. He could breed from Lola again – she was from good stock and he'd get a few bob for the pups. It was something to think on.

John waves at Tim, who's gingerly stepping out of the car, his boots landing in the mud. The other man smiles and then lets his own dogs out of the back. Jumpy critters, those, but they do the job. John can see some of the ewes are getting tired so he calls out and his dog lies down and lets the sheep catch their breath. He steadies himself on the staff, leaning forward, panting; he's not so different from the animals, the dog there with her tongue hanging out like a fat slug.

Most of these ewes will be put to the rams he's rented from Manorafon Farm – good stock that should maintain the hardiness of his current flock, though Alwyn drove a harder price than the year before – perhaps because he's been hit by the poor price of today's meat. But weren't they all? Cheap chicken, cheap beef and lamb and pork so brattish boys and girls could have their processed burgers, breaded thighs and what-have-you, even though some of them had never seen a cow or sheep in the flesh, and even though they'd never dream of doing their own killing. But there it was.

Christ, those rams had been a price. Still, they're good animals. John checked one of them over thoroughly, could see it in the way he stood, the quality of his thick, oily coat. And Alwyn had the kind of philosophy that John appreciated – livestock was either for breeding or feeding, nothing else. It was a life of slaughter, sex and rain and that was just fine with him. No fucking way would you find him sitting on a soft chair, beneath tube lighting, tapping away at a computer. He had that in common with Harri, at least.

He liked doing something vital. What did people stuck in offices really do? Shuffle papers? He didn't know. He didn't care. Though he depended upon them now, was in thrall to them even, in a way his great-grandparents would never have been.

The bankers and the managers and the lawyers and so on. With all their paperwork and their paperclips, biros in the pockets of their dark suits. What did they know about life that he didn't? Nothing is what.

John calls for the dog to stand and she leaps to her paws, eye on him. He whistles low and she pounces towards the flock. Yes, the rams will do nicely this year, though he's putting them to the ladies later than he'd have liked, but that was the weather for you. He recalls one of the rams he'd had some five years back, Biggles, the owners had called it. A big fella with the bollocks of an elephant. But it had done fuck-all, just stood there in the field, looking hopeless, the ewes eyeing him suspiciously. John had watched him for an hour or more, even done a little encouraging: look here's the rear end and there's the hole, you daft lump. But it just stood there, gormless, grazing away. John had given the owners a call, people he'd not used before, and he'd explained the situation and they'd said he'd still have to pay half the fee, which had him exploding down the phone. Listen here, he'd said, listen here. You should be paying *us* for the time we've taken getting him here, the time we've wasted. You've rented us a dud; he's not worth the feed he's guzzling. Well, that had been that. A bent ram. He supposed it happened; he'd seen enough of it in his own animals, though it was rare, mind. His own father had taken a firm view of such things: get the shotgun.

Last year he'd used a few teaser rams to get the ladies ready but they'd not gone for that this time. He was sure once they caught the smell of the fellas they'd be randy enough. He'd been promised high libido, three-year-old rams, so plenty of experience, large testicles that he'd measured with the same green tape his father had used, and John would have the rams for a couple of cycles, which should satisfy the flock. They were lively fellas, certainly, and John was confident things would go as well as they could this year. Better, at any rate, than the year when Rhys had turned twelve and had got charged by a ram and they'd had to take the boy to the hospital to get tetanus jabs and stitches. Hell's teeth, Catrin had been furious. *Where were you? What were you doing?* But it was the boy's fault, as much as his own: Rhys had put his back to the brute and hadn't been in clear line of a quick exit. What had he expected? And how many times had he told Rhys to take care? He should have known better. Still, the lad was a help. More than Harri, at any rate, who'd got that faraway look in his eyes before buggering off to university and then the Army, leaving his younger brother to pick up the slack. Rhys took to it, though. Farming was in him and that gladdened some deep part of John, made him feel as if he'd done at least one thing right in the world.

The ewes are bunching now and John strolls down towards Tim. The two men shake hands.

'Bore da, Tim. All right?'

'Well enough, John. Yourself?'

'The same.'

'And the wife?'

'Keeping on.'

'A cold day for gathering but clear enough.'

'That it is.'

Tim nods at John's dog, who's keeping the ewes in check. 'She's done well.'

'She has.'

'We'd better get the ladies sorted, then.'

'We had.'

As John walks towards the road where the cattle gate hangs open, Tim calls out to him.

'Market's damp, John.'

'I've heard it.'

'It'll be another tight year.'

'Like every other.'

'But we wouldn't be doing anything else, would we?'

John gives a thin smile. 'We wouldn't.'

There's nothing more to be said. They've been fast friends for some decades now; they've both been in it, understand the way of things, how it is up here, how a man can be undone by a single week of rain, and how the skin becomes thicker with each passing year with the work and oil of wool and dogs. You can lose your words in the mountains; the land swallows them up.

Right now, there's the gathering and sorting and the putting to the rams. This is the cycle of his world.

~

It is late afternoon and the men have congregated in the Black Sheep, a favourite haunt. It's a small, loud space, full of smoke; the old, patterned carpet is stained with spillages; there are dark varnished tables and chairs, beer-warped mats, a roaring fire, a dartboard, hook-the-ring and bar billiards. At the far end, by all the tables and chairs, is a fruit machine, its lights flashing, large buttons waiting for the feel of eager fingers. It's the first thing John notices whenever he enters a pub; it's as if the machines have a gravitational force, a magnetism he's almost incapable of resisting. It's easier when he's not alone.

John stands with a cue in his hand, chalking the nib, rubbing some of the green-blue powder on to the skin between his thumb and his forefinger to help the wood slide smooth and true, just as his father had taught him. He leans over the faded green baize, feels his stomach press against the edge, lines his eye along the wood and holds his breath, just as he would if he were shooting. He pulls the cue back, then taps the white ball. It rolls forwards, knocks against the rear wall and hits the red ball, which inches towards the centre pocket, pauses, then, at the last moment, tips into the hole.

'Lucky, that,' says Tim.

John gives a canine smile. 'How many years have we been coming here?'

'Too many,' says Tim.

'And what's the count between us?'

'Who's counting?' asks Tim.

John lines up another red along the line, takes aim. Taps. Tim pulls out a packet of tobacco from his jeans, puts the small white filter between his lips, slides out a Rizla paper, folds it. John taps a third red, misses. He looks up at Tim and shakes his head. 'They'll ban that soon enough as well.'

'Like fuck they will,' says Tim.

'It's what we said about the hunt.'

'It'll kill places like this.'

'D'you really think they care?' replies John. He nods towards the table. 'It's your turn.'

'Give me a minute, will you.'

Tim lights up, releases a cloud of smoke and looks over to the far end of the bar, where the other shepherds and farmhands are sprawled out across three or four tables, laughing, dozens of pint glasses between them, loud and content after a long day's work. Most of them will be picked up by understanding family later in the evening.

'It's your round, I think,' says Tim, eyeing the emptying glasses across the room.

'So it is,' says John, resting his cue and walking over to the table where his coat hangs over a chair.

'Fellas,' he nods. There are the Turner boys and their da, the Jacksons, Hughes, Bryn, the Joneses and a gaggle of the younger farmhands including Simon, who's watching the play at the dart board.

'John, you old dog,' says Alwyn, a shaggy, red-headed bear of a man with a wild beard. 'How's the leg?'

'Christmas is coming early.'

'Like every year,' replies Alwyn. 'We'll have to get you one of those electric wheelchairs.'

'Will you now?'

'Or a zimmer?'

'Which I'd be shoving you know where.'

'Are you putting Tim in his place again?'

'Seems a shame to break with tradition,' says John. He continues to pat down his jacket, then checks his jeans. 'You fellas seen my wallet?'

'Not in here,' says Alwyn, peering inside a crisp packet.

'Lost it again, eh, John?' This comes from the youngest of the Jackson boys, who's clearly had a drink too many. He sits there grinning like he's said something clever. There's a large white-ended pimple on his chin.

'Pipe down, you,' says his father, giving him the elbow.

John keeps his eye on the lad. He'd like to land a fist on the little turd. What the fuck does he know? 'Let me check the car. I'll be back in a tick.'

It's biting cold outside. He opens his car door, shoves aside the *Racing Post* and climbs in. He reaches up to the mirror above the wheel and unclips the notes, counting under his breath. Thirty quid. Not enough to cover the whole round in any case, he tells himself. He slides the money into his pocket and rests his two hands on the steering wheel, at ten and two o'clock, just as his father had taught him. John wishes he could speak to the old git now. Then again, he'd not be able to stomach the shame of it. He can already hear that voice like a rusty hinge, telling him a man always paid his way, that his word was his bond.

He knows the men inside will be talking. They'll be muttering about how he's had trouble paying some of the farmhands, wondering if he'll need to let some of them go, who it'll be and how he'll cope. It'll be a shadowy kind of muttering: unhappy and rehearsed, what with one smallholding following another over the years. They'll be speculating about his land – what it's worth, whether he'll soon have to sell it, bit by bit; the land his father and his father's father had tended. Poor sod, they'll be saying.

But, no, he'll not do that; selling the land is a line he'll never cross. Not for anything or anyone.

John balls his hands into fists. He cannot bear their pity or his shame. He wants to charge in there like a bull, but the truth is that if he were a farm animal, he'd have been put down long ago. He'd be canned up as dog food.

A tap at his window brings him round. It's Tim standing there, hat pulled on against the coming drizzle. John opens the door.

'All right, mate?'

'I'm okay, Tim.'

'Will you come back in?'

'I said I'll be a minute.'

'Don't worry about it, John. I covered you.'

John thinks about telling his dearest friend, godfather to his elder boy, about the thirty pounds in his pocket but something holds him back: a weakness, a terrible, gluttonous, unquench-able need.

'Must've left it at the farm,' he says. 'You're a good man, Tim. Thanks.'

'We're on your side, John. You know that. If you need help, whatever it is, you'll ask, won't you?'

John nods slowly, catching Tim's eyes drifting to the *Racing Post* by his side. That damn paper, cooking his thoughts and filling his head with hope.

'Come,' says Tim, giving John's shoulder a gentle shake. 'Let's finish the game.'

Back at the table, John takes the cue, chalks the tip, lines up the red, aims, shoots. He was always good at this. Three or four years back they'd done a tournament, with the Black Sheep putting up five hundred quid, with a five-pound buy-in, winner takes all. There'd been sixty-plus names in the ring and John had got to the final, where he'd faced one of the lads from down in the town, a young fella, not much older than Rhys was now, who'd had a wispy beard and pale-green eyes and a bum-chin. The whole place had been packed and there was some tension, what with him being the local man, a man who'd spent all his years in the place and one of them, one of the farmers, and this lad, just out of school, who hadn't got his roots in the earth of the place. It had been a tense game and, with all those eyes on him, John had felt a certain expectation, but he'd kept his cool, sinking one ball after another, seeing the score board rise and rise. The lad had kept up well enough, even overtook John on two occasions, but it was John's game. Now, as he remembers the roar of his friends and the pride he'd seen in his boys' faces, he feels that same steely determination settle in him.

The red ball rolls forward, bounces off the back wall and slips neatly into the hole like its one and only purpose had been achieved. John is already lining up the next ball, eyeing the possibilities on the table. One ball after another drops into the pockets and the score builds and builds, the needle on the board sliding along the row of numbers. At one point he nearly knocks over the black skillet and his heart thuds heavy in his chest but the small wooden cross holds fast. He's vaguely aware of Tim whistling between his teeth and calling over the others who drift by. The score climbs above the thousand mark. John wishes Harri and Rhys were here to see him now. Catrin, too.

His back starts to ache and when at last the break ends the

men are nodding like he's done something special. Jackson nods his way, smiling. Tim was right: they were on his side.

Stepping up to the table, Tim smiles. 'Comeback of the year?'

John shrugs, grins.

Alwyn walks over and pats him on the back. 'How are the lads?' he asks.

John can feel ears pricking. 'Rhys's getting by. Exams next summer. His mam's more worried than he is, of course. I'd have liked him with me today but sometimes there's no arguing.'

'Isn't that the truth. And Harri's out there in the thick of things?'

'He is.'

'You've had word, then?'

John shrugs, taking another sip of his beer. It's been two weeks and there's been no contact from their boy. 'Not yet,' he says. 'Not yet.'

~

John shouldn't be driving. And if he was driving anywhere, it should be home. But he felt the familiar tug, the inescapable pull that came with winning, with beer in him, with thirty pounds in his pocket. He'd planned on having only the one, but when did plans ever run as expected?

First, though, he needs something to eat.

Down in Llandudno, he pulls up outside an Indian restaurant that he and Catrin have visited a few times.

Inside, the tables are covered with pink cloths. Fabric napkins are folded neatly next to wine glasses. John is guided to a seat by a young waiter who calls him 'sir'; he's a slight man dressed in a dark waistcoat, black trousers and leather shoes. He offers a polite smile and asks if he would like anything to drink.

'Tap water, please.'

John orders chicken tandoori and rice. While he waits, he studies the paintings on the wall and listens to the soft music, the kind of music you only find in a place like this or in a lift. His order arrives quickly, steaming hot. John tips the lot on to his plate, stirs the rice into the sauce, his mouth salivating. He savours the taste, the light tingle on his tongue. The chicken is soft and tender.

He wonders what Harri would be eating. Ration packs that last years and years. Powdered this and that.

He watches the young man, as well as an older man behind the bar who is polishing glasses with a napkin. He wonders if they're father and son. They look similar and share murmured exchanges, the occasional smile. John swallows. He finds his throat tightening. The father and son share a joke. John puts down his knife. He's worked a long, hard day.

He beckons over the young waiter. 'I don't think the chicken is cooked all the way through,' he says, prodding the remaining few pieces with his fork.

The man looks between John and the plate. 'I'm sorry, sir?'

'The chicken,' John repeats. 'It's not cooked.'

'Our chef is very experienced, sir. He's been here for several years.'

'And where was he before that?' asks John.

'He was in London, sir.'

'And where was he before that?'

'Sir?'

The young waiter removes the plate and disappears through a door into the kitchen. No fuss. No disagreement. John wonders if they have encountered this kind of situation before and the thought fills him with shame.

The older waiter walks over and smiles. He's going silver around the ears. Like his son, he's a slight man. John thinks he could probably lift him off his feet and hurl him across the room, just like he'll grab the twine on a hay bale and fling it high up on to the trailer, ready for stacking in the barns. It wouldn't be difficult.

'I'm sorry you weren't happy with your meal, sir. The chef assures me everything was cooked through but we would like to offer the meal on the house.'

'Thank you,' says John. It's all he can say. He feels the heat rising to his neck, spreading to his cheeks. His hands are bunched and he feels there is, deep within him, a terrible violence.

Outflanked, he escapes to the streets, where his blood cools beneath his skin. Rain spits down. John walks towards the centre of town. The streets are relatively empty for a Monday evening. Ten minutes later, shoulders damp, he sees the establishment, a well-lit Win365, a punter leaning by the door, cigarette between his lips.

John undoes his coat, steps inside. He keeps his hand in his pocket, fingers on the tip of the notes. The fruit machines are to one side and a tall bloke in a puffer jacket stands with his hands on the buttons as he stares down at the barrage of flashing colours. The screens of the other two machines offer a selection of Roulette, Roulette Classic and Multi Bingo. Opposite, the largest screen shows the racing, while the smaller ones display the greyhounds, the football, the latest prices on upcoming events, plus a few with the rolling racing results and special deals. Below these, the wall is covered in the *Racing Post* wall pull-outs. There's an area for the footie and the greyhounds but mostly it's racing and more racing, with scattered slips for bets to be placed. At the far end of the room, two men are laughing behind a glass screen.

John joins the other man standing behind the arcade machines. He'd like to bet on the horses but he's too tired for that and, besides, he's not studied the paper today. And, to be fair to him, he always rings those in the know, people like Mike, who have an ear to the turf. And he always does his sums. That's something, isn't it?

He inserts the notes into the machine. It swallows them whole, adding the credit. The lights on the screen spring to life like something from outer space. He selects Roulette and places his first bet.

The wheel spins and the visual ball bearing rattles around before coming to a stop. Nothing. He bets again, presses the single rectanglular button. So easy. *Push, push, push.* Two quid per spin, more if you wanted. Thirty seconds a spin. He could be done in about ten minutes flat.

John knows that on the side of the machine there's a small white sticker with the Terms and Conditions that outline the return to player, knows it stands at an average of 85 per cent. Not bad, if you were able to walk away. A small loss. But the man who spends a hundred quid will likely spend the eighty-five and then the seventy-two and on it will go until the returns diminish in a vanishing act. For some people it's like trying to keep hold of a fistful of sand. People like him.

Push, push, push. Watch the money disappear like magic.

Yes, it's magical. It's soothing. He can let it all go, forget about Catrin and the fuse burning away, forget about the Jackson lad and his comments, Tim and his kindness, and even what he did at the Indian restaurant, lying like that, just out of spite. Yes, he can empty his mind, let time disappear, his body occupy this tiny space, and everything, *everything*, at the mercy of the gods in the machine.

There's one thing he can't forget, though. And that's Harri.

With his last play, feeling sick and drowsy under the bright lights of the shop, he places everything on Black 22. Harri's age. The digital wheel spins and the shiny metal ball circles the wheel. He's had a good night, hasn't he? He deserves some luck. He presses the button.

The ball continues to spin and it goes round and round, and the thought comes to him that, if the small silver ball lands on Black 22, Harri will come home safe and sound.

And if it doesn't?

He can't unthink it now. It's there, out in the universe.

Black 22. Harri home. Safe.

John hates himself. God he hates himself.

The wheel slows, the ball bounces several times, jumping like a rabbit between numbers. Jumping until there is no more jumping, until all is still.

Red 23.

Well, then, there it is. There it is, you bastard.

John slams his palms against the side of the machine. A dark shape moves towards him. Sound comes from a great distance. Again, John brings his hands down against the machine. Again and again.

'Oi, mate!' He looks up as one of the staff grabs at him.

He's not looking for trouble but he brings his fist down anyway. Gleeful violence rears up within him and his fists fall.

But he's no fighter. Not like his son, not like his boy.

22 November 2004

Dear Mam, Da, Rhys

Thanks for the bluey you sent. Please keep them coming. I'm sorry it's taken me so long to write – I'll try and do so more often but it's not always easy. You know the drill. It's hot out here (21 degrees yesterday) and if it wasn't for the nights (jumpers & trousers territory) I know I'd be missing the cold back home.

How's life at the farm? You should see the livestock out here. Not sure you'd be too impressed, though. A lot of scrawny chickens, goats and some cattle that show every one of their ribs. Often you'll see the larger animals roped up but sometimes they wander about,

*free to roam. The lads have been talking about buying a goat –
already we're pretty sick of ration packs. Civvies don't know their
luck.*

*A few of the fellas have said I should do the honours with the
killing of the thing. That's what us cave-dwellers in the mountains
do, apparently . . .*

*The days are often the same. There are the patrols and a lot of
waiting about. Sometimes I forget what day it is. The waiting's the
worst part of it. Over three weeks in and I'm already a bit sick of
the sand. And the heat. Everything is so flat and dry, although there
are mountains somewhere in this country.*

*I do miss the hills and the cold, thin air that gets into your lungs
and cleans them right out.*

*Sometimes it's a bit intense but there's not a better bunch of lads
to be around. We keep things lively enough. It's what I signed up for
and I have a responsibility to my men.*

*I'd better leave it there – Lieutenant Williams reporting for duty
and all that. I hope this reaches you safe and you can read my
scrawl.*

I love you all. Give Flint a hug from me, won't you?

*Llawer o gariad,
Harri x x*

P.S. Could you please send some more razor heads (Gillette)?

369. During a video conference with President Bush on 30 November, Mr Blair said that Fallujah 'had gone well' and the story of what US forces had found there – including evidence of torture chambers – should be put into the public domain.[*]

370. Mr Blair suggested that the operation had 'sent a clear message that the insurgents could not win'.

– *The Report of the Iraq Inquiry*, Volume VII, Section 9.3

---

[*] Letter Quarrey to Owen, 30 November 2004, 'Prime Minister's VTC with President Bush, 30 November: Iraq, Syria and Iran'.

3

Two important letters arrived yesterday.

One of them was from Harri. When Catrin had seen his cramped handwriting on the envelope, she'd felt her entire body tense, something inside her scrunching up, the light-blonde hairs on her arms standing to attention. She'd called to John and Rhys and they'd stormed the kitchen as she ripped through the seal and her thoughts spiralled: *He's alive, he's alive, he's alive.*

Bored and missing home. But alive, thank the gods.

The three of them had sat at the table, passing the letter around like a flask of whisky before battle, the single sheet of paper being read over and over. And John, sitting there with his purpling face, his hands cupped together, eyes like stone. He'd said he'd slipped and landed against a fence post but Catrin finds it hard to see how it could have left a bruise around the eye like that.

Rhys had looked disappointed after reading the letter, as if he'd expected more. Her two boys still had things to talk through: Harri had upped sticks without much thought of his younger brother and a root of resentment was now growing inside Rhys; she could see it twisting and turning, tapping something deep. It's hard knowing her two boys – who once roamed the farm with water pistols and jokes at the ready – were drifting apart. Catrin hopes that when Harri comes home they'll work things out between them, that white flags will be raised.

The second letter, complete with capital letters and bold font, was from the bank. She'd shown it to John after Rhys had left for school. He'd rubbed a hand through his salt-and-pepper hair and promised to fix it. Catrin almost believed him. But how could they possibly owe *that* much? John had done what he always did – shrugged and told her not to worry about it, that he had everything in hand. She'd looked at him, bruised as he was, and wondered.

'Is that it?' she'd asked. 'Is there anything else I should know about?'

She'd watched as he'd picked up the letter and read it again, looking at the long number at the bottom of the page, the words CONSOLIDATED DEBT highlighted in red. 'No,' he'd said. 'That's it.'

She'd pushed him, made him promise there would be no more surprises and when he raised his hands like a man under arrest and said there was nothing else – 'It said consolidated, didn't it?' – she'd let the matter drop.

Later that morning she'd made a call to Tim. John wouldn't like it but who else could she turn to? She couldn't – wouldn't – ask her mother for help. And John wasn't going to fix things.

They'd pinned Harri's letter to the cork board by the fridge and Catrin looks over to it now as she slides a nail along the brown tape, waiting to feel the slight lip to mark the edge. She's spent all morning putting together Harri's care package. It's helped to keep her mind occupied. She's added a bumper pack of razor heads, a pair of high-quality walking socks, soap, deodorant, sun-cream, a small sewing kit, a deck of cards, AA and AAA batteries, PG Tips, some packets of Haribo and a few paperbacks he'd read for his degree. She's included a letter of her own. She likes to picture him reading her letters: the physicality of the paper, the handwriting that is hers alone; it's a string, something to guide him back home from the war. Her note is censored, of course: no mention of the letter from the bank; no mention of the cracks that seem to be widening and deepening down to the very foundations of their family, their farm; as if the mountainside itself is riddled with treacherous fissures.

She tapes the flaps of the box and reinforces the corners. It seems unfair that these small items will see her son before she does. She scrawls the address on the front of the box and then places her palms on top, looking down at her boy's name. Leaning over, she kisses the paper and then rests her cheek flat against it, ear pressed to the cardboard, as if she's listening for a heartbeat. Flint, beneath the kitchen table, snuffles at her feet.

Anything could happen.

These three words have lodged themselves somewhere inside her, like the barbs of an arrowhead, and, no matter how hard she tries, Catrin cannot shake the doubt, the worry, the guilt. She'd hoped it would ease but it's there, day and night.

Anything could happen.

And still the Earth spins: she'll take the box into town, pick up some shopping, collect Rhys from school, make dinner.

She looks at her list, considers the ingredients of a home. Bread, milk, tea. Her children safe and sound. A husband who can accept the need for change. A dog who gets no older.

She likes writing lists. She feels that all the problems of the world could be solved if she could just write them down.

In the corner of the room is a spider in her web, sitting there at ease, the centre of her small world. The eight-legged creature will have mated by now and in the spring she'll lay her eggs; a month later her little ones will tumble out, scattering on their own life-strings.

The sound of John in the hall interrupts her thoughts. He walks in, his face ruddy, unruly hair poking out from under a blue beanie. In one hand he carries a dead hen, its body swinging from side to side. In the other he holds a carton of eggs.

'Broth for the next week,' he says. 'Unless you want to give it to the dogs?'

Catrin looks at the chicken, its eyes glazed over. 'Both. Leave it there. I'll pluck it later.'

'Bloody cold outside,' he says, voice loud, filling the kitchen. He smells of livestock and talc. As long as she's known him, John has come back from a day out and covered his feet and socks in the powder. His father had done the same. Thankfully it's not a tradition the boys have continued.

John puts the eggs on the side by the microwave and wipes his running nose with the sleeve of his dark fleece. He casts a glance over the box. 'For Harri?'

'I'm heading to the post office soon.'

'Will you wait a moment?' He hurries out of the room and soon returns with an empty bottle of mouthwash.

'What's that?' she asks.

'Something he mentioned before he left,' replies John. He reaches down and takes out a bottle of gin from the cupboard, unscrews the cap and begins filling the old, plastic bottle.

'He said it was an old trick. It gets through.'

'He's not supposed to have alcohol.'

'Right,' says John. 'Which is why he said about this.'

Catrin tries to remember anything Harri had said about drink. She can't.

'He shouldn't be having that,' she repeats.

'They all do it. God knows they'll need something stronger than tea, doing what they do.' He walks over and looks down at the box.

'I've already taped it up,' says Catrin.

'I can see that,' says John, and he pulls out his keyring, takes the edge of a key and slices right along the centre of the brown tape. 'Won't take a moment to put back.'

Catrin wants to say, *But this is from me.* She wants to tell John to do his own care package rather than coming in here and undoing her work and interrupting her like this. She looks over at the hen on the side, its body limp.

'Shouldn't you be at the Shepherds' Meet?'

'Not for another hour.' Gin safely nestled among the other items, Catrin watches as he retapes the box. 'You're not the only one who worries about our boy,' he says.

'I never said I was.'

'No. You just act it.'

And with that he's gone.

How quickly a truce can be broken, she thinks. How carelessly.

Catrin picks up one of the eggs. It's still warm to the touch and she imagines the small life that might have been.

~

Standing in the queue at the post office, Catrin waits behind a short lady whose close-cut hair reminds her of film sets from the 1920s. She wonders what those years must have been like, after the Great War, when all the dead had been buried. She wonders if the survivors felt lucky or if they were hollowed out, cracked up, like shrapnel. At the front of the line, an old lady with a crooked back has withdrawn her weekly pension allowance and is slowly counting the notes to check the sum. Catrin is reminded of her own mum, who'll be waiting for her weekly call.

'*Cat?*' A man's voice she almost recognizes, like the scent of an old perfume. But no one calls her that. Not these days. She turns and is confronted by a man she half recognizes, his sharp blue eyes beaming. 'Cat Williams!' His voice rumbles through her and she feels her body respond, her face glowing. 'Matthew? Matt Edevane? How . . . What . . .'

How long has it been? Ten, fifteen years? Not since Rhys was

50

a toddler. She puts down the box and he gives her a kiss on each cheek. She feels her heart thunder.

There are too many questions, and he does not stop smiling as he tries to answer the flurry.

'. . . down for some exploring. . . the Mawddach Residency . . .'

'You look radiant by the way . . .'

Old memories wash over her.

'A few months . . . my father . . .'

'We're no longer living together but . . .'

Catrin is called forward in the queue.

'Perhaps a coffee once you're done here? I'll wait for you outside.'

'I'd like that,' says Catrin.

Says Cat.

~

The two of them walk over the zebra crossing towards Lisa's, the name painted across the pink shop window with its large display of freshly made cakes and pastries. Matt doesn't stop talking all the way, flip-flopping between questions and answers, charting the last decade, with boyish excitement. It feels exactly like it used to and, although he's older – with greying hair and lines around the eyes – he has the same infectious energy and impulsive smile.

'I've been meaning to get in touch. You've not changed a bit, you know,' he says.

'Liar.'

He laughs and his arm wraps around her shoulder and pulls her close. She can smell his aftershave – the scent of cedarwood.

'You have,' she says.

'Oh, yes?' He opens the door for her. Inside it's warm and the air smells of coffee and pastry.

'Your accent. You've gone southern on us. And the tan.'

He laughs again and then nods at a young waitress who stands behind a large glass counter filled with slices of cake. Catrin guides them towards the back of the café, away from the old gossips who peer at them over their mugs of tea. The waitress walks by and hands them two frayed menus.

'The tan is all Vietnam.'

'Vietnam?' asks Catrin, feeling her parochialism, how small her life is, how limited its vision. Sitting here, with Matt in front of her, she feels herself confronting the life she might have had. A life of travel, culture; a life at the heart of things. Matt.

'I was there for a few weeks. Finishing up some work I'm doing for an exhibition next year. The accent's down to a combo of London and Claire.'

'And you and Claire?'

'We've gone our separate ways. It was a slow growing apart and, as these things go, as amicable as one can hope. No hard feelings and all that.'

'I'm sorry to hear it, though. And the girls?'

'We share weekends but they're old enough to look after themselves. And you? The cattle are lowing?'

'Sheep. But yes. John's at the Shepherds' Meet this afternoon.'

'How is he?'

Catrin doesn't know what to say. She feels the urge to confess but bites her tongue. 'He's getting older.'

'Aren't we all. But he's well? You're well?'

'We've been married a long time.'

Matt's sudden laughter fills the café. A few heads turn. 'I can relate,' he says. 'And Harri and Rhys?'

'Rhys's still in school. And Harri's with the Welsh Guards.'

'The Welsh Guards?'

'On tour in Iraq. Six months.'

'That must be tough,' says Matt, shifting in his chair.

'You don't approve?'

'I'm that easy to read?' He shrugs. 'It's nothing personal.'

The waitress arrives and Catrin watches Matt's easy charm as he orders tea and cake for two. The waitress leaves with crinkles at the corners of her eyes.

Matt takes her hand, gives it a squeeze. 'It really is so good to see you.' He has nice hands, she thinks. Surprisingly long, delicate fingers. Artist's hands, perhaps. A wide span – they'd be good for playing the piano. He'd easily reach beyond an octave.

The two of them stay like that for just a moment longer: her hand enclosed in his. Everything around her feels stripped away, the garish pinks and purples of the wall, the murmur of customers, the bell ringing as people walk in and out, sending waves of cold air into the room. It's just her and Matt, sitting there, something between them, his gentle touch, his kindness, something that seems impossible after all these years. And then he pulls back, the touch breaks and she feels its loss.

'You got out,' she says.

'In a way,' he replies.

'What happened to us, Matt? All those dreams we had.'

'Well, there's hoovering. And the flossing of teeth.'

She laughs. 'What?'

'Daily life has a way of getting between things, people. You know what Claire and I used to argue about? It wasn't the girls or money. It was the fact she never emptied the coffee from the cafetière. And I always left my toenail clippings on the side.'

'Toenail clippings?'

'I know. I'm repulsive. But on the lesser end of the scale, all things considered.'

The cake arrives on two small side plates. Matt picks up a fork.

'Do you remember those stupid rhymes we used to make up?' he asks.

She smiles. 'Cat and Matt were this and that?'

'Pure poetry.'

Sipping her tea, Catrin regards the man opposite her. His white, ironed shirt, blue chinos, brown leather brogues. He holds himself differently now; the mark of success in the weave of his confidence and his clothes.

'Would you let me visit the farm at some point? Take some pictures?' he says. 'I'd like to get in the right space for this residency and it would help to take my mind off my father.'

'Any time,' she says. 'How is he?'

Matt shakes his head. 'Hard to say. Could be next week or next year. Neither would surprise me.'

Their conversation darts and dives between past and present. Catrin recalls their time at Aberconwy Grammar School and how lucky they were to have gone before it changed into a comprehensive. Matt brings up their time at Bangor University, when they'd lived in a damp house next to an old bachelor with seven cats.

'Do you remember how he'd scream at them? You'd hear it through the walls,' says Matt, smiling. '*Ozymandias, get down from the curtains, this instant! Genghis Khan, you naughty pussy, leave the spider alone! Tutankhamun, if you shit in my poinsettias one more time, I'll crucify you! I'll pull your brain through your nose! I'll wrap you in muslin! I'll mummify you! I'll entomb you! Stop, I said! Stop!*'

It's been a long time since Catrin has laughed so much.

When the cake has gone and the tears have been wiped away, Matt asks for the bill and they look at one another afresh, as if all the years have fallen away.

'It's so good to see you, Cat.'

'You said,' she replies.

'Do you still play the piano?'

'Not as much as I used to,' she admits. 'Still teach it, though.'

'Strange to think how different things might have been.'

'Do you regret it?' she asks.

'No,' he replies, looking her straight in the eye. 'You?'

Catrin slides crumbs around with her fork. 'Sometimes.'

They exchange numbers before leaving.

As Catrin walks back to her car, she can still feel the heat of Matt's hand upon her own.

Driving through streets she has known for decades, Catrin understands why Matt left, feels her own wish to scrub her hands, be damned with it all. The two of them had dreamt of it: Matt with his art and her with her music. They'd move to London or New York and become famous. But then, when it came to it, Catrin had wanted to stay closer to her parents and build up a reputation at home; she had high hopes for the Eisteddfod. Matt, meanwhile, had gained a place at the Slade School of Fine Art. He went; she stayed.

Two years later Catrin met John, by chance, while playing a gig at the King's Head. In exchange for dinner and a ready supply of drinks all evening, she had stood in for a local band member who'd taken sick. By then she'd been stuck in her parents' orbit too long and had leapt at the opportunity to leave the house. It had been exciting, being part of a band, playing to an audience. And she'd seen John, sitting with a group of friends, his knee going up and down, keeping time. Afterwards, they'd got chatting and Catrin had sensed his interest, had felt herself responding. It wasn't just his looks – those broad shoulders, the dark, wavy hair – it was the way he seemed so settled, sure of who he was, what he was: a man of the land, born and bred. She can still remember her first time at the farm, seeing him with the animals, the unexpected gentleness and how a thought had come to her, startling in its clarity: *He'd make a good father.* And she had liked – still liked – that he was practical, could fix the engine of a car, didn't mind the dirt and grease of days out in the open. He was different from so many of the smooth-talking, smooth-palmed men she'd known at university, cloistered among the bookshelves, so keen to explain their theories of the world. *He is life*, she'd thought.

In those early days, he'd visit her home and listen to her at the piano, ask about the music, call her a marvel. She'd never had such an attentive audience and it was a thrill to play as he watched, something like love growing up between them.

It hadn't always been easy, though. Catrin's mother had been disappointed. *He's no good. And what do you want to go living up on a mountain for? The rest of your life spent among sheep and what-have-you; throwing away a promising career?*

Her mother was like that. Always arguing. Always thought she was right. Always thought Catrin could and would do better. She still hadn't told her about John, their cash-flow problems, the way the farm was coming apart around them. Her mother had a way of saying *I told you so* that Catrin couldn't stand.

She turns up the heating in the car and peers up at the darkening clouds. November was drawing to a close and the final month of the year was upon them. The shop windows were filled with Christmas lights, fake snow and festive stickers. It will be the first Christmas without Harri. Instead, he'll be under a foreign sun, sand beneath his feet. She'll send him another Christmas care package in a few weeks, wishing she could send so much more.

The school car park is like a game of Tetris with vehicles, teachers, parents and children darting from unexpected places as she creeps along, wedged between other frustrated drivers. Eventually she finds a space and swings the mud-splattered 4x4 into a narrow rectangle before switching off the engine. She hopes Rhys will appear soon, as she doesn't feel like making small talk with other parents. Besides, she's arranged to stop by Tim's house on the way home and she doesn't want to be late.

Her mobile buzzes. It's a text from Matt.

So good to see u. (I know, said that already) Lunch soon? x

She sits there, reading it over, wondering how to reply.

The car door opens and Rhys appears, dumping his school bag on to the back seat.

'What's the good news?' he asks, clambering in beside her.

'I bumped into an old friend in town,' she says, her smile sticking.

'That was clumsy,' says Rhys.

She smiles. 'How was school?'

'Same as ever. Shakespeare. Carbon cycles. Nazis.'

Catrin shakes her head and, catching a sudden whiff of her son's dried sweat-stink, she wrinkles her nose. 'Perhaps they could teach some hygiene while they're at it.'

Rhys lifts an arm and sniffs his armpit. His face contorts into a half-grin, half-grimace. 'Lovely,' he says.

'I'm sure the girls –'

'Smell just as bad,' says Rhys. 'Besides. Pheromones. It's all about the pheromones.'

Catrin feels her brows arching and her lips twitching into another smile. At least he was learning *something* at school. She opens their two windows a crack and starts the car. They inch out of the space, waiting for a gap between the humming vehicles. 'I've got to stop by at the Evanses' on the way back. Will you be okay doing some of your homework in the car?'

'Sure. So who'd you bump into?'

'Matthew Edevane. I went to school and university with him.'

'Didn't you date him?'

She must have mentioned it to Rhys at some point. Strange what kids will remember. 'A long time ago.'

Rhys nods and peers up at the sky as he rubs his hands against the cold. It'll be dark in under an hour and the stars will dance in the wide, dark blanket. As the car moves along the grey road, it begins to snow. Catrin shivers, reaches for the button to close the two windows.

'Does it snow in Iraq, do you think?' asks Rhys, his voice cutting through the silence.

'There are mountains in the north, so I imagine it does. Maybe not so much in the south.'

Rhys is silent for a time and Catrin allows the thrum of the engine to fill the quiet. She tries to go over what she plans to say to Tim but her thoughts keep returning to Matt.

'What would you say if I wanted to join the Army as well?' asks Rhys.

Catrin keeps her eyes on the road. 'Do you want to?'

'No, I suppose not.'

'Well, then.'

'But if I did? Hypothetically.'

'I'd say you should wait a few years before applying.'

'Harri didn't.'

'There wasn't a war going on when he did.'

'You're saying it's okay if people join the Army, so long as they don't actually do any fighting?'

'I'm saying it's a very different thing for someone who's only sixteen when there's a war on, yes.'

Rhys folds his arms. The air has thickened and Catrin reaches for the radio.

'I don't really want to listen to music,' says Rhys.

'You're not the one driving,' replies Catrin. The sound of a violin fills the car as Johann Strauss's 'Morgenblätter' dances through the air.

'Do we have to listen to this?' asks Rhys.

As they drive along the narrow roads, the trees that line the bank sway in the wind and leaves unhook from branches. Catrin spies the flash of rabbit eyes as they dart to their hiding places beneath the ground. Sometimes she wishes she could join them. She'd like to hibernate until spring, when everything comes alive.

Now, though, she lets the music carry her; imagines herself dancing.

They swing up on to Tim's driveway. The Evanses have one of the larger farms in the area and Tim has worked hard to expand it over the years; Catrin hopes he might want to continue adding to his holding. It is a desperate move and John will be furious but they are left with few options. The farm just isn't bringing in enough. As they park outside the farmhouse, a floodlight switches on and Catrin observes the signs of comfortable wealth: the new Land Rover, the hanging baskets on either side of the door filled with late-autumn foliage, and the more subtle things, too – the wooden windowpanes in mint condition, the front door freshly glossed, the driveway free of weeds. There is no sign of decay.

She unstraps her belt and turns to Rhys. 'You'll be all right staying in the car and getting on with your homework?'

'Sure,' he says, reaching behind for his backpack. He switches on the light above as Catrin gets out.

'I'll see you in a bit,' she says. She walks to the front door and presses the bell, listening for the shrill sound. She's rewarded with the sharp yaps of two dogs and the sound of a turning key. The door opens a crack and there's Martha and two black noses at her feet. 'Hello there, Catrin,' she says, opening the door for the two terriers to crowd around, sniffing. 'Tim said you'd be over; he got back from the Meet about an hour ago. I've put the kettle on. Do you want to ask Rhys in?'

'He's fine there. I won't be long. How are you keeping?'

'We're on fine form, thank you. Our Rhiannon is getting back from university next month.'

Catrin pictures the girl with her books and dimples. Rhiannon was a nice, pretty girl and, being an only child, there was the farm behind her. Catrin had always hoped Harri might see something in her but the spark never seemed to catch, though the two were friends well enough. Perhaps that was the reason. Perhaps not.

'It's her last year there, isn't it?' she says.

'It is. You know, it doesn't seem a moment since I was cradling her in my arms. They grow up too soon,' says Martha.

'I couldn't agree more.'

'And how are the boys?'

'John won't like it,' says Tim, sitting in the armchair next to a crackling fire, his legs crossed, hands around a crystal tumbler with a splash of whisky that glints in the light.

'We've got no choice,' replies Catrin, shaking her head.

'It's that bad?'

'It is.'

'I can't say I'm comfortable with the idea. Mixing money and friends rarely ends well. He'll resent it. You. Me.'

'What else can we do? The land will just go to auction; and that's after they've seized the machinery.' They both know a farm without its machines was as good as finished.

'Okay, Catrin. I'll get the guys at Bone & Payne to draw something up for us. John has to agree to it, though, and you know how he is.'

'I know. Too well.'

'I've been telling him for years he needs to straighten things out. Farming's not what it was.'

'I've tried, Tim. I can't say he's listened. Or that he will.'

'He'll have to, sooner or later.'

'He's got his father's pride,' says Catrin.

'He does. But pride doesn't put food on the table. Perhaps I shouldn't say this, Catrin, but right now you and the boys deserve better. You know he's keen on the horses?'

'I know he likes the occasional punt. You all do.'

'It may be more than that,' says Tim.

The air feels taut. Catrin looks at Tim. 'I'll talk to him,' she says.

'I'm sorry, Catrin. I'll do what I can to help.'

The logs on the fire glow and crackle. Catrin looks at her hands. 'Thank you,' she says. Her voice is quiet, smouldering in the heat and light.

Walking back to the car, Catrin spies Rhys with his head down, a frown on his face. She opens the car door and finds him tapping away at her phone.

'What the –' She snatches it from his grasp.

'I was –'

'You were *supposed* to be doing your homework!'

'I left my textbook at school and –'

'What were you doing with my phone?'

'Playing Snake. Jesus.'

'Now's really not the time, Rhys.'

'I'm sorry, okay. And what were you doing in there anyway? You've been like an hour.'

'I can't believe you're acting like this. Now of all times.'

'What's that supposed to mean?'

'It doesn't matter. We'll get home and then it'll be work, dinner, bed. Got that?'

'Heil, Mother.'

Catrin slams the door shut and starts the engine. They drive along in silence, Catrin's thoughts going around and around like a tombola drum, thinking about Harri, Rhys, John, Matt and

Tim. Bloody men. Bloody, bloody men. Why couldn't she have had daughters? Find herself a cottage and live with her dogs?

Rhys opens the drawer in front of him and pulls out a tin of boiled sweets. He puts one in his mouth. Catrin can hear it against his teeth and for the briefest moment she hates her son.

~

It is late. Rhys is upstairs, brooding in his bedroom. John is watching the news, quietly seething; furious that she has spoken to Tim, that she has offered up his land, the land of his father, the land that feels like it's tremoring beneath them. Catrin can sense it now, the uncertain world that seems to be shaking all around her; it's a miracle things don't fly from the cupboards, fall from the walls. She'd asked John about the races, whether it was more than just a flutter here and there, but he'd brushed her off, asked her why she was causing such a goddamn ruckus over nothing.

Because, she'd wanted to say, *lies and secrets cause earthquakes.* Couldn't he feel it?

Exhausted, Catrin holds Harri's letter in one hand, phone in the other. She's finally calling Alice, her mother.

'Catrin?'

She slides down on to the floor, her back against the Aga. Flint walks over, settles at her feet.

'Mum.'

She knows her mother is lonely; after Catrin's father died, she's found it harder to get out, especially as he was the one who drove the car. Her mother natters about the neighbours; there's a dispute over someone's tree that's had half its branches lopped off. Catrin lets Alice rattle through the local gossip and, once she's run out of steam, mentions Harri's letter.

'Well, what are you waiting for?' says Alice.

Catrin reads it slowly and clearly. She imagines Harri sitting at one of the mess tables, biro in hand. She hears his voice as she reads. Her mother doesn't interrupt once.

Give Flint a hug from me, won't you? Llawer o gariad, Harri.

'He sounds like he's keeping busy.'

It's such a generic statement that Catrin almost laughs. 'I just want him home,' she says.

'Oh, love,' says Alice. 'He'll be with you soon.'

'I know,' replies Catrin. 'I know.' She ends the call and then reaches over to her old dog and gives him a hug – for Harri, and for herself.

As Flint nuzzles against her, she pulls out her mobile from the pocket of her jeans, scrolls through the messages and taps out her reply to Matt.

December

Iraq Body Count: 1,129

379. In a note to his No. 10 staff dated 12 December, Mr Blair commented that the situation in Iraq was 'worrying'.[*] Iraqiisation was not yielding the looked-for progress; the insurgent attacks were continuing far beyond what was manageable; there was a risk that insufficient Sunni Arabs would participate in the election; life in Basra had not sufficiently improved; and reconstruction remained a problem.

— *The Report of the Iraq Inquiry*, Volume VII, Section 9.3

[*] Note Blair, 12 December 2004, 'Iraq'.

4

John raises the rifle, pauses as he aligns the scope with the target and holds his breath so that his hands and sight are steady. In the space of half a heartbeat he pulls the trigger. The rabbit collapses to the ground, its feet kicking out as nerves shoot along the length of its legs. It's John's eighth kill of the morning and it's a good clean shot and he feels a cold satisfaction in his skill; this, at least, is something he can do, and do well.

The mountain air is cold and wet, gathering in his lungs, in the gaps between his clothes, between one thread and another. His breath steams before him and he wheezes a little and the noise of it reminds him of his own father. He pushes the thought away. Twilight is just beginning to spread across the rolling hills and between patches of fog; he can see the sheep grazing against the damp green. Clad in a thick Barbour coat, woolly hat, gloves and mud-splattered gumboots, he moves on, his feet sinking into the soft grass, wet with the recent rain. The land is swollen and the sky is heavy. This is the way things have always been around here, with the living pressed between the cold earth and dark sky.

Striding forward, John finds his kill. The rabbit lies lifeless on the ground, the eyes vacant and bloody. He removes his gloves and picks up the animal by the ears. With his free hand he slides his thumb down its body in order to expel the urine, cold skin against warm fur. Next, he wraps it in a plastic bag, ties the two handles into a knot, takes off his large backpack and places the package inside. After wiping his hands clean on the grass, he slips on the backpack and both his gloves; stretching, he feels the weight of the load pressing against him as he tightens the straps of the pack around his waist. Marching on, rifle broken and resting in the crook of his elbow, John scans the land, listening to the murder of crows that looms in the distant copse. They caw loudly, muttering among themselves. He shakes his head in frustration; he'll have to clear the birds come spring or they'll multiply, dark beaks and talons menacing the lambs from above. They'll be back the following year, though, the bastards.

He looks out at the land. His land. His father's land and his taid's. One day it'll belong to his boys, which is why he cannot accept what Catrin has done, even though there's a voice telling him it would be the easiest thing in the world. To sell up. Sell out.

But no. He loves Tim like a brother but the land is not for him or for anyone else. The land is sacred and it's for Harri and Rhys. Even with the creditors knocking on the door, he knows he'll find a way, no matter what.

He can't shake the picture of Catrin holding the damn letter from the bank and asking him if that was all, if there was anything else she ought to be aware of. And he'd stood there like a boulder and said yes, that was all. He'd lied to her face and she'd accepted his word like she always did because deep down she thought him a good man, and because she'd put her trust in him – many years ago, when they'd made their vows. And he'd been a good man once, but then the damn disease had struck at the animals and he'd taken to the races and the machines and soon he couldn't stop; he just couldn't. Money had a way of disappearing. Abracadabra. Alakazam.

The truth is that there are other credit cards, other companies, other debts. Soon enough they'll come calling as well. He's already keeping an eye on the post, waiting for the letters, ready to squirrel them away from Catrin's accusing eye.

But then what? Loans to pay loans? Perhaps he'll be forced to sell after all; his father's legacy and his boys' bequest gone like frost in the early sun.

Bastards, all of them. And he was the worst of the lot.

His feet sink into the soil. The dead rabbits weigh him down.

John reaches the quad bike, secures the backpack with the bungee cords and then swings a leg over the seat and switches on the engine, listening to the roar as he presses down on the throttle, sensing the thrum of speed. The vehicle hugs the land as it slopes and John keeps his head high as if he were galloping, the wind whipping past his ears, eyes and nose streaming in the cold while he surveys the curve of the mountain leading to the valley. He follows the path through the fields towards the farmhouse, which is nestled among the large barn, stables and kennel. Further to the right is the lake and beyond that are the woods where Catrin roams with the dogs each morning. The mist is clearing and the lake catches the light so it looks silver. He'd taught Harri the basics of fly-fishing in that lake. He remembers sitting by the bank, showing him what to do with the fly line, leader and tippet; pointing at the flies, nymphs and streamers, explaining why they were different and when to use them. And John remembers standing by Harri, no older than seven or eight, the two of them with their feet at the edge of the lake, casting out, arms going back and forth, back and forth, the sounds of the lines zipping through the air.

At length, he approaches the yard, slowing the vibrating vehicle beneath him, and studies the new car parked next to his own. He's seen it a few times now: it belongs to Catrin's old schoolfriend Matthew Edevane. Catrin had invited him up to take some photographs; she said he wanted to do a portrait of farm life before he set off for Snowdonia to do something or other. John knows there's history between them, although it goes back a long way; Catrin has never said much about it and he hasn't asked but he knows enough to find the man's presence like sandpaper to the skin.

Rubbing the cold from his fingers, John picks up a heavy diesel canister that sits against one of the outbuilding walls and funnels it into the quad bike as it cools. He breathes deeply, enjoying the mixture of machine and animal smell. He's always liked the stink of diesel. A little of it splashes on to his gloves, the red dye seeping into the fabric, and he brushes at it until it disappears – not that he has anything to hide. He's always been careful when it comes to using the stuff, knowing how easy it is to put the wrong fuel in the wrong machine and have inspectors knocking on the door, issuing writs and warrants and what-have-you. John was guilty of plenty of things but he wasn't a crook, didn't go in for petty fraud. And he well remembers the incident with Michael Horsefield some ten years ago. The man was caught selling red diesel at near-cost, mainly to the Travellers who would come to the area in the spring. He'd made a tidy profit, so it was said – until someone grassed – and then the authorities came down like a sledgehammer, seizing his farm equipment and levying a hefty fine. They didn't approach the gypsies, though, the cowards. Authorities were always like that, went for the easy targets, the low-hanging fruit; meanwhile millionaires in ivory towers got away with murder.

Untying the backpack and hoisting it over his shoulder, John walks out into the yard. He can hear the hens clucking, which means Catrin or Rhys must have just scattered their feed. He peers over the doors of the two stables to see if the hay has been put out for the horses but both are empty. The horses stand watching him, long lashes blinking.

He enters the kennel and smiles when the dogs leap up. At the far end, the two large chest freezers hum and, lifting the lid of one, he begins to transfer the dead rabbits into the cold, placing each sealed body against the other, stacking them tight, cousin against cousin. The dogs aren't fussy; they eat the rabbits whole, fur and all. As he crams in each one, he recalls the support package from the Army that had contained brief information about the repatriation of the dead; morbidly curious, John had gone online and read detailed accounts about the process of returning a human corpse to its home country.

Its? Strange, how quickly the dead become things.

It is a difficult task, what with all the documents to be signed and the body needing to be embalmed. The casket has to be lined with zinc so that it can pass through the security checkpoints at the airport. Yes, John remembers reading about all this, years ago, when it did not seem to matter. A time when the idea of his son joining the Army had been something he had slowly come to accept as a temporary departure, although three years seemed like a long time for his son to find his feet. No, he hadn't been happy about it but he'd given his signature in the end, hadn't he? And then Harri had done exactly what he'd said he would: gone and got the scholarship, one of a hundred, been awarded his bursary for university. John had to admit, he'd been proud. It was the start of the millennium and things had seemed so positive. And then the unthinkable happened: the Twin Towers came down and the country went to war. Harri got his degree, spent his year at Sandhurst, became an officer, and by then the US and the UK had moved from Afghanistan to Iraq. And the Army demanded its blood: three years in return for those sweet thousands. And now his son, the boy he has raised, the boy he loves, is in a foreign land, where the threat is unrelenting, where the scratches of life have become so much more dangerous, so much more horrifying, and they cannot be kissed better by his da or his mam.

It has been over two weeks since they last heard from Harri but he must be alive because no one has come from his regiment. No one has driven here in the early hours of the morning, their expressions flat as marshland. No one has called. But John is awake before dawn each day, listening for the sound of tyres on the gravel outside their house – harbingers of the worst kind of news a parent can receive.

In this mood, with the weight of Harri on his thoughts, John decides to avoid the farmhouse. He's not ready to see Catrin or Matt, this man who once had his wife's affections. Instead, he heads to the lake and kicks a stone, watching it bounce at one angle and then another before landing on a tuft of grass by the gate that leads down towards the still water of the lake. The rocks and the mountains will outlast them all; perhaps there was something in that. And, yet, how pointless it made the whole business of war seem. How brief and pathetic.

The lake is dark and deep, with thrushes circling the edges like a crown. Bubbles rise up here and there. John casts his mind back to when he and the two boys had bought dozens of small fish from an aquatic centre, bringing them to the farm in large bags of clear water that they'd dangled in the lake, allowing the slim silver bodies to become familiar with their new home. After a short while, John had reached down with a knife and slit the bags open and the fish had rushed into freedom, their bright scales quickly disappearing into the depths. He remembers Rhys – four or five at the time – and his little squeal of happiness; the sound had made John's heart light, marvelling at how small a thing could bring such joy.

Over time, the fish had grown and multiplied, and soon they became sport. It wasn't the same as fishing in a river, knee-deep in water, waders pulled up tight, the whisper of current around you, but it served its purpose. The three of them had spent hours together, in companionable quiet, sending their lines out. To begin with, Rhys was more hindrance than help but it wasn't long before he also had the knack of it, seemed to enjoy the weave of motion followed by the silence and stillness.

John had liked seeing his boys working in tandem, nets and rods, watching the way they depended on one another.

It was a good few years before the heron arrived, standing on the edge of the island, its long beak angled down. A skittish thing, much like the moorhens, up and away the moment it heard or saw something like danger. It was a skilled hunter. John had watched as it took fish after fish, tails flapping uselessly in the grip of the bird's yellow-tinted bill. He'd done his best with three plastic herons, two on the perimeter, and even one on the island; he'd stripped down and swum out, hammering the things into the ground. They were said to be solitary birds and, for a few weeks, there were no haunting shadows from the sky. And then there it was again, supping each morning.

At one point, John had almost taken the rifle to it but Catrin hadn't been happy with the idea. She'd even quoted the law at him. 1981. For a farmer's wife, she had a lot of the town still in her. And so the fish were eaten, one by one, until there were none left and the heron moved on.

He'd like to replace those fish – likes the thought of standing there with Harri and Rhys, the three casting their lines once again.

Picking up the stone he'd kicked just moments ago, he skims it across the lake, low and fast, watching as it bounces one, two, three times, before disappearing from view, leaving a spread of ripples. Turning back, John walks up the path towards the farmhouse, a shiver in his step. His leg aches. He knows it will snow tonight. Listening to the ewes in the fields, he wonders if he should bring some of them further down.

John pauses at the door of the farmhouse, feeling a peculiar reluctance to step inside. Before he can turn away, the door opens and he's suddenly face to face with Catrin, who looks surprised to see him.

'John,' she says. Catrin glances behind her as another figure looms up. Matthew.

'Bore da,' says John. He offers his hand. Matthew, he thinks, is a handsome type but he doesn't look like the sort who appreciates mud. 'You'll want to change your shoes.'

'That's what Cat said,' replies Matthew, smiling. A large camera dangles around his neck. 'She's given me a pair of boots.'

Cat? No one calls her that. John peers round the two of them and sees Rhys's gumboots ready and waiting.

'I hope you don't mind my taking a few snaps,' says Matthew.

'Fine. But not in the house.' John doesn't know why he says this but now it's there in the open and he can't take the words back.

'I understand,' says Matthew.

John gives a tight smile, wondering what there was to understand exactly. Just as he's about to give some more advice about shutting gates, there's a sound of crunching gravel behind him and the young farmhand Simon appears.

'Morning, all,' he says. 'John, I've seen a stray wandering out on top; thought I'd better come find you so we can bring her down.'

'Good lad,' says John. Damn things were always getting themselves lost and lonely. 'We'll take out the quad; can you get one of the dogs from the kennel?'

He turns back to Catrin and Matthew. His wife is smiling and John wonders when he has last seen her like that. 'Well, then,' he says. 'Nice to see you.'

∾

John revs up the engine of the quad and Simon slides on to the seat behind him. They've attached the trailer, which Lola now occupies, her tongue hanging between her teeth. He can feel the warmth of Simon behind him. The engine leaps into life and John reverses it out of the barn. He glances back at his wife and Matthew.

'Have you heard from Harri recently?' asks Simon.

'Not for some time,' replies John.

Earlier in the morning he'd switched on the TV and the news had shown a burning vehicle outside the Green Zone, an area that should have been safe, an agreed off-limits space. Thirteen dead. But it was war, wasn't it? Who could say what the rules were when it was a matter of life and death and simmering hatreds? Still, it was impossible not to think of Harri, even though he wasn't anywhere near the car bomb and its wreckage. Small mercies.

The wind picks up. A scattering of leaves falls from the quivering branches. John eyes the farmhouse. The trees have been shedding thick and fast in recent weeks and the gutters need clearing, the waterways getting clogged with soggy red matter.

'John?'

'Sorry, Simon. I was away with the fairies.'

Simon's mouth opens briefly, then closes. There's a hint of something there, a smile maybe, but the lad holds his tongue.

'Shall we?' says John, turning the key, eager to be off. What was that poem Catrin likes? No time to stand and stare at sheep and cows? Damn bloody right.

The quad bike pulls forward, the tyres gripping the cold, hard ground. At each of the gates, Simon hops off. John hates the inconvenience of gates but God forbid anyone leaves one open.

'Did I ever tell you about Old Henry?' John shouts.

'Henry Lewis?'

It was some years ago. The old boy had taken his quad and chased after a group of ramblers who'd gone a mile, maybe more, up one of the hills. He had a shotgun on his lap, telling them in no uncertain terms that they'd left a gate open down below. There was no livestock about at the time but it was the principle of the thing, so said Henry. And it was a matter of respect. Well, they'd tried to reason with Henry but he'd just sat there, on his bike, shotgun in his lap, until one of the fellas agreed to walk down, close the gate and walk all the way back up. Henry didn't offer the fella a lift – let it be a lesson to them. There was no arguing with Old Henry. They'd complained, of course, and a pot-bellied man from the local council came to give him a slap on the wrist. Old Henry had sat there at the kitchen table, cleaning the shotgun and saying nothing, until the man ran out of words and returned to the safety of his square, air-conditioned office.

'Seems about right,' says Simon.

In the lower fells, the sheep look content as can be. John and Simon talk through the need to check their feet this week, a task John generally enjoys; he always feels like he gets to know his sheep a little better around this time, when they were closer to the farm and he was with them each day. That, and lambing season, though spring was some way off and pray God Harri would be home by then to lend a hand. The lad will be missing Christmas this year, which gives John a feeling he can't quite make out. Rhys was around, though, and the boy was usually willing.

The ewes stare at them as they pass by, the backs of the ladies stained by the red raddle from the rams. Fine rams they'd been, working with a real appetite, going from one to the next, sniffing the vulvas, the ladies urinating, the rams snuffling at their watery offering, curling their lips lustfully, nudging them with a foreleg until they stood for them, their heads turning to the ram as if to say, well, what are you waiting for.

He'd known a few girls like that, before he'd met Catrin, as eager for it as he was. He'd never forget Linda Boyle. She went around some, that was fair to say. Disgraced her parents, who were all kinds of conservative. Had to go on a holiday to visit relatives for a few weeks, so they said. Still, he'd heard she was happily married with kids of her own. Sex was nothing to be ashamed about. Not having sex, now that was the unnatural thing, though he might as well be the Pope when it came to Catrin. He couldn't remember the last time they'd done it.

'You got a girl yet, Simon?' he shouts.

'No,' replies Simon, a shake of his head.

'Well,' he says, 'plenty of time yet.' He feels for the lad, an only child with a father too sick to stand; John knows the boy's da – a good sort by all accounts, a lifelong man of the land who'd been honest in all his dealings. And he'd raised his son to be the same.

As they climb higher, the wind picks up and John hunches his shoulders, lowers the gear as the incline increases. The trailer rattles behind him. Eventually they reach a suitable vantage point and look about for the stray ewe. John wonders how the damn thing has managed to evade being seen for so long. Even with the land as endless and rolling as it is, it's usually easy enough to see the white marks against the dull ground. But there is always one, isn't there? Ninjas, Rhys calls them. Managed to blend into the mountainside and would emerge when you least expected it. And so it is now, the ewe appearing suddenly from behind a small fold on the terrain. John whistles and the dog leaps out of the trailer. Simon and John climb off the quad. Simon walks to the back of the trailer, slides the bolt across and brings down the ramp. John sends the dog chasing after her quarry. Lola works quickly, needing little instruction, an old hand who knows what's what. The ewe is unusually stubborn but gradually works her way towards the trailer. She seems to look John up and down, as if she knows he's the cause of her rude disturbance, before clattering forward up the ramp, which Simon lifts and bolts shut.

'Mission accomplished,' says Simon, smiling.

John clambers back on to the quad. His hands pause on the key. 'Catrin says you've written to Harri?'

'A few times.'

John nods. 'You're a good lad, Simon.'

He's about to get going when his mobile starts to vibrate. It's Mike.

'John!' the voice rasps and John can almost smell the tobacco through the phone as details come through quick as gunfire: 'Tip of a lifetime – but you'll have to be fast – Lingfield Park – tomorrow – noon. Smithson runs two but it's going around the red-hot favourite has been coughing for two weeks and hasn't been pleasing at home. McKay rides him, but The Joker is the fancied one and the stable is going for a touch. He put two lengths on the favourite in their last piece of work. He's eighteen to one but don't let that put you off, and the price will soon be gone once word gets round. You'll need to move ASAP.'

~

Money. Raising the glass of water to his lips, John chugs down water. He needs money. He can feel the heat of his body, the way his clothes stick to his skin. There's dirt under his nails. He needs to shave. And he needs to find some damn money. He pops two tablets from their foil and slugs them back with more water. His leg is aching. He knows he should see a doctor but there are a lot of things he should be doing. And a lot he shouldn't.

Catrin's still out with Matthew and so he climbs the stairs, ignoring the throb in his leg, and hurries to the bookcase. He slides out *Miller's Antiques*, picturing the stash of money, his fingers trembling. Catrin will kill him – but he'll pay her back. Course he will. He just needs something to tide him over. He pulls off the elastic band binding the covers and opens the book.

The money's gone.

John slaps the book shut and begins pawing through other hardbacks. Where would she have put it? He rustles spines, flips covers, shakes volume after volume. Nothing. He hurries to the bathroom and checks the cabinet under the sink, goes through the small grey bag that contains her lady things. Again, nothing. To the bedroom. Her bedside cupboard, under the bed, in the shoe boxes in the wardrobe, the socks, beneath her folded jumpers, inside pockets. Still, nothing! All he can think about are those odds. Eighteen to one.

Downstairs, he rootles through the cupboards in the kitchen, opening cannisters and boxes while Flint stares at him reproachfully. As he opens an old tin of Bisto, he keeps one eye on the window, worrying that Catrin will be back with Matthew at any moment. The kitchen yields nothing. She must have at least five hundred. At those odds, he'd be looking at a return of nine thousand. Nine thousand! Could he ring her? But she'd never agree.

The last place he searches is Catrin's piano. He knows it's Catrin's special place, that he's trespassing on hallowed ground. He looks at the polished wood, the small stool tucked underneath. She tried to teach him once but he never got the knack of it. Fat fingers and thin on patience.

He lifts the lid of the seat. Nothing. The lid of the piano. Still, nothing.

Feeling the opportunity passing by, John bites his lip.

There was the clock. The one in the spare bedroom on the mantelpiece over the fire. It had been his mother's and he knows it's worth something. He could pawn it; buy it back at a later date.

The door of the guest bedroom creaks open and John hears his father's voice: *Needs some oil, that does.* His father had said that about almost everything, from tractor engines to beating hearts.

The clock sits on the mantelpiece above the fireplace, opposite the bed. It's a squat, solid Victorian piece. The gold-rimmed face is set in green marble, two classical columns framing the device. Long hands point to Roman numerals. The wind-up keys are taped behind it.

He lifts the clock carefully and is surprised by the weight. He puts it down on the bed. There is a large rectangular space on the mantelpiece where it has been resting; a perfect dust outline. He takes his sleeve, wipes along the top, lifting the other objects – the candlesticks, two ornaments – and then rearranges these so the gaping hole disappears. He wonders if Catrin will notice and what he'll say if she asks. But it won't come to that. Mike was usually on the money.

Clock in arms, John hurries back down the stairs, listening for the sound of Catrin or anyone else who might come upon him, red-handed; caught in the act.

He'll take it to Benny's.

As he drives past Matthew's shiny silver car, he notices with distaste the flashy, personalized number plate. He imagines the two of them, Catrin and Matthew, arm in arm beneath the hardening sky. He wonders what they're up to, if they're taking their fill of the land and the grazing animals; if they regard the endless rolling hills, or if their vision is arrested, each of them reflected in the eyes of the other.

Benny offers him one twenty, which is less than John is expecting but it's still over two grand if everything comes off good. The pawnbroker sits there in his warm shop, dressed in his green cardigan, smiling – the look of a man who doesn't need to make money but knows he will. While he waits for Benny to count out the notes, John notices the newspaper on the counter. The front headline has a quote from George Bush saying he'll pursue Saddam to the ends of the Earth. Underneath is a cartoon of the President and a speech bubble filled with the logos of oil corporations: Shell, BP, ExxonMobil, Amoco.

Now, as he walks along the street with cash in his pocket, he pictures The Joker, McKay in the stirrups, the thunder of hooves on the ground, the finish line in the distance, getting closer and closer, the horse pulling forward into the home straight. He imagines the horse breaking away into the lead, pictures the steam from its nostrils, the froth at the bit, the pounding of its heart, the tension in the muscles of its legs, the ground being swallowed up, compressed by those four lucky hooves and there, the finish line, head dipped forward, victory within sight. John's own pace picks up and he portions out the money in his mind, again totting up the take-home. It's a tidy sum.

After getting barred from Win365 earlier in the month, he's forced to find an alternative chain in town. Two men stand outside the bookies and one of them sips from a can. Their eyes are dull, lips flat. They glance his way as he passes by, opening the door. It's warmer than the pawn shop and John unzips his coat. He touches a hand to his eye; the bruising has almost faded. John moves over to the papers on the walls, finds the upcoming fixtures and traces his forefinger down the options until he finds what he's looking for: Lingfield Park, 14 December at noon, The Joker. The odds have already started to move, but not much: 16/1. Goddamn, that would be a tidy sum. He scribbles his request on the slip and walks over to the counter. He recognizes the cashier on the left.

'Diolch,' says John.

The man takes the slip, scans the writing, taps the keys. John passes over the cash and is given the receipt. His hands tremble. He feels as if he's already won and the rush, the excitement, of placing that much money with the potential of the win gives him the sweats.

Outside, John wipes the clamminess on his jeans. He stands

there, dreaming of all the things he can do with two thousand pounds. He'll be able to replace Catrin's teaching money that she used back in November to pay wages. He'll have enough for Simon for the next few months, no doubt. And he might even be able to pay off some of the debt and cards Catrin doesn't know of. He would work out a plan. Who knows, he might even get Rhys a pup for Christmas.

He buys a sausage roll and tea at a café nearby and watches as darkness descends and the streetlights come on. His mind turns over the newspaper headline he'd seen in Benny's. He thinks about oil, the barrels of it on the tankers, the rivers of it running through the pipelines, the lakes of it beneath the ground. That's why Harri is out there while those in power are prepared to rip apart the seams of a country and its people, just to dip their goddamn paws in the filthy stuff.

John licks his fingers clean and wipes them on the scratchy paper napkin.

He thinks about the farm and his wife, about Black 22 and Red 23.

This time, he thinks, this time he'll win.

392. The Cabinet Office described a JIC paper on Iraqiisation issued on 15 December as 'grim'. It described 'high levels of dependency on the MNF-I until 2006', 'serious structural weaknesses within the ISF' and 'an assistance programme that, while making progress, will take considerably more time to deliver significant impact'. By contrast, the MOD's paper had suggested that the Petraeus Plan would deliver, given time.

– *The Report of the Iraq Inquiry*, Volume VII, Section 9.3

5

Catrin sits on the toilet with her knickers around her knees and thinks about Matt. She's surprised by how easy it is to compartmentalize, to separate the woman she is at home from the woman she is with him. She's surprised how easy it is to lie to John and she's surprised by how little she cares. She's surprised by how much she enjoys not just Matt's company but also his body.

They've only been seeing each other for a few weeks and already they've had sex more times than she can count on two hands. The first time was in the barn, of all places. Like animals. Matt's hot breath in her ear telling her how *fucking beautiful* she was beneath him. She hadn't felt so electric in years. After the first time, they had agreed to meet elsewhere – John would kill Matt if he ever found out and, besides, it made things easier. They could enjoy their time together if they didn't have to worry about discovery. And there was so much to enjoy! Matt was happy to do things that John had never shown much interest in . . . He was obsessed with turning her on, loved using his tongue, and the things he could do with his fingers!

Oh, gods, why was she so obsessed with his fingers? Was it a fetish? Did she have a finger fetish? Is *that* what it was?

Catrin wipes and flushes, picturing Matt with a hand against her cheek, the other trailing down her abdomen, tousling her pubic hair. His long, beautiful fingers playing upon her body. His fingers . . . so different from John's.

She washes her hands, splashes water on her face. She is about to join Rhys in the car and within the next hour or so they'll be at her mother's. Now is not the time to be wondering if she has a finger fetish. That can wait until tomorrow afternoon, when she'll be seeing Matt again. Until then: compartmentalize.

Downstairs she finds John in the kitchen making his tea, humming to himself. His clothes and hair are wet from the recent rain. He turns and smiles. The bruising around his eye has at last faded and for the past four days he's seemed more like his old self. He says he's restructured the debt with the bank, that he's settled the outstanding wages for the farmhands they'd let go, and also paid the remaining suppliers. He's even bought some more fish for the lake. It would seem like a miracle but she'd seen his jottings in the *Racing Post* with today's races circled in black biro: Fontwell Park, Uttoxeter and Wolverhampton. Still, he'd won, hadn't he?

'We'll be back just after lunch,' she says. 'Soup's in the fridge. Fresh bread on the side.'

'Thanks,' replies John. He walks over, a swagger in his step. He pauses as he reaches her. 'You smell different.'

'New shampoo,' she says.

∼

Catrin fishes out a dog biscuit from her Barbour jacket. She throws it into the boot with Flint. He sniffs around and then gobbles up the treat before lying down. She reaches forward, tousles his silky soft ears, wondering why everything must grow old.

Rhys, meanwhile, has hopped into the driver's seat.

'Scoot,' she says.

'Just to the end of the drive?' says Rhys. 'Da lets me.'

The boy's been driving on the farm for years and Catrin knows he's itching to turn seventeen and take his test, to have the freedom of the roads.

'To the end of the driveway. Then we swap.'

She climbs into the passenger side and looks at Rhys, who gives the thumbs-up. He starts the engine, makes a performance of checking the mirrors.

'Rhys,' she says. 'It's not a pantomime.'

They pull out of the yard. The lad has one hand on the wheel, the other on the gear stick.

'Do you think they'll get away with it?' asks Rhys.

'Concentrate for a moment, will you?' says Catrin. He's become obsessed with the bank robbery in Belfast that was plastered over the news a few days ago. More than twenty million pounds stolen in a single swoop. 'It's unlikely,' she continues, keeping an eye on the road ahead. 'You can't easily hide that sort of money.'

'Unless you can afford tax advisers?'

'You're too young to be so cynical, Rhys.'

They pass through the gates and he moves up a gear. 'Are you sure we'll be back in time for Molly's birthday drinks tonight?' he asks.

'We'll do our best,' says Catrin. She looks at Rhys and smiles.

'What?' he says.

They switch seats and Catrin drives along Pendle Way, passing the many grey pebble-dashed houses with their red-and-blue doors and square patches of garden. The rain has followed them and comes down in buckets. The wipers beat back and forth. Christmas has arrived and with it a week of foul weather. The farm has been turned into a mud-bath and John has been working day and night to bring the ewes down to shelter, their thick coats heavy with damp.

'How long has Nan lived here?' asks Rhys.

'Over thirty years,' she replies. 'I was about fifteen when we moved.'

'Did you like living here?'

'On the whole, yes.'

As she turns right on to Singleton Avenue, Catrin smiles. Flint stands up and shakes his head.

'Singleton Avenue,' she says. 'My friends used to joke about that.'

'And then you met Matt,' says Rhys, as casually as if he were talking about a ram at an auction.

'A long time ago,' says Catrin. She peers at the house. Home, in its own way, even though she no longer lives here. There was a sense of order to the place – her mother had always been house-proud – something that simply wasn't possible on a farm. The dust, mud and muck found their way in, no matter how often you scrubbed and hoovered and mopped.

'Da says you were together for two years.'

'Yes, well. I was very young.'

'Da said he proposed to you.'

She wonders what else John might have said. 'I was twenty. Not much younger than Harri. It wasn't serious.'

'Why did you break up?'

'We went our separate ways, I suppose. He went down to London.'

The old dog sneezes against the back window and releases another whine.

'All right, Flint,' repeats Catrin as they pull up on to the drive. She grabs her hat and coat from the back seat.

'Will you bring the dog in? I'll get the door.'

Catrin rings the bell and turns to see Flint hurrying off to the corner of the front garden, stretching out his two legs and releasing his bladder in a large puddle near a rosebush. He no longer has the strength to lift a leg and has decided to piddle like a puppy.

Rhys joins her at the door, just as it opens. Alice must have been waiting; she'd always been a bit of a curtain-twitcher.

'Mum,' says Catrin, stepping in. Flint barges past, happy to be out of the rain.

'He'll traipse his dirty paws through. Put him in the conservatory. And take your shoes off.'

'Nice to see you, too, Mum.'

'Yes, well, you're all soggy, aren't you?'

'Got the kettle on?'

'What am I, a heathen?'

'Something like that.'

'Worse,' says Rhys with a grin. 'You're English.'

'Get on with you!' replies Alice.

They kiss and hug and Alice looks Rhys up and down and then beams. While she's never taken to John, she's always adored her two grandchildren.

'I know I say it every time I see you, Rhys, but you must have grown at least a foot! And what a handsome lad you are!'

They wander through into the kitchen and Catrin finds herself relaxing at the familiarity of everything. There is a comfort in the constancy of it all. The two table lamps in the hallway with their enormous pink shades, the Meissen figurines underneath that were always removed when the boys were young, in case they knocked them over while running and leaping about. There are the small rows of collectables from the magazines. The portraits of Mozart, Beethoven and Chopin; the music scores in neat stacks resting on almost every available surface.

Catrin walks through into the conservatory, where Flint is already lapping up water from a bowl. His dog bed is at the end by the door. The rain comes down on the glass, the sound like galloping horses.

'I brought you something,' says Catrin, returning to the kitchen. 'Rhys, have you got it?' He hands her the paper bag and Catrin, in turn, offers it to her mum, placing it on her upturned palms. Fingers, now riddled with arthritis, stretch out.

'Oh, lovely,' says Alice, opening her eyes and peering into the bag. 'A walking stick. Yet more evidence of my infirmity and impending doom. Thank you, daughter of mine.'

'I thought you'd like it. It's better than that big weapon-like thing you use. See how light it is? And it's got roses on it and folds nice and neat. Perfect for getting about.'

'I love it. Really, I do.' Catrin isn't entirely convinced but then it was never easy to tell what her mother was thinking, unless she wanted you to know – and then you really knew, whether you wanted to or not.

'Well, then, the kettle's all ready, what are you waiting for? I want to hear what's been going on. And you, too, Rhys. Take a seat, dear. We can be busy bodies in a bit, can't we? How is Harri?'

Before Catrin can reply, her mother is talking again.

'I'm not convinced by this Blair–Bush nonsense. Oil and money. You see if I'm right.'

Catrin shakes her head. 'Perhaps we can skip the politics for today?'

'You don't think it matters? You think it's okay that your son is out there because some knucklehead wants to sit on the lap of the American President? What's he doing? Sucking his little . . .' She holds up her pinkie and wiggles it. The old woman looks at Rhys, who's trying to hide his smile behind a hand. 'I'm sorry, dear, but your mother has always been too accommodating.'

'We've been over this,' says Catrin. 'And I didn't drive here to be lectured.'

'I just find it impossible,' says Alice, '*not* to be furious about the whole thing. He's a precious boy and the idea that he's among all those poor devils who probably have no idea what the Americans are doing there in the first place –'

'Mum, really. Please.'

'How about you, Rhys? Are you going to join the Army or are you going to do something sensible?'

'Rhys has got his GCSEs next summer,' says Catrin. 'And then he'll need to take his driving test.'

'And I'm sure Rhys can answer for himself.'

Rhys sits half off his chair like he's looking for a quick escape. 'I'm not sure,' he says. 'I guess I'll probably work the farm, like Da.'

'You guess? What do you mean, you guess? You can't go around guessing, Rhys. That's no way to live. You might as well roll some dice. One: work the farm. Two: become a librarian. Three: join Greenpeace. Four: train as a lobotomist. Five: write erotica on the internet. Six: start a cult and have twelve wives and twenty-six-point-nine children.'

'Mum, please give it a rest.'

'Give it a rest? I'll be dead in a few years, what do I want to give it a rest for? Don't pout like that, Catrin, it's not an attractive look.'

'Why must you *always* be so combative?' says Catrin. She doesn't want to argue, especially with Rhys here, but she can't help it – the day is already feeling too long.

'Combative? I didn't raise you to be a wallflower, Catrin. Sticks and stones, remember. Just ask Harri. I'm sure he'd be the first to tell you that words are just so much air.'

'Mum.'

'All I'm saying is the world is a tough old place and you've got to work hard and be resilient. Now listen, Rhys, dear. There are three boxes in the attic – labelled FARM in black pen on the sides – why don't you bring them down and put them in the car for us?'

Once Rhys has escaped, Alice turns her attention back to her daughter.

'What's happened?'

Catrin's surprised by the question. 'What do you mean?'

'I'm your mother. I can tell when something is wrong.'

Catrin knows what her mother is doing. Asking questions to fill up the space and time so she won't have to talk about herself. Won't have to talk about the stairs, the visits to the doctors, the arthritis in her hands, the loneliness of the house.

'I'm worried about Harri.'

'I'm sorry, Catrin. It's difficult, I know,' says Alice, keeping her eyes on her daughter, letting the moment hang, suspended in the grey space of silence. And then she reaches across the table, places her palm gently over her daughter's own hand, her old arthritic fingers holding on to all that's precious. 'There's something else, though, isn't there?'

Catrin wonders what she should tell her mother. The old woman will ferret it out of her one day, she knows. But not today.

'Nothing,' she says. 'I've just been sleeping poorly.'

'You know, after you disappeared to university, I sometimes slept in your bed? Much more room not having your father sharing the mattress. No snoring, no wriggling, no toilet trips throughout the night. Not that I blamed your father for that, of course. We all have our problems when age creeps up on us. Though, in his case, it was less creeping and more like a great leap of a thing. But there it is. I do miss him, you know. You'll think I'm mad but when I come down in the morning he's sometimes there, sitting in the armchair reading his newspaper.' Alice stops a moment, her eyes lingering on some invisible space in the conservatory next door.

'I'm sorry, Mum,' says Catrin. There's something dreadful about seeing her mother like this, suddenly so vulnerable.

'It's not your fault. It happens to all of us.' The old woman tightens her grip on her daughter's hand. 'You can tell me anything, you know.'

Rhys appears in the doorway, looking flushed. 'Everything's in the back.' He looks at his watch and gives Catrin a meaningful look.

'We ought to get going soon,' says Catrin. 'I promised Rhys I'd get him back for a party.'

'Heavens, I miss those!' says Alice. 'Well, perhaps before you do, you could play for me? I'd like to hear how the old piano sounds. I've not listened to her for quite some time, given these crummy old hands of mine. They're more like claws, these days. Please, dear. Just the one song.'

Catrin turns to Rhys, who shrugs. Who can deny an old, lonely woman such a simple request?

'Anything in mind?'

'Chopin,' says her mother. 'Something relaxing – a nocturne?'

The trio wander into the living room, where a large grand piano stands, the three wheels on wooden cups. An antique Bösendorfer. It's a beautiful instrument and certainly worth a small fortune. Catrin takes a seat on the stool, adjusting the height a few inches, feels for the pedals at her feet while her mother sorts through a box of sheet music. Lifting the polished mahogany lid, Catrin lets her fingers slide along a few black and white keys.

'Don't sit there smiling. Warm her up,' says Alice, walking over, sheafs of paper in hand.

Catrin goes through a couple of Hanon Exercises, conscious of her mother studying her hands, her posture, the very rhythm of her body, while ears, trained over decades, catch the rise and fall of notes. When her fingers grow still, Alice sighs.

'I wish you'd come to visit more often,' she says softly.

'I'd like that,' says Catrin and is surprised by how much she means it, longs for it even. Those days when she could just lose herself in the music. Looking at her mother, Catrin wonders at the agony of having this instrument in view every day but no longer the ability to play it. She hates what the arthritis has done.

Taking the score, Catrin rests it on the music stand and closes her eyes, breathes deeply three times and begins. Her mother turns the pages and the piano sings, sound travelling from the strings. Rhys sits on the sofa, hands clasped in front of him. The piece lasts almost seven minutes and, although there are a couple of slip-ups, Catrin maintains form.

'You've still got it,' says Alice. 'Rhys, do you want to take a turn?'

'Not for me,' he says, getting to his feet.

'Boys!' says Alice, shaking her head but smiling. 'Obstinate brutes! Would you grab my suitcase from upstairs, then?'

'The carthorse is yours to command,' replies Rhys and then he flexes his bulging biceps beneath his jumper.

'He's going to be a heart-breaker, that one,' says Alice, as her grandson walks out of the door. 'Bit of a mouth on him, though.'

'I wonder where he's got it from?' says Catrin.

'Well, it's no bad thing. And, Catrin? There *is* something else, isn't there? Something you're not telling me?'

~

'Rhys likes this girl Molly, then, does he?' asks Alice, as the car speeds along.

'You're a terrible gossip.'

'I'm a nan interested in her progeny. What did you expect?'

'He's sixteen,' replies Catrin. They've dropped Rhys off at Molly's and are just a few minutes from the farmhouse.

'More than old enough, if the *Daily Mail*'s anything to go by. And Harri's still single, is he?'

'Iraq doesn't offer much in the way of long-term prospects.'

'Unless you're a jihadi and then I hear you're eligible for seventy virgin brides if you play your cards right. Did you read the news yesterday?'

Catrin shakes her head, hardly able to believe it herself.

Another car bomb. Eighteen dead. 'All I could do was thank God it wasn't him.'

'You and me both, love. You and me both.'

'Did I tell you I was working on something?'

'Composing?' asks Alice.

'It helps, somehow. Would you look it over?'

'I'd like that.'

The car pulls up into the farmyard and for once Catrin's mother doesn't pull a face or make a comment about the smell, although Catrin can't help noticing all the things that could do with a spruce.

Just as the two of them are making their way into the house, Catrin spots Simon in the stable. She ushers her mother inside the house. 'Make yourself at home,' she says. 'I'll be with you in a moment.'

Simon smiles as she approaches. 'Afternoon.'

'Hello there, Simon. I won't disturb you long but I was wondering if you'd heard from Harri recently? You asked for his address, and I thought perhaps he might have returned a letter or two?'

Simon slides the brush along the rump of the horse. 'I got one about a week back,' he says. 'He seems well enough.' Catrin feels the weight lift. She hopes for more but Simon offers nothing and instead resumes his brushing, the dark, loose hairs of the horse drifting through the air. She gets the hint but lingers, unable to let the matter go.

'Anything else?'

'Not a lot. Says it's hot for this time of the year. A bit bored; finds the American lot a mite, well . . . *American.*'

She wants to read the letter for herself, to see Harri's writing on the page, hear his voice in each sentence. It doesn't seem right that Simon should have heard from Harri so recently, while she, his mam, is kept in the dark.

'Would you let me know if you get any more? I just want to know he's all right. That's all.'

'Sure,' says Simon. 'I can do that.'

'And if I could just see them, see his handwriting . . .'

Catrin knows what she's asking, that a letter is a private thing, that sealed envelopes are like lips closed against the spilling of secrets. But she can't help herself. It's her boy, her little one. She'll cross whatever line there is to cross.

'I'd have to ask Harri,' says Simon, removing hair from the brush. She can see he's unable to say no but unwilling to say yes. They'd been forced to cut down his hours and no doubt he was worried there was worse to come. But they'd not do that to the lad; he was as much a part of the farm as any of them.

'No need,' she says. 'I shouldn't have asked.'

Simon smiles, puts a hand on the horse.

Catrin regards the lad as his mother would, wondering if indeed she understands her own son half as well as she ought. There was something there that made her worry. She gives her goodbye and as she walks back to the farmhouse she considers how her own mother was wrong, that parents don't intuitively or even intimately know their children – or at least not as well as they might wish. A person was a closed box. Sometimes the lid lifted and you were given a rare glimpse inside but then the lid came down with a thud, and all you could do was hope that the contents you recalled were close to the individual's truth.

16 December 2004

Dear Mam, Da & Rhys

Thank you for the care package the other week. Mam, could you send me Nan's address? She sent something and I'll write to her soon.

Strange not to be home for Christmas. First year without Da's famous bubble and squeak. Jesus, I'd die for something that's fresh from the ground. Not a great choice of words that . . . Well. Gallows humour has a certain flavour out here.

We've had a lot of gifts come through this month – plenty from church groups and charities and the like. I've now got ten razor heads stashed away. Is Rhys shaving yet?

Things are getting hot, so anything that can boost morale is welcome. Even a card can do wonders out here. Speaking of, some more thick socks wouldn't go amiss next time, if you can rustle up another pair of those for us.

You may have heard the news by now, but one of our guys triggered an IED last week at one of the FOBs. It's been tough. I wasn't there and it wasn't fatal but a few of the fellas will be going home. I don't exactly know how quickly information gets through if it's not critical.

It's tough to be missing Christmas but we're all making the best of it. Some of the guys have got decorations and we've put a pair of velvet reindeer antlers on the front of one of the trucks. Wilson's been going around in this big Santa beard & hat shouting out Christmas-cracker jokes. It makes people smile.

Thanks for the mouthwash. That's another thing that can, in measure, keep the spirits up. More is always appreciated.

There's a rest day next week, which will be good. I'll do some exercise and maybe play some cards or read a bit.

How are all the 'ladies' on the farm? Mam, have you done your famous church window again?

I miss Flint as well, so give him another hug from me, won't you?

Your son,
Harri x x

399. Mr Blair visited Baghdad on 21 December, where he commented to journalists: 'I tell you exactly what I felt coming in. Security is really heavy – you can feel the sense of danger that people live in here . . . coming from terrorists and insurgents . . . Now where do we stand in that fight? We stand on the side of the democrats against the terrorists.'*

– *The Report of the Iraq Inquiry*, Volume VII, Section 9.3

---

* BBC News, 21 December 2004, Blair's statement in Baghdad.

6

The saddle sits on the kitchen table like something hibernating as John carefully applies the leather conditioner. Last week he'd spent an entire evening washing off the dirt and the grease, working away with a ball of mane hair, just as his taid had done. For the fiddly bits, he'd wielded an old toothbrush and several toothpicks for the bridle pieces and stirrup leathers, where the dirt had congealed. He'd been careful not to widen the holes in the leather, which would have made them as useless as a clipped bird. It took hours and he was dog-tired by the end of it; his nostrils had been filled with the smell of saddle soap, the water was dark and grimy, his hands wrinkled. But it was a job well done and he'd felt the keen promise of the hunt building in his belly. He'd towelled off the saddle and then placed it with the others to dry, near but not too near a radiator in the hall; if the leather was forced to dry too quickly, it would become hard as rock and was a bastard to loosen. It was a lesson both Harri and Rhys had learnt as boys, just as John had when he was a lad.

Presently, he dips the cloth into the conditioner and applies another layer. He'll have to get to polishing in the morning. He should have done all this earlier, of course, but things were always a rush around this time of year, when there was so little light and there was the feeding of the animals taking up all the hours of the day. It would have been much better if Jesus had been born in July and then there would have been ample time to fit in the feasting, singing and gift-giving around the work. As it was, the days whipped by, rains lashed, legs ached, and all the while you had to keep a sodding smile on your face because it was the season of goodwill. He looks over at Catrin, who's standing by the Aga. In her hand she's holding a slip of paper he'd left in the pocket of his trousers. She's frowning.

'I know you like a punt, John. But this? Two hundred pounds? On a single race?'

He continues to rub at the leather. Perhaps he should tell her? In some ways it would be a relief. To have the whole truth of it out there in the open.

'Look,' he says. 'I was given another tip and I thought it was worth a flutter.'

'A two-*hundred*-pound flutter? You've spent all winter worrying about whether we have enough cash to cover the extra feed we need over the coming months but you spend two hundred on a *flutter*?'

'And if it had come good like the last one, we'd have had it. More than enough.'

'But it didn't. And we don't,' says Catrin. He risks a glance. She looks hurt, confused. Guilt and shame roll through him, over him. But he cannot tell her. Not now. If he told her, he would lose her.

And he cannot lose her.

'I'm sorry,' he says and is surprised to find the words catching in his throat, a damn betrayal. And she is there, a hand on his shoulder. Perhaps, he thinks, perhaps . . . 'We've not been making ends meet,' he admits. 'I thought that with a few well-placed bets . . .'

'How long has this been going on, John?' Her voice is like the shattering of old stone.

There are so many different answers to this question, so many half-truths he could say; white lies to keep what little peace they had. 'Three years,' he says, adding the tenor of certainty that always seemed to work, even as the sound of it scraped at his own insides.

'And how much are we talking about? What else do we owe?'

He waves his hand at her, pushing her questions away.

'How much, John?'

It doesn't matter what he says. How can it?

'John?'

He picks a number. 'About three thousand,' he says. One cowardly lie follows another.

He hears her sharp intake of breath, feels the removal of her hand.

'Oh, God,' she says. 'You didn't think to tell me? When that letter arrived . . .'

He wipes his hands on the cloth and dumps it on the table. He cannot look at her. 'I didn't know what to say.'

'You never know what to say,' replies Catrin.

'No,' says John, closing his hands. 'I suppose not.'

She is moving away from him and there is nothing he can do. She's right: he never was good with words. In fact, he's not much good at anything. But he's always been faithful. There is that.

'Catrin,' he says.

'I need some air.'

'Catrin?' he repeats, staring at the saddle. He has to cling to something.

Alice walks in, a novel in her hand. 'What's all the fuss?' she asks, looking first at John and then at Catrin.

$\sim$

John had woken to a slight headache. He'd fallen asleep in the living room, his last waking moments spent picturing horses racing down a track, a winning slip in his hand. This is his reality: his first and final thoughts of the day are not about the land, they're not about his animals; they're not even about his family – they're about odds, accumulators, winning and losing. There is no escape.

He looks about him, at the deep gloom. The hackles of the house are raised and the building quivers. There are coiled words in the corners of rooms and there is something bitter dripping down into the foundations, disturbing the soil, weakening the stone and wood. But what can he do? What can he do?

He ignores the tremors of his world and enters the bathroom, squinting in the forensic light. He lathers up his face and slides the razor along his jawline. His face contorts as the blade sweeps along skin, cutting through the stubble that lines his jaw. He turns his head this way and that, checking his work. Satisfied, he splashes cold water over his features and wipes away the last of the foam. When he looks again, he sees a small nick on the trunk of his neck, a bead of bright red blood pooling. He reaches for some toilet roll and dabs until the bleeding stems.

In the bedroom, John regards the pressed clothes spread out on the duvet and a growl escapes his lips. Catrin should be here but she has taken off in the small hours of the morning with Alice. He doesn't know when or if she'll be back.

He pulls on his cream jodhpurs, which cling to his legs. He rearranges his own tackle before tucking in a crisp white shirt, taking his time because this is one of the few days of the year it matters. Today, presentation is a mark of respect; it's about honouring the men and women who worked the land and marking the traditions of the past. It's important, on today of all days, because, what with the hunting ban, who in God's name knows what the future's going to look like? Not John. He doesn't have a fucking clue. All he has is shame and guilt and a twisting anger.

He grinds his teeth as he pulls on his father's old hunting coat. It's a tad tight around the shoulders but it fits well enough. The elbows have been patched more than once and there are lines of thread where cuts and bruises have been stitched but John wouldn't replace it, not for anything. He fondles the polished buttons, tries to take comfort in their solidity. Each has the three initials of the hunt's name looping across the metal in precise, cursive script. After all these years, there's still a pride in wearing the uniform, in the memory of being awarded his buttons by the joint masters and the look in his father's eye.

He checks the rest of his uniform: his stock and gloves. Everything is old and worn but that in itself is a mark of distinction. He picks up his riding hat and stands to attention before the mirror.

And thinks of Harri.

Pictures his son pulling on his own uniform: combat trousers, jacket, boots. And helmet – a different kind of hat for a different kind of protection.

Christ, John, you old bastard. Don't think of that.

Out on the landing, he thumps Rhys's door and the boy appears, ready and waiting. He's also dressed in his hunting uniform and John gives him a nod, a flash of pride in the way his boy's turned out. Still, he can't help notice the clouds beneath the lad's eyes and John wonders how much he'd heard last night. Whether he'd been woken by Catrin slamming the front door like she wasn't coming back.

'Just you and me, then?' says Rhys.

'Will you help me get the horses in?'

John opens up the trailer. The horses are dressed in the appropriate tack, with the traditional breastplate, martingale and girth. In the twilight hours of the previous days, the two geldings have been clipped and brushed until their coats gleam like polished wood. The tails have been picked and cropped and plaited, while the manes have been given equal attention. Rhys has even oiled the hooves until they shine as smart as silver cutlery.

They're working their way through some bacon sandwiches and slurping down coffee when Simon arrives. John gives the young man the keys to the quad bike and quickly runs through the schedule for the dogs and the sheep. Simon nods along, confident in what he's about. They exchange a few pleasantries about Christmas. The lad seems quieter than usual.

'Everything all right?' asks John.

'You haven't seen the news?' says Simon.

John's heart stalls: *Harri*, he thinks. *Not Harri*.

But no. There's been a tsunami in the Indian Ocean. It's caused carnage along the coast of Indonesia, Thailand, Sri Lanka and elsewhere. Whole families have been swept away.

John and Rhys finish loading up and, once they're settled in the front of the Land Rover, John turns on the radio. They listen to the news as the car hurries along the small lanes.

'Christ,' says Rhys.

At length, John turns it off, his mind drifting elsewhere. In one of his pockets there's the twenty quid he'd taken from Alice's handbag one evening when the rest of the family had gone to bed. The two tens feel like they're burning a hole in his pocket. 'It's the King George Day,' he says.

'Da,' says Rhys.

'I thought we'd make a quick call.' He pulls up outside a Win365. It's still early so they should be at the hunt in plenty of time. 'You coming?'

The two of them enter the shop. He spends five minutes scanning the free copy of the *Racing Post*. His hands are clammy as they fill out the slips and hand over the money. As John gets back into the car, he feels his relief mix with shame.

'Da,' says Rhys.

John reaches over and puts his son in a headlock, scrubs his knuckle against the boy's skull. 'Come on,' he says. 'Today's going to be fun.'

It's a good day for hunting. The sky is silver-grey but it's cool, and the hounds are eager and the horses are alert. It's one of the largest meets John has ever seen, with a sizeable field of fifty riders, as well as the usual handful of whippers-in, and a throng of locals and supporters – some of whom had travelled a fair wind to watch the old tradition one last time. Men, women and children stand about dressed up in coats and scarves and gloves. They watch, whisper and even cheer as the Masters confer; there are four this year and John feels a fierce joy at the thought of a long day in the saddle – it's almost enough to make him smile. If only Catrin were here. He's already been forced to lie so often about her absence that his pleasure feels marred.

It was the first year in almost two decades that his wife hadn't been with him. He'd told the other riders that she had to take Alice back to her home; a half-truth but one he'd had to follow up with further assertions that, yes, his mother-in-law was well enough and there was nothing to worry about. It grated but he was used to lying, wasn't he? It wasn't hard: you just said whatever seemed most likely; on the whole, people didn't like to dig, they had their own lives, their own problems.

He scratches at the skin beneath the strap of his hat and brushes at his jacket, feeling for the flask in the inside pocket; a little fire for the ride always helped. He takes a swig and sees Tim talking with a few of the local landowners. The two have hardly spoken; the air between them has become too thick. Tim is one of his closest mates, his neighbour and godfather to his elder son but the man knows too much and might just say too much. And so John has kept his distance, although he worries that, in trying to protect his friendship, he might be ending it.

John watches Tim from beneath the shadow of his hat's brim; the man has always had the knack of conversation, whether it's with the landed gentry in their ancestral homes or the guys in their caravans.

A couple of hounds start sniffing around at his horse's hooves and John places a hand on the beast's neck, even though he knows his mount needs no steadying; the gelding has been John's stalwart companion for over six years and has never let him down. Still, he doesn't like to take chances – it takes only a single, frustrated kick for a dog to find itself facing death. And the rider's reputation with it.

One of the Masters of the Hunt, Jack Harrison, urges his horse towards him until he's next to John. He holds a whip with its thong and a small walkie-talkie hangs from a cord around his neck. John feels his stomach sink beneath the saddle. He knows what's coming.

'Good weather for it,' says Jack. 'Your boy, Rhys, will be in the second flight this year. He'll need to take the gates.'

'I'll speak to him,' says John, nodding. Rhys had remained quiet on the rest of the journey to the meet but as soon as he was saddled up and was able to join his friends his spirits had picked up.

'I'm sorry about Catrin. We could have used her help today. You'll give her my best?'

'Will do,' says John.

'Secretary's still taking caps and speaking to some of the landowners – but we should be away soon.'

'That's good,' says John. He shifts in his saddle.

'The country's extensive today, so we'll be working off the Christmas pudding and red wine.'

'Even better,' he says.

'One other thing, John. It's about your membership.'

'Yes?' says John, raising his brow, hand tightening on the reins.

'It's lapsed. We have written.'

John frowns. 'I don't see how that could have happened. I've always been up to date.'

'An oversight, I'm sure,' says Jack. 'In any case, you may wish to settle up with the Secretary before we head off.'

John looks up at the heavens and bites his lip as if deliberating. 'Look,' he says. 'The truth is, I've got this damn tax bill: end of the month.'

'That's what you get for being a Labour man, John.'

'And I've been wondering if the club might offer a loan of sorts? I'm in a bit of a squeeze, see.'

The Master shakes his head. 'I don't know about the club, John. We're not exactly Coutts. That said, I'll have a word with a few of the others. There might be scope for some private arrangements. We can discuss it later.'

'I'd be grateful,' says John.

Jack nods, the matter put aside. He looks around at the gathered crowd. 'It's a good turnout. One of the best I've ever seen. It's a damn shame, what they've done. A damn shame. Few things better than the chase and watching the hounds draw.'

'No man can deny it,' says John but his mind is on other possibilities. What private arrangements? And how much will he be able to borrow? How long can he keep the wolves with their teeth from his door?

∾

The hounds are working deep within the heavy scrub and John's ears ring with the sounds of the hunt: the thrashing of bracken, swishing of tails, snorting of beasts, his heart beating wildly. Twigs, branches and leaves snap and crack as the horses and riders thunder after the hounds through the winter-crisp copse. Ancient trees, young saplings, thick briars and thistles block and yield passage; branches snap back and forth as muscles ripple by. Snouts, paws and hooves press into the cold ground, the layers of millennia – moss and earth, rock and bone.

There is a slowing and a momentary pause, a collective breathing in and out. And then the Master calls out and there is a sudden speaking of hounds and, as John leans over the neck of his horse, he watches them drawn as if pulled by some powerful magnetic force in a long line as the horn peals in unison with the chorus. There is lightning in his heart and in his stirrups. He follows another rider and they emerge from the tangle of growth into a wide pasture with a stone wall that rises before him and for a moment horse and man are airborne, arcing up, up, and up! And then over! They thud down and along, not a pause in the step of the horses, and there is excited chatter and laughter and marvel at the chase, whose point and very joy is not the death of the fox – for there are many ways a man can kill – but rather the pleasures of the chase itself, the marvel of being at one with the horse, the hound, the land and even the prey. It is the raw reality and energy of everything connected in the wild chase and underpinning it all a strange feeling of riding through time, of being both modern man and something less evolved but more alive.

The hounds converge on another covert and once more there is a moment of seeming stillness; perhaps the scent has vanished? The cunning of foxes is well-enough known and even admired; John has seen foxes circle round a flock of sheep to hide their scent.

The hounds hustle, commune with one another, passing the secrets of smell back and forth. It's possible the fox has gone to ground. There is a flutter of movement. Perhaps it has doubled back? John breathes deeply, feels the sweat beneath the starch of his uniform. A wind picks up, rustles the trees, the elms, horse chestnuts, oaks, hawthorn; it tousles the bushes with their winter berries, the cotoneaster, buckthorn and dogwood. Birds dance in the trees, rise and land, watch expectantly.

Briefly, John wonders how Rhys is doing. The lad will be frustrated not to be nearer the front but he's got his place and his responsibilities and John's glad to see his son getting some respect. He's a fine rider and has the trophies and rosettes to prove it.

He thinks, too, of Catrin and wishes she was here with him now to enjoy this moment, to feel the excitement, the belonging, the communion.

There! They spy the fox, breaking covert and making a dash. The field follow after the Huntsman. Some of the riders have fallen behind now, the way being difficult, with jumps aplenty. John rides a few places behind the Field Master, the muscles of his horse rippling with power and pride. Ahead, the fox is a beautiful red against the landscape; it looks round just the once, its eyes alive with craft and intelligence as it speeds away, its great tail vanishing through a thick hedge as the pursuit follows in full flight. Nearby, there is a path where a group of foot-followers whoop and shout. The rider behind curses – is it the fucking antis, he wants to know. But there is nothing to stop the hounds and riders, who are a whirl of movement, slicing and snorting through the air!

As he passes the group of spectators, he spies a face he recognizes, and his surprise almost sends him from his saddle as his mount leaps over the hedge. It was Matthew Edevane! He's sure of it. Matthew fucking Edevane. What is *he* doing here? But there is no time to ponder because the chase is on and they must follow the fox – the wondrous roll of hooves against the earth, a tumbling, rumbling thrumming; a dash of cavalry in their pinks and blacks. Onwards! Every obstacle crossed by the fox must also be conquered by hound and horse. Over and under and along they travel and it's in the pursuit that the hunter learns, too, a respect and sympathy for the prey – for its drive and its daring, for the way it denies, as long as it may, the inevitable that must come to all things. Onwards!

The skies begin to scrunch up and discolour and then it is spitting; wet mud sprays and splatters. Soon, all that was cleaned, dried and polished, all that was starched and ironed, is damp, ruffled and spotted. John cannot stop his thoughts spinning. Spinning and spinning like a fucking roulette wheel. Catrin! Matthew! Harri! Rhys! Fox!

And now, as the day's damp and sweat begin to work their way through the thread and his thighs burn, he begins to feel the awful ache of age. He's not the young man he used to be. He is not the *man* he used to be.

And perhaps it's this, or the rain, or simply the way his body is positioned as his steed plunges onwards and takes a difficult jump, catching its hind legs, that sends John sprawling and twisting through the air to land, with a deafening thud, on the ground. He releases a wild groan as the air is forced from his lungs. He has fallen! He clenches his fists and jaw, makes to stand. Pain darts along his left leg. He pauses, pants, tries again. Another rider comes up behind him and John crawls to the side to avoid being trampled beneath the heavy hooves of oncoming riders.

'Watch it!' he shouts.

He looks down at his leg and thinks of his own father, trapped as he'd been beneath the tractor.

John closes his eyes, his head against the cold, grassy ground, the rain beating down upon him. The old man would be giving him an earful now, telling him to get up and on. A man always gets to his feet.

And maybe he should have listened more to the old bugger, given how things have turned out. But there it was. The old sod had got himself killed, hadn't he? Driving that damn tractor when he shouldn't have been, when the light was coming down too quick. Always a stubborn bastard, he was. Claimed to know the land as he knew his own skin. And yet. A February evening, the damn machine tipping on that ledge up by the south entrance and leaving him trapped there, legs wedged, head bruised and bleeding. And how many hours had the old man been stuck there, confused and in pain, the cold creeping in, before they'd thought to go looking for him? When they'd found him, his voice was gone from all the shouting and his body was as cold as anything and he'd just shaken his head, knowing that was it. They'd got help, managed to lift the vehicle and slide him out and he'd been rushed to hospital. Later, they'd propped him up in bed, his whole body banged and bandaged up. When John had seen him, sitting there as useless as a broken spade, the old man had smiled the kind of smile you never want to see in someone you love and he'd said, *Well, that's it, John.* He'd said this while looking down at his legs, that smile on his face. Two days later he died. The doctors had said it was pneumonia but John reckoned it was knowing he'd never be able to walk the farm again, that he'd never roam his own land on his own two feet. His mam had followed inside of three years, her body riddled with cancer. Both buried before the age of seventy. It didn't seem fair.

John was left the farm. But he hadn't wanted the farm. He'd wanted his parents.

'Da?'

He growls, rises to his feet. He puts some weight on the leg; it's not as bad as he'd feared.

'Fucked my leg,' says John.

'Here,' says Rhys, lending an arm. With the help of his son, he casts about for his ride, but the horse has wandered off, one of the herd. He pulls his flask from his pocket, unscrews the lid and takes a long draw and then another.

'Easy, Da,' says Rhys.

'You're driving,' says John. He tips the flask higher.

On the way back, John demands that they stop off at the Win365 and he tells Rhys to stay in the car. As he limps into the shop, he knows his body smells of old sweat and his breath has the stink of booze but he doesn't care. Harri has left. Catrin has left.

Soon, no doubt, Rhys will leave as well. He checks the results of the King George. His own horse finished fourth. Rhys's fared better, clinching victory. John collects the winnings – a crisp seventy quid. The bookmaker counts out the notes, three twenties and a ten. John fans the money. An older guy in a black leather jacket gives him a conspiratorial nod.

'Chelsea game on Tuesday. Against Portsmouth. Easy money,' says the man.

John nods. Over the years he's built up his rituals – he bets only on the horses. Horses he knows. Horses he understands. Sometimes the rugby if there's a sweepstake, which there usually is. That, and the fruit machines, because he likes the roll and spin of things and the way he doesn't need to think. But football? Fuck-all he knows about football.

But why not?

He takes two further punts on races coming up in the following few days, knowing the beginning of January will be dead quiet. And then, because he's feeling lucky – because there must be another win around the corner soon – he has a go at the Lucky 15 with a two-pound stake across the board, thirty quid all in. Above him, screens flash and races run.

Rhys accosts him as soon as he clambers back into the car. 'What took you so long? I was starting to worry.'

'I got chatting to the guy behind the desk.'

'And?'

John shrugs. 'You going to sit there talking?'

'It'll be dark before we get back.' The statement is riddled with accusation.

'Then get. The sooner we're off, the sooner there.'

Rhys switches on the engine. 'So? How'd we do?'

'Fourth and fifth,' says John.

Rhys shakes his head. 'Fuck that for a game of soldiers.'

It's dark when they reach the driveway to the farm. John hopes Simon has managed with the animals. As the car swings into the yard, he's relieved to see Catrin's car parked by the kennel. She's back.

'Will you see to the horses?' asks John.

'Again?' Rhys rolls his eyes.

'Again.'

John limps to the farmhouse listening to the sound of the trailer being opened, the horses being led out. The boy deserves more. He knows that most of the lad's friends find themselves holiday jobs and the like, temp working on less than minimum wage but still earning something. And what do they pay Rhys for all the work he does? They hadn't given Harri an allowance either but that was hardly an example to go by, what with him signing up to the Army and getting that damn scholarship when he was only sixteen. Sixteen. Old enough to buy tobacco, get married and have a child. Old enough to join the Army. Old enough to make life, to take life and old enough to lose it. Christ, his boy, but he misses him so.

In the living room, Catrin is lying on the sofa, a blanket wrapped around her. Her eyes are closed and air whistles through barely parted lips. She hadn't showered in the morning before she'd left and now the curls of her hair stick to her skull, a little greasy, greying at the sides. Flint lies curled up asleep. The electric heater is on, the filaments inside glowing orange, the fans purring softly. His father would hate to see something like that running in the house, costing an arm and a leg.

The TV shows a row of trees bending at right angles, their branches being pulled back, rain slashing down. Flint opens his eyes, flaps his tail. John treads carefully into the room, raises his palm at the old dog, who makes to rise, and then he lowers the volume until it becomes a gentle hum. Chaos continues to flash on the screen, the devastation of the tsunami still being counted.

The kitchen has been cleared and tidied. He notes Catrin's handbag on the side and a leaflet on the table. John picks up the glossy piece of paper, scans the list of questions.

Question One: Do you ever borrow to finance your gambling?

John's leg thrums and he reaches down, massaging the knee. Outside, he can hear Rhys with the horses. The boy was right: they should have got back while it was still light.

He walks over to the sink, washes his hands and drinks a glass of water, gasping at the cold. He opens the fridge. They can microwave the bubble and squeak for dinner. With a bit of cold turkey, it will do the job well enough.

Question Two: Do you ever gamble to get money with which to pay debts or otherwise solve financial difficulties?

He turns and makes his way to the handbag, his right foot dragging. Rhys is still outside. Catrin is asleep.

His fingers go hunting through the darkness of the bag, searching for the feel of notes, the weight of coins.

His leg aches. His heart is heavy.

Question Three: Is gambling making your home life unhappy?

He sees himself tumbling from the horse, his body landing like a puppet. And in the darkness the house quakes and whispered questions that have been hiding in the corners and cracks come snaking out, winding their way towards him.

How often can a man fall?

And how far?

2005

January

Iraq Body Count: 1,222

414. On 11 January Lt Gen. Fry, Deputy Chief of the Defence Staff (Commitments), submitted advice to Mr Hoon on prospects for 2005.* In his view a 'strategic watershed' was approaching in Iraq: 'The prognosis for the security LOO [Line of Operation] in '05 is stark . . . The Sunni insurgency will grow in scale and intensity . . . Kurdish and Shia violence, recently quiescent, may be sparked by intractable constitutional discord over federalism . . . The recent alignment of AQ and Al-Zarqawi has formally established Iraq as the central front for radical Islamic terrorism . . .'

– *The Report of the Iraq Inquiry*, Volume VII, Section 9.3

---

* Minute DCDS(C) to APS 2/SofS [MOD], 11 January 2005, 'Iraq 2005 – a UK MOD Perspective'.

7

She's arrived at the pub early and excited.

It's been ten difficult days since she last saw Matt and she's already feeling the relief of shrugging off the role of Catrin the mother, Catrin the wife and Catrin the daughter. Once again she can be, simply, Cat: carefree and desirable.

With time to spare, she looks in the sun visor's mirror and applies another coat of lipstick and some mascara. She gently tugs at her skin, eyeing the wrinkles around her eyes and deepening above her brows. When she was younger, she'd always worried about her appearance. Her feet had seemed too big and her breasts too small. She'd constantly felt too hairy and was always scraping away at her skin; she hated the small mole on her neck that sprouted long black hairs that she'd routinely plucked, all the while worrying that such frequent, violent disturbance of the mottled brown would trigger skin cancer. It was only after she'd had her boys that she stopped caring what she looked like. There was too much stretching and ballooning and cutting of the body, in addition to the terrible ripping apart from bearing children. Years of sleepless nights and being constantly *on* put things like plump lips and 32B into perspective. She wasn't especially beautiful, Catrin knew that, but she was more confident now; she was round in some places, thin in others, and knew enough about makeup and clothes to be presentable. She could turn up at a dinner or a parents' evening and look scrubbed, which was something of an accomplishment when she'd likely been shovelling horse manure all day.

She was happy to learn that seeing Matt – *sleeping* with

Matt – hadn't brought any of those insecurities back. On the contrary, she'd never felt better about her appearance. Being called beautiful and sexy at every moment did that to a woman, even one of her age. Thinking about him now sent her insides quivering.

Catrin wonders if all this made her a bad mother. She didn't feel like one. She'd brought her boys up well, hadn't she? She wasn't even a bad wife. All those years with John, being at his side, supporting him, doing her best to help him, keeping the farm going, even when things had got so bad she'd sometimes wanted to take her passport and go. And didn't everyone know, secretly in their heart of hearts, that it was possible to love more than one person, that in a world of six and a half billion people there were probably thousands of individuals who lit the spark?

Was she in love with Matt? And, if she was, what was she supposed to do with it? She had children. So no thinking about love. Love made things complicated. She didn't want complicated. She wanted carefree. Think about anything. Think about fingers. Yes, fingers! Matt's fingers! Matt's fingers undressing her. Matt's fingers on her skin, Matt's fingers in her –

She hears the wheels of a car crunching on the gravel and recognizes Matt's estate as it swings round the corner. He flashes his lights and beeps his horn. She smiles and, before she has time to take stock, Catrin finds herself hurrying out of the car. Moments later, she is being enfolded, engulfed in his warmth, his arms around her. He holds her tight and then draws back and they kiss and she can feel the slight sandpaper skin of his cheeks, catches the scent of aftershave, and whatever else it is that makes him *him* and sets her whole body on fire.

'Oh, God,' she breathes.

Matt laughs. 'I've been called many things but not that. It's good to see you again, Cat.'

Catrin smiles but, before she can say anything, she's pulled back into another warm embrace, Matt's face nuzzling at her neck, his lips right by her left ear, his hands sliding where they shouldn't. She feels appallingly exposed. Here in the cold, outside, where anyone could see. Appallingly, delightedly exposed.

'Ah, there it is,' he whispers.

'Stop,' she says at last, more of a moan than she intends. 'We should go in.'

'Or,' says Matt, 'we could drive to a hotel that's not far from here.'

Catrin's stomach groans in reply, loud and long. He laughs and releases her.

'Well, there's our answer.'

Inside, there's a gaggle of old smokers by the bar, muttering through the fog, amber dregs in pint glasses. They nod as the two of them pass. The large stone fireplace is roaring with the crackle of logs. There's a group of six white-haired ladies at lunch and a good-looking lad is at the bar tapping at his phone. There are old signs from the railway station on the wall and pictures of Llandudno from the past, photographs of Victorian ladies and gentlemen strolling the promenade, decked in hats, brollies and canes. The carpet is a dark red, complete with old spillage stains. The tables and chairs are an assortment of polished wood.

They take a seat by the window and for a moment look down at the menus before them, momentarily awkward after the long week and a half spent apart and the high of that initial rush when their lips and tongues had touched.

'You look nice,' says Matt.

Catrin's smile wobbles. It was exactly what John had said to her that morning, word for word, and it had sent a tiny pang of guilt running through her. Relationships were two-sided, she knew. When was the last time she'd dressed up for John?

'Well?' says Matt, spreading out his hands like he's about to receive a gift. 'How was Christmas?'

'Good,' she replies, hearing the lie. But she doesn't want to lie to him, of all people. If she can be honest with anyone, it's Matt. Still . . . some things are best left out. She tries again: 'Different.'

'Different?'

'First year without Harri,' she explains.

'Of course.' He nods and then looks back down at the menu. Catrin knows he's opposed to the war – *illegal occupation*, he calls it – so they generally avoided talk of the Middle East. When it came to Matt, it was the one thing Catrin struggled to square.

'My mother was the same,' she adds. 'Difficult as ever.'

'Your mum never lacked an opinion.'

'You'd think by now she'd trust me to cook the turkey. But there's always something not quite right. Her perfectionism used to drive Dad up the wall.'

She doesn't mention John or the debt or the fact that deep down she is absolutely sick with worry. That she's beginning to get a sense of all that her husband's been up to.

'And you?' she says, turning the conversation. 'I think you said you'd be with Claire and the girls?'

'Not this year,' replies Matt, his expression pained.

'I thought –'

Matt shakes his head. 'Claire decided differently.'

'I'm sorry,' says Cat. She wonders if she ought to ask about the divorce. Another topic they tend to avoid. Mercifully, the young lad from the bar saunters over, pulling out a pad of paper from his back pocket, a pen from his ear.

After they've given their orders, Catrin catches Matt watching the young man as he walks away and she wonders if the rumours that had circled at university had any substance. But what does she care? She can still feel the tingle of their early kiss.

She asks about the residency at Snowdon and his face lights up.

'Where to begin?' he says. He talks about the work he's done there – capturing the life and landscape on film and canvas.

He's been reading *I Bought a Mountain* and has acquired a new appreciation for farming and what it used to be like in the old days. He digresses to the flora that sprinkle the land, surviving even now against the cold winds, the rock-hard ground. Catrin listens with half an ear, enjoying the sound of his voice, smiling along as his almost childish enthusiasm mounts as he warms to his topic.

'The chickweed, campion, saxifrage, rockcress . . . there's such poetry in the names. And there's something so . . . *heartening* about it all? I'm not sure that's the right word. Something awe-inspiring, comforting, to see that no matter how hard, how cruel the environment becomes, life struggles on. When you think about it, when you get down close on your hands and knees, and really *see* things, even a blade of grass seems miraculous. I don't believe in God but that's as close as it gets.' He laughs suddenly and scratches behind an ear. 'I'm sorry, I'm rambling.'

'You've become a worshipper of nature,' replies Catrin.

'Oh, I was always that,' he says. 'There's something about being here, about you. You've helped me more than you can know.'

Catrin is rescued from her embarrassment by the arrival of their food. The conversation meanders back to their children, gossip about old friends, the places that Matt has been.

She lets him do most of the talking and asks about his exhibition. He recounts his trip to Vietnam, narrating his journey to the north of the country in a night bus, a strange double-bed situation that seemed precarious to say the least but passed without major incident. From Hanoi he reached Sapa, where he spent several days trekking through rice paddies in the mountains, the endless terraces of green rising towards the sun, and the workers, backs bent, cone-shaped hats protecting their necks from the heat of the day.

Down from Sapa to Hội An, with a final stop in Saigon. He describes the semi-hatched egg he ate on one of the food tours.

'It was the slight crunch,' he says, pulling a face. As he talks, Catrin finds her mind drifting to her own travels. The furthest she has gone is Provence, and that had been for her honeymoon with John. With the farm, the boys, the money, it just hadn't been possible to go more often or further afield.

'I've never been much of a traveller,' admits Catrin. 'But both the boys have the bug. Difficult not to these days, what with the TV and all the places of the world beamed about. Rhys's been talking of a Euro-trip for the last six months but I've said he'll have to pass his exams if he wants to go.'

'He might not return. I've friends, old and young, who never looked back after boarding their first bus. The younger ones tend to be running *to* something – adventure, excitement, the exotic. The older ones tend to be running *from* something.'

'It sounds –'

'Irresponsible?'

'Different,' says Catrin. 'Just . . . different.'

Matt nods wistfully and then his eyes crinkle in sudden anticipation. 'Before I forget,' he says, 'I have something for you.' He dashes from his chair and returns a few minutes later with a plastic bag that he hands over. Inside, there's a square item wrapped in decorative paper. 'I meant to post it to you in time for Christmas but the days went by so quickly. And I'm sorry about the paper; cartoon reindeer wasn't the look I was going for but it's all they had in the local shop.'

'Thank you,' says Catrin. 'Do you want me to open it now?'

'No time like the present?' He offers a theatrical wink.

Catrin gives him a look and pulls against the tape. She slides out two vintage records, the first of which gives her pause.

'Matt,' she says.

'I know. But I couldn't resist.'

Frédéric Chopin: Nocturnes 1 à 19, performed by the legendary Samson François. Although vinyl isn't the best medium for classical, with its pops and crackles, this one's in near-mint condition.

'Matt,' she repeats, shaking her head, knowing what the record would have cost.

'What about the next one?'

She turns to the second record and gasps.

'I thought it would bring back memories!' says Matt, laughing.

'My God. Duran Duran! We used to play this *all* the time, driving around in that tin-box Ford of Charlie's. God, this takes me back.' The five band members with their floppy hair stare back at her. They look so much younger than she recalls.

'I have a permanent memory of Sylvia singing "Girls on Film" but never quite getting the words right.'

'I used to think they were the bee's knees back then,' says Catrin. 'Thank you, Matt.' She scans the list of songs on the back.

'There's also a note on the inside, which you can read later,' says Matt. 'It's an invitation.'

'An invitation?'

'You'll see,' he says, grinning.

As she slides the two records back into the bag, Catrin marks the time on Matt's watch. There's a good few hours before she needs to be getting home.

Excusing herself, she heads to the toilet. The bathroom is cold and smells of artificial flowers and old bleach. The floors and wall are decked in red tiles and a single window opens out on to the back garden, letting in a cold flow of air. Catrin looks at herself in the mirror and brushes a few curls behind her ears.

She wanders over to the cubicle door and grits her teeth in anticipation but the small space is mercifully clean. She wrinkles her nose, lowers her knickers and hovers. On the door someone has scratched SEEKING LOVE CALL 07737495736. She wonders what kind of person writes something like that; whether they're having a laugh or if they're so desperate for money – it must be for money, surely – that they're forced to spread their legs for others. She wonders what she'd be willing to do for three thousand pounds. Finished, she flushes and washes her hands, smoothing out the wrinkles in her jumper.

Back at the table, she tells Matt about what she's seen – the desperate number carved into the door – and how it makes her sad.

'It's the oldest profession around,' he says. 'We should legalize it, of course.'

'*Of course?* Why do men always give opinions as if they're obvious facts we should all be aware of?'

'I didn't realize I was debating Germaine Greer.'

'You don't think it debases women?'

'Some say it empowers them.'

'You don't really believe that, do you?' says Catrin, surprised.

'I'd forgotten you could be so square,' says Matt.

Despite his grin, the comment nettles Catrin. 'We can't all float around being artists with wild friends and wild ideas.'

Matt laughs. 'I've had more jobs than you'd think. Perhaps it's living in London; you grow accustomed to seeing and hearing things.'

'But as a *father*, doesn't it concern you that men can pay for sex? That women sell themselves?' There's an edge to her voice she can't keep back.

'Sure it does,' says Matt, spreading his hands wide and then bringing his palms together with a shrug. He looks uneasy, as if they're stepping on sand that might, at any moment, quicken.

'I suppose you've never had to pay for it.' Catrin isn't sure why she says this, but coils of anger and desire have been turning inside her. Matt with his ready answers to everything; his certainty about everything; his confidence – it all makes her hate him just a little but also want him. A rush of heat rises inside her. She puts a warm hand on the cool wooden table.

'I've never had to pay for it, no,' says Matt. His voice is even and he doesn't smile as he looks her in the eye. His body seems to be poised, ready.

Catrin looks away and absently slides her knife and fork together. She's thinking about the hotel again – she knows the one he mentioned – the big double bed, the closed door. And she knows he's thinking the same.

Matt insists on getting the bill and, as he pays, Catrin wonders if he's using her because she is here, because he is getting divorced, because she is willing, because her warm body is better than a cold hand.

But no. If anything, she thinks, she's the one using him.

Later, they're in bed together and the pale afternoon light filters its way through the window and Catrin feels the weight of her guilt pressing down on her and she knows the hours have slipped away and that she ought to be getting back to the farm. But she still wants to stay here for all time. She's sleepy and dreamy here in bed, the sun falling. Matt turns on his side and traces a finger from down below and up to her chin, finishing on her lips, which he leans towards and kisses, and then whispers just loud enough for her to hear: 'I love you.'

And Catrin kisses his lips, her tongue working to silence him.

He pulls away. 'You don't have to say it back. I just wanted you to know.'

She rests against his arm, says nothing.

'What are you thinking about?' he asks.

She lets out a long sigh. 'Everything.'

'That's a lot to be thinking about.'

'I should be getting back.'

Matt nods and reaches down to the side of the bed for his trousers, fishing out his mobile.

'No signal. I suppose it adds to the charm of the place, doesn't it? Space to breathe, to think.' He leans towards her. 'To fuck.'

She gives him a playful shove.

'I'm used to it,' she says.

'The fucking or the lack of signal?'

She gives him a long look. 'There's reception in the kitchen and a few other spots. Otherwise, you're better off with carrier pigeons at the farm.'

'You were always something of a rock,' says Matt, absent-mindedly.

Catrin turns to him, her earlier irritation returning. 'What am I? Mrs Ramsay?'

'Mrs Who?'

'*To the Lighthouse*? Virginia Woolf?' says Catrin.

'I remember you as a reader,' says Matt. 'The stacks of second-hand books, the smell they gave off. Musty.'

'That was the damp from the bathroom,' Catrin replies, waving her hand in frustration. 'And you, never opening your windows.' She pulls herself out of bed and heads to the bath-room, looks at her profile in the silver mirror. More and more, she has started to see her mother in her reflection, a fact she's beginning to make an uneasy peace with.

She returns to the bedroom, sees the time on the radio clock. She has to get back. Dreams, she knows, don't last.

~

'Seems a daft present. We don't even have a turntable,' says John.

The records sit on the side by the kettle.

'It was kind, nonetheless.'

'You'll be putting them in the raffle prize cupboard, though. Or you could plonk them on eBay. Get a few quid for them.'

'I'm too tired to argue,' says Catrin.

'Who's arguing?' replies John. There's gravy dribbling down his chin. Rhys sits silent and awkward between them, staring at his plate.

The sound of tyres on gravel interrupts her reply. Lights flicker in the yard, the dogs bark at the intrusion. Flint clambers to his feet, lets out a low, disgruntled growl. Catrin shakes her head at John's raised eye. They're not expecting anyone. She gets up and peers through the window at two men. Her heart shudders. Are they here about Harri? Have they driven up here late in the afternoon bringing with them the most awful news, ready with their kind sympathetic eyes and supportive tones? But there's enough light to see they're in civvy clothes, as Harri would say, and Catrin can make out the lanyards swinging from their necks, the clipboards in their hands. Her brief relief is pushed aside by a thunderous knock at the door.

Catrin looks at John but he just shrugs. Perhaps they're men from the bank, come to serve possession orders on their home. 'Will you put the plates in the Aga to keep warm, love?' she says to Rhys, marching to the hall, squaring her shoulders as if she's about to do battle. She can sense John moving swiftly in behind her as the hinges of the front door groan. Both men stand there in the cold, looking tired and serious.

'Mrs Williams? Mr Williams?' says the shorter of the two men. Older and portlier, too. His cheeks are red from the cold and his lips are turned down at the corners, while his ears stick out, rat-like.

'Yes, what can I do for you?' says Catrin.

'My name's Conrad Heatley and this is my colleague, James Richardson. We're Fuel Duty Officers here on behalf of HMRC, in order to investigate a report on the misuse of rebated fuel in the area. May we come in?'

'We're in the middle of dinner,' says John, his voice rolling out deep and dangerous behind her. She shoots him a glance, her eyes pinpricks of anger; being rude isn't going to help anyone.

'I'm sorry,' says Richardson, piping up in an unusually high-pitched voice. 'You're our last stop of the day. It's just some routine tests. Assuming everything is in order, we won't be long.'

'Everything *is* in order,' John states, while Catrin opens the door wider and ushers them in.

'Please, come out of the cold,' she says, wondering if John has crossed yet another line, if things have got so bad he's stepped beyond the letter of the law. Surely he wouldn't be so stupid?

'Can I get you gentlemen a cup of tea?' asks Catrin as they make their way into the kitchen, where Rhys is finishing off his stew. The lad looks up as they enter, his eyes glittering with hidden thoughts.

'As I mentioned,' says Heatley, 'we've encountered reports of the misuse of rebate fuel in the area and we're investigating all bodies in the local vicinity who have been issued with a rebated-fuel licence. We'll need to see evidence of up-to-date records for the last twelve months, including all registrations and payments to and from suppliers; copies of your tax statements; a list of all vehicles, both with and without a Statutory Off-Road Notification; and the whereabouts of your oil tanks. We'll be testing all vehicles and taking samples of oil to check for re-colouring, and inspecting measurements to ensure fuel consumption is within the expected standard use.'

'Christ,' says John. 'How long did you take to learn all of that? I thought this was only supposed to take a few moments.'

'It does, Mr Williams,' says Heatley, turning his dark eyes on John. 'If establishments have their paperwork in ready order, in line with the law.' There was an imperious note to his tone, something dangerous; he was the sort of man, thought Catrin, who would kick a dog because he could. They would have to be careful around him. If it wasn't the fuel he objected to, he was certain to find something else.

'Milk? Sugar?' she asks.

Heatley takes five sugars. Catrin drops in the teaspoons one after the other and stirs.

'My colleague will start with the oil tanks,' says Heatley, nodding in the direction of his lankier companion, who is busily slurping down the steaming brew. 'I'll be going through the paperwork.'

'John can help outside, and I'll make sure you have everything you need here. Rhys, now that you've finished dinner, why don't you go upstairs, love?'

As the boy makes his exit, Heatley lays his clipboard on the table. 'And I'll need you to sign these first,' he says, pulling out a black biro from his pocket and placing it across the front page of a form filled with small text.

'What's that?' asks John, leaning towards the table.

'It's a consent form, granting access to the property, outbuildings and equipment. If you need me to go through anything, please just let me know.'

Catrin reaches for the clipboard and scans the bullet-pointed items.

'And if we don't sign?' says John.

'Then we'll be back with a court order.'

'There's no need for that,' says Catrin, signing in one of the small rectangular boxes at the bottom of the page. She hands it to John, who barely reads it over before scrawling his own signature.

Heatley takes it back, lifts the top piece of paper and pulls at the yellow carbon copy underneath. It comes loose in a single, perfunctory rip. 'Here you are,' he says, resting it on the table. 'Well, we don't want to take up any more of your time than we have to. Are you ready, James?'

The younger man nods and removes the torch clipped to his belt.

With John and James in the yard, Catrin begins ferrying files from the study area in the corner of the living room to the kitchen. Once she's brought Heatley everything she can, she takes a seat next to him, feeling anxious at the way his finger methodically skims through papers and slides beneath lines of letters and numbers. There's a slight odour to the man, as if his profusive sweat has mixed with his antiperspirant to form its own particular musk. His pudgy finger stops in the middle of a page, which he taps three times.

'I see,' he says and stabs the pages again, three times over. *Stab-stab-stab.* He then turns to Catrin just as she's about to ask him what the matter is. 'Could I trouble you for another cup of tea perhaps?'

'Of course,' says Catrin, almost jumping out of the seat. 'I'm sorry, I should have offered.' John and the other officer are still outside. It's been almost an hour and Catrin is beginning to feel twitchy. As she gets to her feet and turns away, she feels a hand on her rear, fingers giving a sudden squeeze. She gasps and turns to see him smiling. He taps the paper with his fat hands. *My God*, she thinks. *In my own home.* She fills the kettle and turns again to face the piggy little man, her heart raging.

He sits, watching her with his dark little eyes. He's smiling.

'Five sugars,' he says.

415. Lt Gen Fry judged that 'only additional military effort by the MNF-I as a whole' might be able to get the campaign back on track. He identified three possible courses of action for the UK – increasing the UK scale of effort, maintaining the status quo or, if it was judged that the campaign was irretrievable, accepting failure and seeking to mitigate UK liability. The second two options carried an inherent 'acceptance of probable long-term campaign failure', which could destabilise the Middle East, create a safe haven for international terrorists and damage the reputation and morale of the UK defence forces.

– *The Report of the Iraq Inquiry*, Volume VII, Section 9.3

8

They didn't find anything. Tweedledee and Tweedledum had searched the farm like hounds on the scent but there was not a mark of misplaced or misused oil to be found. Course there wasn't. Not something he had ever done. Not something he would do.

They weren't the only people to end up empty-handed. The damned Americans with their excuses. Couldn't find this, couldn't find that. Not a single weapon of mass destruction in sight. A bit fucking awkward, it was, given they'd sent people overseas to kill and be killed. They might at least have fabricated some evidence. Wasn't that what they always did? Isn't that what the CIA had done not so long ago?

Empty-handed, under-handed, red-handed.

John looks at his own hands, wide and lined and strong. Hands that had seen good, honest work. He looks at the ewes before him and feels a moment of rightness.

The ewes watch him, knowing nothing of his roiling thoughts, and that's just how he likes it. Earlier in the week he had separated the rams from the ewes and presently he stands with a number of his ladies penned up, their rumps red with the ram's dye. In his hand he holds the injector gun, which he now carefully assembles, placing the needle on the front and then taking the sterimatic cap and slowly pushing it down, before removing the guard by twisting it clockwise, feeling the release of the seal. The ewes are bunched up, their calls ringing in his heart. He grabs the nearest of them, with just the right amount of force so that she can't get away, feels a sense of inevitability, and, in that, a peace and docility. He places the end of the gun against the ewe's neck, a few inches beneath the ear, feels the needle slip under the skin, and squeezes the trigger. And, with that, he's done his duty, marvelling for a moment at the ways in which modern medicine and machines have changed the world of farming but also how, in its essence, it is the same work that Moses himself did all those thousands of years ago. He slips the gun into his breast pocket, pulls out the blue dye and marks the head of the ewe to show she's had her vaccine. It's not an absolute preventative against foot rot but it should help. With the wet conditions of the place, the disease was always a danger, no matter how careful a man was.

The ewe gives him a long look but John's not finished with her yet. He raises the back leg of the ewe and in one swift, practised movement he flips the lady over, holding her two front hooves in one hand. He checks the nails aren't too long and runs a palm over the pad. He then slides a finger between the digits, making sure there's no reddening of the interior where bacteria can get inside the tissues and cause foot scald. But this lady is fine. He lets her go, smiling grimly. No stink, no rot, nothing deformed. He prays to whoever is listening that it remains that way.

There was no forgetting the outbreak a few years back, a terrible time that, in which he'd had to spend all the hours of the Earth bringing the ladies in, mixing the copper sulphate solution, the powder turning the water blue. He'd poured the liquid into an old gumboot and then set about dipping each foot in the solution for a minute. Endless work he didn't need. And all those visits from the vet seeing over the treatment plan, costing him each time. He was a good vet, though, Cai Bracken. John wasn't so sure about the new fella they'd taken on: young, up here from Cambridge or Oxford or one of those, his voice as soft as butter, southerly; not experienced enough yet to know a farmer will swing the lead this way and that way, that recommendations will be ignored, that between two choices they would always go for the cheaper because, after all, they're recommendations only. If he was a sensible lad, he'd watch the way Cai laid down the law, which wasn't strictly how things were supposed to be done, but it worked, didn't it? Do as I say, or find someone else to traipse all the way here in the cold and the rain, boots caked in mud, eyes watering and nose running.

John injects the next ewe, marks her, flips her. This one needs a trim, if not more. He takes out his shears with the serrated edge, checks with a finger – sharp, well-oiled and disinfected, just as they should be. He pares back the nail, the ewe bleating and the others, crowding behind him, starting up. He cuts quickly; some blood appears and he whispers a soothing 'sorry'. He may send them all to slaughter eventually but he doesn't like to cause them pain, not if he can help it. Keeping her in place, he reaches in another pocket and pulls out the blood powder and sprinkles it like salt on to the area. It'll help the clotting and cleanliness of the thing. After seeing to the other legs, front and back, he helps her up, checks the way she stands, nice and flat, all four feet on the floor. She bleats softly, eyeing him. John breathes heavily and wipes a sleeve across his nose, which is beginning to run. It's going to be a long day and his leg aches in the cold and he wonders if he should have kept on the other farmhands. If he just had some more money . . .

One of the guys on the hunt had given him the name and phone number of a man who had a small lending business. Said that he should be careful, that it ought to be used only in an emergency, but that if he played by the rules it might get him out of a tight squeeze. John has the scrap of paper tucked into his wallet. Sooner or later, he'll have to make the call.

He looks up at the clouds gathering in the sky. He wonders if it will snow today or tomorrow. He can cope with rain well enough. But snow was the enemy. Snow was death and disease. Snow was horror.

He mouths the names of cloud formations, high and low: cirrus and stratus, cumulus and nimbus. But thoughts of Catrin invade, arrest his attention. He can't fail to see the way she now keeps her distance. He wasn't totally blind. He'd noticed the makeup, the dresses, the time spent away with *friends*. Yes, she was closing herself off from him. Before, he'd still felt her warmth, the way she'd briefly place a hand on his shoulder, a smile here and there, made his tea in the morning. And he'd thought maybe his worries were all in his head, that maybe he was the one who'd walled himself off. He knows he's always been a little remote. It's a remote kind of life and attracted a certain type but she'd always been okay with that, respected it even.

But there was none of that now. She went through the motions. She was present in some ways but totally absent in others. He was losing her. And he senses the stoking of the furnace inside him, the burning hiss of a fury that it is not just a something but a someone who is coming between them.

And, despite this, despite everything, he can't shake the feeling that if he were able to work just a bit of magic, if he could line up his horses in good order, he'd be able to set everything to rights. He could pay off the interest, pay off the principal, pay off the arrears on some of the farm accounts, settle all the personal and professional debts . . . If he could do all that, all the worry, all his fear and stress, would disappear. And he'd stop. Of course he'd stop. He'd have no reason to keep going.

It was possible. On one of his first big punts, he'd used an accumulator and won £18,853. Since then, he'd chased that single win with hundreds and thousands of losses. But all it took was a single victory and he'd never fall again.

He moves to another ewe and puzzles over the news that had come through earlier in the day: the BBC confirming the

US were no longer looking for weapons of mass destruction in Iraq. John had stood there in the living room, watching the box, incredulous at what he was hearing. He couldn't get his head round it. The whole sodding justification for the war had been built on the foundations of that threat. The whole fucking thing. He could hardly contain his bitter rage. It was one thing to gamble with money you could never pay back; it was another thing to play roulette with the lives of whole families. John had stood there, knowing he would never forget today: 12 January, the day he lost faith in politics and those in power – not that he'd had much to begin with.

The truth was he hadn't been surprised. Not really. Unlike Catrin, who'd sat there, wringing her hands, saying she couldn't believe it. He'd almost had a go at her then. Felt that she was being wilfully ignorant, when they'd all known it was only ghosts and shadows being hunted, evidence to excuse the act of aggression. Everyone had secretly known that, deep down, hadn't they? Ever since that weapons inspector was killed, found with that vein cut open. And, even if he had killed himself, he was probably pushed to do it. What the fuck was his name? Kelly? It was all a world of mist and misdirection; nothing had changed for hundreds of years. But the rich and powerful didn't give a damn. Their sons and daughters went to private schools and ended up working in politics and finance, just like their parents.

Meanwhile he was out here, cold and furious, his younger boy facing an uphill climb, no doubt about it, and his elder one stuck in some godforsaken land. Sometimes John was on the side of Guy Fawkes: he'd like to see the whole lot go up in smoke.

Yes, he'd nearly raged at Catrin. Perhaps he should have done. He knew the guilt that was twisting inside her because it was inside him as well. They'd let their little boy go, too young, and who was to say what might happen to him, so far from home, from the people who loved him? Who was to say the ball wouldn't land on Red 23 once more? That's it. That's the lottery of life, that's the gamble you've made and, well, son, it's not paid off. Not this time. And the debt must be paid.

And so John, silent as a shadow, had kept his lips shut and his ears to the news as a man with a grey face, wearing a grey suit, stood facing the camera, shaking his head. We knew all along. We were there all that time, just going through the motions, justifying. But we knew all along. There was nothing to be found.

Some hours later, John discovers the carcass near the border fence, lying there with its eyes glazed, fleece ripped away, red and raw. It is a sickening sight and for the life of him he can't make head nor tail of what has happened. It wasn't the work of a predator, that was for certain. All he can think is that the sheep somehow got her skin caught on the fence wire and in a desperate attempt to break away she must have pulled off her own fleece. It is a hell of a thing and he can see from the terrible violence that it must have caused her considerable pain. He sits down on the cold-hard ground and places a hand over her eyes. Poor thing. What happened to you, he wonders. He doesn't like to think of her suffering out here, alone, separated from her flock. She'd have been cold and desperate, her feet would have kicked uselessly beneath her as the threadbare frozen land embraced her. It was a small mercy that it was so cold – she would have suffered but not for too long. He rests his palms against the earth as if he might feel something of her last moments, allow for some communion between the land, the dead and himself. Scores of animals lay beneath him. The sweat and blood of his own family was soaked into the soil.

Mid-afternoon sees the sky darkening outside. The clouds have continued to gather, and the temperature has dropped yet further. John brings the quad bike to a standstill next to the stables. The ewe's cold body lies in the trailer behind it, covered by a tarpaulin.

In years past they'd have buried the poor beast but ever since the EU had stepped in there'd been a significant tightening of the rules and regulations. The red tape was a nuisance and an added cost but he couldn't complain. They needed the subsidies.

After bringing the bike round to the site's carcass bin, John slides off the metal lid and peers inside. With its 1,600-litre capacity, it could easily store several large bodies. He sniffs to make sure it's clean. He'd given it a good wash down last time but it always paid to double-check. Satisfied, he uncovers the ewe, lifts her up by her legs, her stomach resting across his shoulders, then tips her into the grey container, her carcass hitting the floor with an echoing clunk. It was a small mercy that she hadn't been tupped. At least there weren't any other lives forming inside. Just her, alone up on the mountain, separated from her flock.

He reaches in, gives her a pat on the head. 'Rest easy,' he says. He then slides the lid back in place and clamps it down.

Back in the farmhouse, John removes the clingfilm from the plate of sandwiches, and checks his hands for grime and grit before taking a bite. Egg mayonnaise in fresh bread – few things are better. While he waits for Catrin to come back, he walks over to the small pile of Harri's letters. His son's handwriting is bunched up, as if he wasn't sure all the words would fit on the page. Their boy will be home at the beginning of February for two weeks of leave. Not soon enough and not long enough.

John puts the kettle on, his mind filling with the rumble of the water. Catrin comes through, dressed in jeans and a thick fleece. She looks flushed, as if she's been carrying bales of hay. He knows her body is going through all sorts. He'd noted the new, lighter duvet but hasn't said anything, not wanting to embarrass her, thinking it was better to let her speak to him in her own time. Was he wrong?

He notes her lipstick, the earrings. Could he be wrong about this, too? Was it even possible to be so wrong about the woman he's shared a roof and a bed with for more than twenty years, the woman he married and pledged his life to? Perhaps he shouldn't be surprised, given the things he's hidden from her.

Under Catrin's arm is the thick-volumed Holding Register, its cover scuffed red leather. She lays it on the kitchen table and raises a ready biro, her behaviour and tone damningly to the point.

'Okay, 12 January 2005 . . . Identification number?'

John pulls the yellow tag from his pocket. 'UK2228469.'

'One of the Welsh Mountains?'

'Yes.' He listens to the scratch of pen on paper, takes another bite of his sandwich, fills a glass with water.

'Notes?'

'Dead on discovery.'

'On its back?'

'No. Found her fleece ripped from her, caught on wire or something.'

'Poor thing.'

'I'll have to check the perimeter later.'

'We've kept up the NFSC membership, haven't we?'

'As far as I know,' replies John.

'Do you want me to contact one of the collectors? The maggot farm was helpful last month.'

'If you can. I still need to deal with some of the sheep and finish up with the vaccines and foot check,' says John. He takes another mouthful, watching Catrin as she flips between the pages, counting the deaths in the last few months. No more than usual.

John scrunches up the clingfilm into a tight ball and throws it into the bin. He places the plate in the sink, runs the water. He watches as Catrin reaches down and fondles Flint's silky black ears.

'I need to go to town,' she says. 'And I'm dropping Rhys off at the cinema. Will you pick him up later? He said he'll call you.'

Flint licks her palm, looks at her with large eyes that follow her as she disappears without another word.

The two records are still on the side and John picks one of them up, turns it over. His parents hadn't been music people. There was enough noise outside. When they came in at last, after a hard day's physical work, his parents wanted the peace and quiet. He pulls the record from the sleeve. Something falls to the floor. John bends down and picks up a rectangle of white card.

It's from Matt.

An invitation to his exhibition down in London at the Sunny Art Centre.

Darling Cat, he'd written. He'd be honoured to have her. And she can stay a night or two. *With love, Matt.* There are three large, flamboyant kisses.

John's hands shake as he methodically rips the invitation in half, and then does it again and again. It's thick card and he must bend it in the middle first, weakening it. Eventually there's a pile of irregular white squares, like snow or confetti, a miniature mountain on the worktop.

John leans down and looks at Flint, rubs behind his ears.

'I can't lose her,' he says. 'I won't lose her.'

Once he's deposited the remnants in the bin, John returns to the kitchen with one of his shotguns and the cleaning kit. He refills his mug of tea and, keeping an eye on the time, methodically dismantles the gun and sets about cleaning and polishing. As he works, he thinks about Matt. He's seen him only a few times up on the farm but it's a clear enough target, and, while he cleans the barrels and oils the mechanism, John thinks about the kind of mess that can be made of a man.

When he is no longer shaking, John returns the gun to its locked cabinet. He then finishes his work with the sheep, checks on the chickens and the horses. Feeds the dogs. When he gets home, the phone is ringing. It's Rhys.

'Da?' says Rhys, his voice like slurry. 'I need help.'

~

Christ alive, thinks John, what was the boy thinking, alone out here? And where were his damn friends, leaving him on a night like this when not two years back a man had been found in the morning, his eyes frozen wide? Fucking sixteen-year-olds. It was a rite of passage, he knew, but not like this. There was something cheap and miserable about being left here on the pavement in the dark, nothing but the big shopping markets lighting the sky.

Cineworld lies ahead and John brings the vehicle to a quick stop and hops out. He marches towards the glass doors that swing open at his approach. He spots Rhys almost immediately. The boy is holding a paper takeaway bag, his head bowed towards his knees, a hand over his eyes. There are two bottles of water on the table. He nods at a man standing behind the counter, who shrugs as if it's not his problem or it's something he's seen a hundred times before.

'Rhys?' He places a hand on his son's shoulder.

'Da? I'm sorry. I'm so sorry.'

'We'll get you home, okay? Do you think you can make it to the car?'

'Yeah, yeah, I feel sick.'

'Have you chucked?'

'Yeah, outside.'

'Just the once?'

'Yeah. But. But –'

'You might need to again?'

'Yeah, I'm sorry.'

'What were you drinking?'

'Cider.'

'Okay.'

'And some vodka.'

'Anything else? Any pills? Did you smoke? Rhys, try to stay awake. Can you tell me that, lad?'

'No. No. I mean. I mean some of the guys were smoking.'

'Marijuana?'

'No. I don't know. I don't think so. Da. I feel sick.'

'Do you need to be sick now or can you wait until we're outside?'

'I don't know.'

'Well, stay here and keep that bag at the ready.'

'Okay.'

John strides towards the counter, where the server watches. 'Thanks for looking after him,' John says. 'Did you see what was happening? He was supposed to be at the cinema with friends.'

The other man shakes his head and crosses his arms. 'The only thing I've seen this evening is the puke covering the toilet.'

'Christ. See anything?'

'Look, I'm not here to babysit.'

The man is staring at him with the same kind of expression that Catrin had been wearing earlier. He's middle aged, round and has deep smile lines. His badge says his name is Colin. Colin doesn't look like the kind of man who smiles much and John wonders if there's someone at home, if he's a different sort of man when he leaves the grind of serving customers fizzy drinks and sandwiches and having to put up with the general crap of a job like this.

'Where's the mop?' says John.

The man deflates, his arms dropping to his sides. 'Don't worry about it. Put a few quid in the charity box there,' he says.

John digs in his pockets and finds a few coins. It's for survivors of the tsunami, connecting families with lost ones. The money rattles and clinks.

'His first time?' asks Colin.

'That I know of,' says John.

'Always the worst.'

'I remember mine.'

'Well, you can bet it won't be his last.'

'No doubt. I'm sorry for the mess.'

'It's fine. I've three kids of my own. They can be a handful, I know.' Colin smiles at this and his whole face lights up. There he is, thinks John. There's the different man.

Walking back over to Rhys, he lifts his boy up on to his feet. 'You good to go?'

'Uh-huh,' says Rhys.

John grabs the sealed water bottle and offers an appreciative nod to Colin.

In the car, John unwraps the bottle and hands it to Rhys. 'Drink this.' He then lowers the window so the lad can lean out and get some fresh air and upchuck if he needs to. He calls Catrin, who picks up on the first ring.

'Where are you?' she says.

'It's Rhys. He's a bit wobbly on his feet but he's conscious. Nothing a good sleep and a bad hangover won't sort. Yes, we're in the car. Just about to head off. Yes, will do.'

He puts the mobile away and switches on the engine. 'Your mam says you're a bloody idiot.'

'Uh-huh.'

'If you need to be sick, do it out of the window. And face behind you. I don't want it blowing back in.'

'Mmm.'

Rhys stinks of sweat and sick and cider and a lingering tobacco musk. John opens his own window. He remembers the first time he'd drunk much too much. He'd gone along to the Young Farmers' Club and one beer had followed another until he could hardly walk. He was fifteen and foolish. A friend, also drunk, had driven him back home. His father had seen him walk through the door, shaken his head and said see you at half six. And John, he'd said, a man holds his drink.

Different times.

'Da?'

'I'm here.'

'Are you and Mam going to get a divorce?'

John's hands tighten around the steering wheel. 'No,' he says. He wonders if this is the reason behind tonight. There's only so much that can be hidden, muffled. The walls are only so thick.

'I miss Harri,' says Rhys.

'Me, too, lad,' says John.

The boy will forget this by the morning, thinks John. He glances over at his son. Rhys has his eyes closed and his cheek is leaning against the side of the door and he's clutching the bottle of water, like a raft at sea.

18 January 2005

Dear Mam, Da, Rhys

    How was Christmas?

    I'll be home sooner than you know it. Just a few weeks until I get to place my eyes on your ugly faces once again. Sooner, by the time you get this.

    I've been pretty damn tired these last few days. Definitely not getting enough shut-eye. I'm on duty again in a few hours and we'll have to stumble our way through.

I've been thinking a lot about Gramps and Nan recently. I don't know why. I think maybe it was because I ended up in this house the other day and there was this smell that came from – I don't know where – and it was just like the way their house smells. I guess everyone has their own sort of smell and if you live somewhere long enough it just seeps into things. They say it's what you eat, don't they? Which means by the time I get home I'll smell of ration packs – an aromatic mix of All-Day Breakfast and Steak-and-Vegetables. Not the sort of scent you'd buy at Christmas, is it?

Do you remember how we'd go down to those beach huts on Penmaenmawr and go digging in the sand? I miss that. The two of you laughing about me asking if we'd ever be rich enough to buy one for a whole year. I still remember filling my bucket with all kinds of things, sand and water and a few crabs. I found some of those sea worms or whatever in a rock pool and put the whole lot together. A few hours later the crabs had chopped the worms into pieces. It was fascinating and horrifying at the same time. Reminds me of that time I found Rhys popping ants with a magnifying glass when he was four or five.

Do you remember when there was all that frogspawn in the lake? It had somehow survived the ducks and the moorhens and the fish. One late afternoon, I caught one of the young frogs and took it with me up on the fells. I carried this small leathery fella and then put it down on the grass and watched it hop and hop and hop. I must have been there for an hour. The little frog got slower and slower and started to struggle with its hopping. At that point I realized the guy needed to be getting back in the water. I ran to the lake and carefully put him back on the edge where he could hop in. But he wouldn't move, just stood there gazing out at the water. I gave him a push, gentle as I could, and he fell in. Tumbled, really. His head was down and his belly was up. He just lay there floating. I could see his eyes open and I watched, waiting for some kind of miracle to happen, thinking I couldn't have killed him. I'd never intended for that to happen; I'd just wanted to play. But his body just hovered there on the surface of the water, so still, like he was doing a circus act. People say that when someone's dead they look like they're sleeping but I don't think so – there's a stillness and an absence, a void if you like, that you see when someone's no longer there, when it's just a shell, a husk, a mortal coil. Anyway, I'll never forget that. The way I'd killed this little creature because, what, I wanted to see it hop? Because I wanted to be entertained. Not a single damn thought for the life of something else.

When I went back inside you asked me what the matter was and I couldn't tell you. I just couldn't tell you. I worried you'd think I was some kind of monster and, in my own head, I was. So I just wiped my snotty nose on my sleeve and said it was nothing and I sat there eating jam sandwiches, listening to you talk about the new baby that was due soon. In a few weeks, you said, I'd have a little brother. You and Da were still debating the name, going back and forth between Rhys and Dylan. You asked if I'd help look after him and I'd nodded, all the while worrying I might hurt him by accident. I think that was one of the most miserable days of my life and it's not something anyone else would suspect or know about. And now here I am.

Strange what happens to your head out here. You have these long stretches when all there is to do is think about things. And then there's too much going on and not enough sleep. You remember stuff you thought you'd forgotten.

I love you and I'll see you very soon. I'm looking forward to being among the green hills and being able to sleep in a room with a door and food that fills you right up and not having any responsibilities.

Two weeks at home. What could be better?

Your son,
Harri x x

440. Mr Blair and President Bush spoke by video conference on 25 January and discussed messaging around the imminent election.* Mr Blair considered that talking publicly about withdrawal would smack of defeat. Rather, he suggested that: 'Our aim was to make our role redundant.'

– *The Report of the Iraq Inquiry*, Volume VII, Section 9.3

* Letter Phillipson to Owen, 25 January 2005, 'Prime Minister's VTC with President Bush, 25 January: Iraq'.

9

It's still dark and the sun sits beneath the mountain but Catrin wakes early, her body clammy against the white sheets, faint chords trilling at the back of her mind. She reaches for it, tries to solidify the sounds, repeats each note, but like morning mist they clear and leave only a sense of what remained. For a while she stays tucked up against the cold of the room, listening to John breathe in and out, his body rising and falling like waves against a beach. She runs a tongue along her bottom-left molar, which has been throbbing on and off in recent months. She can't remember the last time she went to the dentist. Rolling on to her back, she stares up at the ceiling and tries to play through the chords again but the notes have lost their shape. She sighs, restless. Years ago, she used to keep a voice recorder by the bed and would quietly hum melodies that came to her in the half-dream state that seemed so perfect for conjuring new ideas, with enough lucidity to lend structure and pattern, but not so much that insecurities and distractions interrupted the creative spell.

Doing her best not to make a noise, Catrin slides from the bed and pulls on her dressing gown. Shivering, she hurries downstairs to the hallway gloom and pulls out the stool by the piano. She quietly lifts the lid and settles her fingertips on the cold keys. She is careful not to press down, lest she waken the whole house. Instead, she closes her eyes, lets her fingers brush intuitively, meditatively, along the surface of the keys as the notes play in her mind. She tries to find the pattern, the pace and mood of it, until – there! – she hears the rightness of the songscape. Pausing, Catrin smiles and retraces her fingersteps, dallies, repeats, tweaks and returns.

She opens her eyes, goes through the small piece again, committing it to memory, before reaching up for some paper and a pen. As she makes her marks on the manuscript paper, watching the pattern appear, she feels happy in her solitude; right now, she could be the only person in the world, yet content in the full.

Catrin doesn't know where it comes from, this ability to weave sounds; it is a strange thing because when she is channelling the magic, and it does feel like a kind of magic, she is most herself, most alive, but also the least; because she is a conduit through which some greater force seems to flow. Composing something new is different from playing music. She can get lost at the piano easily enough but that is more of an ecstasy of sweet sound and the delight of reflex. Making something wholly and wonderfully new – something the universe, in all its immensity has never known before – feels like a shout of joy and defiance; it's a creative act that says *I exist*. More than that, thinks Catrin, it is a hymn to life itself, to the miracle and strangeness of living.

Sitting here, something else pushes at the edges of her consciousness – other recollections – of Harri, sitting here when he was twelve or thirteen, composing his own song for the school talent competition; memories of Rhys going to the Eisteddfod when he was twelve, the seriousness he had shown as he played before his audience. She pictures Rhys last week, stumbling into the house, groggy-eyed, reeking of vodka and vomit. Catrin's concerned it's part of a more worrying trend and even though John had shrugged it off, said it was bound to happen sooner or later, she'd seen the way his eyes had watched Rhys, how he'd placed a hand on the boy's back as he climbed the stairs and then put a waste-paper basket by his bed. She'd noticed how John had checked on Rhys three times in the dead of night. Catrin knew that, in their own ways, they worried about Rhys, about both their boys. But what could they do?

Pushing aside this viscous question, she tries to follow the music, the melody inside and out, whispering the markings as she makes them: her own spell that ballets around the five lines of the staves. But the question sticks.

And, as she works, Catrin becomes increasingly aware of two things. The first is the cold that has begun to seep through her dressing gown, despite its thickness. There was never any getting away from the weather, even indoors. It would steal upon your skin, setting the little hairs on end and over time settle in your bones.

The second disturbance is the growing ache in her back. Catrin knows she has a tendency to hunch but she's always liked to get eyes and nose close to the piano or the paper as she works.

She presses a few more keys but the mood and moment are rapidly disappearing. It's already getting lighter outside, the black of night replaced by a glowing purple. The solstice had passed over a month ago and, while they were still in the heart of winter, it was comforting to know the days would be lengthening into spring – her favourite season, when the small flowers raised their heads from the earth and hibernating creatures yawned and stretched and pulled themselves from slumber. The ewes would tread along the mountain, their bellies swollen, ready to give birth.

A third disturbance breaks the spell of her work for good – Rhys coming down the stairs, peering past the door, watching. A small sigh of disappointment escapes her. Magic, she thinks, is a private thing.

'You're up early,' she says, letting out a sudden yawn, feeling her body shiver as her skin begins to soak up the terrible chill. Flint walks over, his tail wagging. He nuzzles at her and Catrin rubs behind his ears.

'Couldn't sleep,' says Rhys. He's already wrapped up in a scarf and a coat, a rifle in his hand. 'Thought I'd do Da a favour and get us some rabbits for the dogs.'

'Making amends for your performance the other week?'

'I didn't tell you?' he says. 'Hollywood was on the phone.'

Catrin gives a half-smile but there's something in the way her boy stands there in the rising light that makes her feel as if everything is slipping through her fingers. 'Is everything all right, Rhys? Really?'

For a moment it seems as if he's about to tell her whatever it is that's been troubling him but then he shrugs. 'I'm just tired,' he says.

'You don't need to go out. Your father can take care of it.'

'I'll manage,' says Rhys. 'Besides, it's the old man who needs his sleep. You must have noticed?'

Catrin nods slowly but in truth she hadn't, and she wonders what this says about her, about them. The farm wore everything and everyone down; there was truth enough in that but over time you stopped being aware of the slow decline of the body.

'Your father's forty-eight, Rhys. Hardly an old man.'

'Nearly an antique,' replies the boy.

Catrin rolls her eyes. 'You'll be back for seven thirty, won't you?'

'Latest,' replies Rhys. He picks up the rifle and nods – so like his father, thinks Catrin. She looks down at the sheets of music before her and tidies them away. Over an hour has passed. Walking to the other side of the room, Catrin turns on the TV, places it on mute and switches to the news channel. John has refused to watch it for the last few weeks, insisting instead on *Bill Oddie's How to Watch Wildlife*, saying he can no longer stomach the news. And so, sometimes, when she's alone, Catrin puts it on, wondering what new horror she'll be confronted with. When she'd told him about Bush being sworn in again, he'd shaken his head in disgust, saying it was hardly a surprise. Men like that, he'd said, were above it all. They brought ruin on the people below them but somehow they swam above it. You mark my words, he'd said, Blair will be made a 'Sir' by the end of it. And when it's all brushed under the carpet and he's moved on, he'll start raking it in on the speaker circuit, working that black book of his, writing his memoir, playing the statesman, smiling benevolently and telling us how hard it was for him to be sending boys and girls to battle. He's a goddamn criminal but they'll ply him with honours for service to the country. And meanwhile our boys and girls will lie dead and buried, suffering inside and out, and in twenty years they'll be forgotten – no one will remember the names of the fallen, apart from the poor bastards directly affected, the families like us. But everyone will remember Tony Fucking Blair.

Catrin had been taken aback by the outburst, but this morning the news seemed to confirm everything John had said: a helicopter crash has left thirty-one US marines dead. According to the report, to date in the war, it was the largest loss of American life from a single incident.

The screen cuts to Bush. 'Obviously, any time we lose life,' he says, 'it is a sad moment.'

A sad moment?

The death of a parent or a child isn't *sad*. And it isn't for a *moment*.

It is an agony. It is an endless, present-tense trauma.

~

The bruised sky stretches far above and the mountains feel like an embrace as Catrin walks towards the coop, one hand buried deep within her coat pocket, the other clutching a small wicker basket, as they would have done in the olden days before the invention of cardboard and egg cartons. John has said his own mother would have gathered eggs like that, piled them up against one another in the hollow of the basket, carried in the crease of an arm. Sometimes Catrin likes to imagine she's from another era, a simpler, less noisy world. The hens cluck as she approaches, hopping about on their feet beneath the mud. She silently collects their eggs and offers her quiet thanks, wondering how the dim-witted birds could possibly be related to the titans of the past, the Tyrannosaurus rex and the Velociraptor.

When she gets back to the warmth of the Aga, John is up, boiling the kettle. She pauses, watching him from the door. He shifts from foot to foot, still favouring his left leg after the fall he'd taken on the hunt at the end of last year.

And what of Matt? Where does he fit in to all of this? Catrin doesn't know and, if she was honest with herself, doesn't care. She's able to separate him from the equation and, although it requires emotional and intellectual gymnastics, she's prepared to cartwheel and somersault.

At the end of February, Matt's residency will finish and he'll be back down in London, preparing for his exhibition. She never found the invitation among the two records but he'd given her another and begged her to come. It would be difficult to arrange but she'd agreed. How could she not? A whole weekend in London with Matt. Her old friend Sylvia would provide the perfect excuse and Catrin has already started to sow the seeds with John.

'Morning,' she says. Flint looks up from beneath the table, flaps his tail.

'You two were up early,' says John.

'Rhys is out with the rifle. Wanted to let you rest.'

'He's a good lad.'

'He has his moments.' She's still upset about the other week when John had brought him back. She'd stayed up all night, wondering if she ought to call an ambulance to have his stomach pumped. She hands John two of the eggs, which he gently lays in the boiling water before returning to the job of spreading his slice of toast thick with butter and then cutting it into strips.

'Don't you think it's strange,' he says, 'how we call them soldiers?'

'Never really thought about it,' says Catrin, kneeling down to stroke her old dog, whose eyes seem sad this morning. 'Do you think Harri's okay?'

'We can hope.'

'I don't like that last letter. Something not right about it.' Catrin looks over to the kitchen table, where the two folded pages sit by the newspaper. For reasons she can't precisely pinpoint, they disturb her.

'He'll be home in less than a week. If the transit vehicles and the corridor or whatever they call it are working properly.'

'Yes, but do you think he'll be okay until then?' asks Catrin.

'I can't say. It's not a playground out there,' says John.

'But what do you *think*?' says Catrin.

'People change. Inside, outside. Sometimes for better. And sometimes . . .' John shakes his head. 'Well.'

Catrin brings a finger to her lips, chews the end of a nail. The man wasn't making sense. She looks at the small plastic hen counting down the minutes. 'I just hope he's all right,' she says.

John takes a seat, two boiled eggs and the soldiers lined up on his plate, like they're on parade. 'Humpty Dumpty sat on the wall and Humpty Dumpty had a great fall,' he chants. On the last word, he brings the knife into the side of the shell and cracks through it. 'All the king's horses and all the king's men, couldn't put Humpty Dumpty back together again.' With the final line, he cuts through the crown of the egg and lifts it clean off.

It was something the boys used to do when they were little before arguing over who had the best yolk for dipping.

'Catrin?' says John, the tone of his voice putting her on edge. 'Are we still okay?'

The question is so unexpected she finds her tongue tied. At least, that is what she'll tell herself later.

John lifts a slice of bread, eyes on his plate. 'I know it's not been easy,' he says. 'What with everything going on. But this. You and me' – he waves his buttery knife around, taking in the farm, the two of them – 'it works, doesn't it? I'm doing enough?'

Catrin walks over to him and places a hand on his shoulder.

John says nothing as he eats but she can feel the muscles beneath her fingers like tight knots. She stands there, massaging his back, trying to undo the cords until her hands begin to feel the pressure. When at last he's finished with his breakfast, John stays in the chair, leaning back into her warmth. He tilts his head back, his eyes on her, and he lets out a long sigh and smiles. 'That's nice,' he says.

'You're tense,' says Catrin. 'Muscles hard and knotted like old vines.'

'Well, you know how it is here. There's always something that needs doing.'

'No rest for the wicked,' says Catrin.

'None,' says John but he doesn't smile. 'Are you still planning on going to see Sylvia?'

Catrin looks into John's deep, serious eyes. 'Yes,' she says. What else can she say? She is too close to him now, the touch of him is unsettling her thoughts and she doesn't trust herself to say the right thing. She can even feel the tug of confession. But she bites her tongue, keeps her secrets.

'You'll have a good time,' says John. 'It'll be good for you to have a bit of a holiday.' He reaches up and takes her hand, kisses it once, twice.

Catrin feels the roughness of his skin, their two wedding rings nestled close – the tarnished gold still catching a little of the light.

Catrin walks slowly around her piano. She takes in its angles and smooth polish; she lets her fingers glide along the wood. Placing her two palms on the flat surface, she feels the heat and subtle contours of her skin against the cool top. When she lifts them, the imprints of her two hands remain, then slowly fade. Raising the cover, she looks into its heart, the bass and treble strings running from the bridges to the pins. The instrument really was too big for the space, almost filling the entire hall, but there was nowhere else in the farmhouse it could fit. Despite the impracticability of having a grand piano in the entrance to their home, it was the one thing Catrin had insisted upon. For better or for worse, Catrin had reminded John. He'd grumbled about it but agreed in the end. Richer or poorer, he'd said. She'd laughed about it back then.

The doorbell rings and Catrin checks her watch – Sophie is always bang on time. She goes to open the front door and the girl is standing there, dressed in her school coat and rubbing her hands. Light-brown eyes peer up from beneath a woolly hat that hides a tangle of blonde hair, a replica of her mother, who is waving from the car.

'See you in an hour or so,' shouts Sarah, winding up the window and tooting the horn, sending the dogs in the kennel howling. Catrin waves back, wishing the other woman wouldn't set the dogs off like that.

Catrin ushers Sophie into the hall and tells her to get settled at the piano, to warm up her fingers and go through some of the scales. 'I'll bring your hot chocolate through in just a moment,' says Catrin. She watches as the girl smiles and settles herself down on the stool, back straight, and blows warm air on to her outstretched fingers. She's only eleven but Sophie has always seemed older than her age. Catrin would have liked a daughter and has always been a bit envious of those mothers who have someone on their side, someone to conspire with, to share intimate experiences with, in a way she couldn't with her sons.

'Here you are,' says Catrin, placing the brimming mug on the side table.

'Thank you,' says Sophie. She has a cute smile that shows a neat row of pearl teeth.

'I was wondering if you'd like to choose your exam piece today?' asks Catrin. She reaches behind the practice book to bring out another, opening it to Section B, where there's a list of six pieces, from Reinecke's Prelude, Op. 183, No. 1, to a short piece by Tchaikovsky. 'I'll play them all through a few times and then you can narrow them down to some favourites, how about that?'

Each piece is under two minutes and Sophie seems particularly drawn to a composition by Cornelius Gurlitt called, rather strikingly, 'Sea Pink', one of twelve from *Kleine Blumen*, or *Little Flowers*.

After Catrin has played the composition for the final time, she tells Sophie that she can select two pieces and then choose the one she wants to play next week.

Catrin guides Sophie in the opening, starting in B minor, moving to F-sharp major, before returning from the dominant to the tonic, explaining to the girl about the ternary form and asking if she can think of any other compositions that follow a similar pattern. Once they've gone through the piece a few more times, Catrin shows Sophie how to break the music down into block chords, taking three chords at a time, to help with hand position and heighten anticipation for each subsequent note, building in muscle memory. Sophie sets her fingers in place and slowly mimics Catrin, her little hands shadowing.

Once they've reached the end of the middle section, Sophie stops and takes a sip from her mug. She looks at Catrin and then back at the piano. 'My cat died yesterday,' she says.

'Oh, Sophie,' says Catrin. 'I'm sorry to hear that, cherub.' She puts a hand on the girl's shoulder and gives it a rub. 'Was he a good age?'

'No. Just two,' says Sophie. 'We found him on the side of the road. Someone had run him over. He was called Sprinkles. We buried him at the back of the garden, next to Jumbo.'

'I'm really so sorry, Sophie. Would you like to talk about it some more? We can sit here and you can have a rest? I can make you another hot chocolate? Or would you prefer to keep playing?'

Sophie sits straighter in the seat. 'Keep playing,' she says.

As Catrin watches the young girl work patiently through the bars, she sits in wonder at the resilience of children. Or was that an excuse parents used because it was easier to pretend kids were strong, could recover from whatever invisible scars their parents caused?

When Sophie reaches the end of her piece, Catrin puts an arm around her and gives a comforting squeeze. She thinks about Harri, hoping that her son still has something of the child in him, that there remains something of the little boy she once held close.

～

There's a thunderous knock at the door and Catrin, buried under admin, jumps at the sudden noise. She's not expecting visitors. It's some hours since Sophie left and Catrin's been busy replying to emails from local schools looking to arrange trips to the farm in April. The knock comes again and Catrin rises, calling to Flint. Who could it be? And what could they want?

The dogs in the kennel are quiet and this sets her further on edge. She doesn't like it when they are silent. It reminds her of the farm down south that went through all that trouble, one of those big estates with fancy paintings on the walls, the frames alone worth more than a new car. Thieves had stolen almost two million pounds' worth of items, the police calling it a 'sophisticated operation'. What Catrin remembers most clearly, though, is the pair – husband and wife – saying over and over that it wasn't the jewellery or the antiques that upset them but the dogs; that what the thieves had done to the dogs was unforgivable; later, the newspapers reported they'd been given raw chicken coated in methomyl. In total twelve dogs had been killed in order to stop them doing what was in their nature, what they'd been doing for thousands of years: protecting their home, their pack.

The knock comes a third time. Catrin thinks of Harri and her heart thunders. She knows how things work, that the Army like to send people to the door when there's bad news to deliver. Flint, now at her side, lets out a long, low growl.

Please, she thinks, *not Harri*.

Feeling sick, Catrin peers through the hall window.

And breathes.

She doesn't know who they are or what they want but they're not in khaki. She wonders if it's related to the fuel inspection from a few weeks ago; but, as Catrin opens the front door and is confronted by two burly men with shaved heads, wearing high-vis jackets and lanyards, it's clear they have a different agenda.

She remembers the last time two men stood at her door, remembers Heatley with his piggy eyes and his wandering, intrusive touch.

'Mrs Williams?'

'Yes?' she says.

'We're working on behalf of the High Court and have been issued a writ to seize goods in order to cover the principal sum of £14,891.' He holds up a piece of paper. 'May we come in?'

The writ is too small to read from behind the shelter of the door and, even if she could make out the words, Catrin's not sure she wants to.

'There must be a mistake,' she says. 'We spoke to the bank.'

'We're not from the bank,' he says.

'They restructured the debt. And it wasn't a third of that.'

'We're not from the bank.'

And then it drops. John. But he'd said only three. Three thousand. That's what he'd said. And now there were men at her door demanding almost fifteen.

'You'll have received a notice. At least a week ago.'

John, she thinks. *What have you done?*

'Please,' says the bailiff. 'We need to come in.'

The man exudes patience and, despite the chill, he stands with such ease that he could be on a beach somewhere warm and exotic, watching the sea lap against the shore. She's tempted to shut the door, slide the bolt across, but knows it won't achieve anything. The other man is already looking left and right as if he's gathering evidence, weighing up the cost of the various vehicles, her 4x4, the quad bike. Everything is second-hand and old as rust. How are they going to make up almost fifteen thousand pounds?

She opens the door wider and the two men step past the threshold, eyes roving. They stop in the hall and Catrin puts a hand out to her piano.

'No,' she says. 'Not this.'

'Is there someone you can call?'

'It was a wedding gift from my father,' she says.

'I'm sorry. I understand this can be difficult but we've got the writ. We're obliged to seize possessions up to the value of the principal. Is there someone you can call?' He turns to his colleague. 'Daniel, would you mind waiting in the car for a moment, please?'

The one called Daniel nods and leaves and the hall seems bigger and lighter than before. Somewhere in the back of her mind, she's aware that these are just two men doing their job, and doing it as well as they can.

'John, my husband, will be back in forty minutes. He's collecting my son from school.'

The man looks at his watch. 'I'm not sure we can wait that long.'

'Let me phone him,' she replies. Catrin dashes to the kitchen and punches in the digits, her hand shaking. The call rings through. She leaves a voicemail. She's not quite sure what she's saying but the words tumble out and her hand grips the phone too tightly. When she returns, the bailiff is studying the piano intently and she begs him to wait for John. She wipes a hand across her eyes.

'Please,' she says. 'Please wait.'

She runs into the kitchen, opens the large cabinet where the silver set is kept, each knife, fork and spoon engraved with her grandparents' family initial. Their good plates, which they rarely use, except for special events like Christmas, are also here. They have a gilt-and-royal-blue edge and she still has the full set. Catrin tries not to think about what she's doing but the feeling of stripping away her house, of pulling at the threads of her home, makes her eyes sting. But there's no stopping – she cannot, will not, lose her piano. She carries the items through into the hall and places them on the floor to one side.

'Take a look at these,' she says. The man walks over, shaking his head. He knows. He's seen it all before.

She brings the guns, old and new, the over-and-under, the side-by-side and the rifles, carefully leaning each against the wall, not caring what John will think. Next comes her vanity box with her rings, necklaces and bracelets, which she sweeps up in her arms, each piece with its own sparkle, its own history and weight. They must be worth something. They mean something to her; they are precious to her.

But the bailiff's look is jaded: sentiment is cheap; the world is already too full of feeling.

She hunts around the house, pulls paintings off the walls, whisks away small ornaments, heaping them up in a panic as if there's a fire at her heels. The items are piled together in a sporadic web, as if she's about to do a flash sale, a car-boot offering. This is what it's like when people die, she thinks, this gathering up of things that mean so much but are worth so little.

She is breathing heavily and about to make another round when the bailiff walks over and very gently touches her shoulder. He shakes his head and his lips are curled inwards, as if he's resisting the urge to say it out loud. But she knows. She knows.

It's not enough.

'It's not something you can just pick up,' she says, looking now at her piano. 'You need to know what you're doing.' She's not sure why but she begins explaining it to him. She points to the screws that need removing, the key cover, the end blocks and the front board that lifts up.

The bailiff nods silently and then calls his colleague, Daniel, back into the house.

Catrin continues with her explanation, hoping that it might buy her enough time for John to get back, although what will he be able to do? She is already beginning to say goodbye. This is what she's really doing. She's saying goodbye to her piano. To each small part of it. And it's his fault. John's. It has to be. It's all coming together now. The way the farm never seemed to make enough, no matter what they did; Tim's gentle nudge; the betting slips. How had she not noticed? How could she have been so blind?

And this was the price.

She points out the action, explaining that it's the hardest step and where mistakes most commonly occur; the hammers breaking off. She talks on, trying to distract herself from what's really happening. Trying to hold herself together while something she loves is taken apart. She highlights the care needed with the soundboard, the piece of wood inside that amplifies the sound of the strings; it's like the heart of the piano, she tells them, and is all too easily broken.

Daniel nods, like he's agreeing with her. 'May I?' he asks, directing his eyes to the stool. He has a soft voice and, when he sits down, Catrin can immediately tell that he's an experienced pianist. He plays through a couple of scales and then sighs.

'She's beautiful,' he says, stroking the wood as one might a beloved pet. 'Don't worry, we know what we're doing. We'll take good care of her.'

Unable to speak, Catrin nods.

'Is there no one else you can call?' says the other man. 'Any other family?'

Exhausted, she lets out a long, tremulous sigh. 'Give me five minutes?'

'Take your time,' he replies. She knows he doesn't mean it.

Catrin goes back to the kitchen. All this time, Flint has stayed in his bed by the Aga. He rarely gets up these days. Just to stagger about in the yard to relieve himself.

Taking a deep breath, Catrin phones her mother. Perhaps Catrin ought to have called her to start with but the shame of it had held her back. There was no escaping it.

'Mum,' she says.

There's a long silence after she's finished speaking.

'I'm sorry,' says Alice, at last. 'But no.' The words come out as hard as a knuckle rapped against oak.

'No?'

'You know John has already borrowed from me? A few years

ago? Almost eight thousand pounds. And he's never paid back a penny.'

Catrin stands in the middle of her kitchen, feeling like the walls are coming down around her. 'I didn't.'

'I agreed not to tell you, which was stupid, really. But I had you in mind and he convinced me to keep it quiet, said it would upset you no end. Marriage isn't easy and I suppose I thought it might help things. I know cash-flow can sometimes be a problem. Strange to say I don't even know what he spent it on.'

'And you won't help now?' Catrin hates herself for asking like this.

There's another long pause and Catrin can hear her mother's breath.

'Please,' says Catrin. 'We'll pay you back. He'll get help.' She hates herself as she says this. She hates John. She hates that she has to defend him.

'No,' says Alice, at last. 'I'm sorry, my dear, really I am. But I think I've done enough.'

When Catrin returns to the hall, all she does is shake her head. The two men get to work. They're kind and careful, apologizing as they begin. And for some reason she can't explain, this makes her all the more upset. It empties her out.

Catrin hears John before she sees him.

'What's going on?' he shouts, his voice like a ripped page.

Rhys hurries in behind his father, his school backpack slung over his shoulders.

'What do you think?' replies Catrin, her words like acid.

'They can't take it,' says John.

'They can. And they are.' She is on her feet now. Her voice fills the hall but she doesn't care. She is tired, sad and angry.

'They can take something else,' he replies, balling his hands into fists, looking back at the bailiffs. 'Anything else.'

Rhys shakes his head and escapes to the kitchen.

'What can they take?' says Catrin. 'The quad bike? What's that, five hundred quid? The cars? The tractor? How are you going to run the farm without the equipment? You're not thinking. You never think. You just wait until the consequences come marching home. Why didn't you tell me, John?'

'Let me call Tim. He'll help.'

'Just like my mother, you mean? Eight thousand, John?'

'I didn't –'

'This morning,' Catrin cuts in, 'when you asked if you were doing enough – well, here's your answer, John: you're not. Not even close.'

John's face contorts, becomes ugly with pain and fury. 'You're hardly the symbol of virtue,' he growls.

The house seems to quake, cracks in the foundations widening.

'What do you mean?' hisses Catrin. She's ready now. Let it all come down.

John looks at her but he won't say it. He doesn't dare.

In the pause that expands between them, Rhys walks in, a piece of buttered toast in hand. 'Jesus,' he says, looking at the two of them, the cavernous space between. 'And you wonder why Harri left?'

February

Iraq Body Count: 1,297

457. The JIC judged that: 'the military campaign is not effect-ively containing the insurgency in Sunni areas. Law and order, the pace of economic reconstruction, the availability of jobs and general quality of life have not matched expectation . . . Sunni "hearts and minds" are being lost.'

– *The Report of the Iraq Inquiry*, Volume VII, Section 9.3

10

Harri stirs and feels the flash of panic at unfamiliar surround-
ings, his body as electric as a live wire, fingers tight around
his bedsheets. But no. He's cocooned by four walls, wrapped
in peace and privacy, cushioned by silence and safety and
the smells of his childhood. He is home. His eyes adjust to the
gloom as he reaches for his watch. It's almost half five at base
camp; he'd be able to hear locals making their *salah*, their reci-
tations directed at Mecca, to their God and Prophet. But here,
in this dark-green patch of northern Wales where Druids once
wandered, the world still feels aslumber. He yawns and closes
his lids, luxuriates in the thickness of duvet and mattress, enjoys
the chill of his room, and then lets his dream-filled thoughts
enchant him away from wakefulness, content at the thought
of being able to satisfy himself later in the morning, not a soul
to disturb him.

Later, outside, he delights in the cold and the wide, open
sky, which is bursting with blossoms of grey cloud. All around
there's a wealth of soil and vegetation and so much that's green
and so many gradients of green that an artist could spend a
lifetime painting a single branch of oak or birch; although it's
still winter, it feels like colour has been poured over all things.
Harri walks over to the lake and marvels at the glistening water.
His da has restocked some of the fish in the deeps – and Harri's
seen the great bird already circling – but perhaps there are too
few to make sport for the heron.

He'd heard of people fishing with hand grenades in Iraq.
They'd lob one into the centre of a body of water and wait for

the explosion to send the fish up into the air like a fireworks display. The men would then send boys out in skiffs, nets and buckets in hand. Harri wasn't sure if it was true. He'd heard plenty of crazy shit. About the British, the Americans, the Iraqis. About people at home and abroad; about things private, public and political. Last week some of the American lads had told him Bucky Bush, uncle of George, had made half a million dollars from the sale of stock in a firm that supplied equipment to the US Army. Was it true? Harri had no idea. He'd heard enough to think it might be. Seen enough, too. But there was no point in dwelling.

Harri casts an eye up the hill and squares his shoulders; his da would be waiting on him. He'd briefly left one war but it felt like he'd stepped into another. The farm had always thrown up its challenges but right now it seemed like there was one drama after another, and, although his parents were tough, they weren't trained to meet conflicts head-on.

But Harri was. And right now there were things to face, to fix.

As he climbs, he marvels at the distance he can cross. No need for a VALLON here; no trudging behind the guy with his metal detector sweeping over the ground, its halo pressed close to the earth like a dog on scent. He didn't have to keep watch on the locals, who seemed to have a sixth sense when it came to disturbances, knew when market day was best avoided, when things were likely to get hot. He didn't have to obsess over body language, tone of voice, or keep eyes peeled for smoke signals and kites. He didn't have to worry about explosives hidden under the freshly turned earth, baked hard in the sun. Christ, you had to be careful. All it took was a single misstep.

He passes dozens of sheep, many of them carrying, teeth idly chewing. In a few months the ewes would take themselves off, find a private space where they could be alone and vulnerable as they gave birth. He thinks about the local farmer he'd recently met near Fallujah. What would he make of all of this? He'd say it was paradise. He'd ask Harri why he would ever want to leave such a place as this. And, after three long months away, it seems mad that Harri ever had, and crazier still that he'll do it again.

He sees his father up ahead by a long stretch of drystone wall that has collapsed and will need extensive repair work. In some sections, they'll have to remove the exisitng stone and rebuild it from the bottom up. His old man's looking down at the ground, studying a selection of rocks. Lola, his da's favourite dog, watches nearby. Harri takes a moment to observe his father: to get the measure of the man who once seemed a giant to his young eyes.

'Harri.'

'Morning, Da.'

'Rest well?'

'Like a lamb,' replies Harri.

'I've sorted some of the stones into size already,' says John, nodding towards the separate piles. Harri nods. A drystone wall needed planning if it was to last.

'We can finish sorting and then lay the foundation stones into the earth,' says Harri. 'Where are the tie stones?'

John points to another small pile further off.

'Good. And there's the hearting and capstones. Looks like we should make good headway and finish up tomorrow morning. What do you think?'

'I think you've brought some of the officer home with you,' says John.

Harri smiles. 'We're joining Mam and Rhys at the Black Sheep after?'

'She thought you'd like to visit some of your old watering holes.'

'Not wrong there.'

They get to work and Harri watches his father, who pants and wheezes while he weaves back and forth between the stones, swapping one for another as he searches for the best fit. It's been such a long time since he's worked with his father like this, father and son, just as people had been doing for generations on the farm. The work is physical and soon Harri feels sweat under his arms and running down his back. Stripping off his shirt, he catches his father staring at him.

'The tattoo?' asks Harri, stretching his skin where the motto of Number Two Company, 'Gwyr Ynys Y Cedyrn' – 'Men of the Island of the Mighty' – is written in black ink.

'No, there,' says John, pointing.

It's a recent scar running up his side towards his armpit. Harri shrugs. 'Nothing major,' he says. 'Things get a little cheeky sometimes.'

They set to work. At one point John takes a seat but Harri keeps at it. He's always liked manual labour. Even at university he'd spent most of his time in the cadets, playing at being a soldier. That, plus rugby and the gym. He liked to feel healthy, to feel strong. Didn't hurt to look the part either.

'Are things easier now that you're out there?' asks John. 'Between you and the other lads?'

Harri scrapes the grit from his hands. After university, he'd started at Sandhurst with a load of posh boys from Eton and Charterhouse. It had presented challenges; he'd not had the right education, accent or lineage. But things were harder for those who served under him, men from the farms, steelworks, pits and valleys. They were okay taking orders from the upper classes because that's just how things were; it was expected. But he was an upstart, someone who was an officer but not an officer-sort. They'd not liked it; called him an 'impostor' and worse. Still, he'd worked harder and drunk harder than any of them, picked them up and backed them up enough to change minds. They were Welsh Guards, after all. It had taken time and some things had changed, though some hadn't.

Harri wipes the sweat from his brow. 'It's better.'

'I'm glad,' says John. 'You know your mam worries about you.'

'She worries about you as well,' says Harri. He looks at the wall. There's another few feet to go. This, he thinks, is the sort of thing they should be doing out in Iraq. Instead, for every wall that's built, several are torn down. Developmental money was pouring into the country. Schools were being built but left empty. The infrastructure was crippled. He looks back at his father, who's taken out a knife and is scraping out the dirt from under his nails.

'You should have told me there were problems,' Harri says, determined to persevere, knowing there's conflict on the horizon that they can address now or later; either way, they'd have to meet it.

'We didn't want to burden you,' says John. 'Not under the circumstances.'

'I'd have coped,' replies Harri. 'Whatever it was. That business with the piano, Da. It's bad.'

'I know,' says his da, clouds building on his brow.

'I'd have helped.'

'Damn it, Harri! How could you?' says John. 'You weren't here. You left.'

The simple accusation cuts through and Harri feels his hand tighten around the rock in his palm. He squeezes it tighter, and the sharp end digs painfully into his skin but still he tightens his grip. 'How much do you need?' asks Harri.

The old man turns and flings a small stone at a crow that's been watching them. Lola leaps to her feet.

'You're a good lad,' says John. But there's something else gleaming in his father's eyes and Harri turns away so he does not embarrass his proud, old man. As he picks up another rock and studies where to place it, he thinks he hears his father's thanks but it could easily have been the wind. The weather is picking up and the clouds are congregating. A storm is coming.

They work for another few hours and the wall grows a few hands at a time.

The rain starts to fall and John calls it, saying they ought to be getting washed up and ready for lunch. As they stride down through tumbling fields, the dog bounding before them, John leans on his son a little because his leg has started to hurt. The knee has been bad for years now and, with the fall on Boxing Day, it's worse still. As they approach the farmhouse, Harri feels his father's fingers grip his shoulder, part comfort, part hindrance.

'Mam ever mention a fella called Matthew Edevane?' asks John, coughing up a glob of phlegm and spitting in the cropped grass.

Harri shakes his head. 'Why d'you ask?'

'It's nothing,' says his old man, steadying himself.

'Nothing?' says Harri.

~

He marvels at the roads and the speeds at which shining cars zip by. Nine days before he leaves all this behind. He turns away and crosses his arms. This was the trouble with sitting around: too much time to think.

'Everything all right, Harri?'

His mam has one hand on the wheel, the other resting on her lap. She wears a burgundy dress and a little makeup; her hair was cut yesterday and, although she says she wants to look her best for her boy, Harri can't help but wonder.

'Fine,' he says at length.

'You seem quiet,' she says.

'I'm fine,' he repeats, and then shakes his head. 'I've been to the bank.'

'The bank?'

'I want to help you and Da.'

His mother says nothing for some time; the silence is filled by the gentle whirr of the heater. The sky looks calcified. Behind them, Flint stirs and stands, licks his lips.

'It's your da who needs the help,' she says at last. 'He's . . . He's a . . .' Her words buckle under bitter weight but he doesn't press.

Eventually the car makes its way on to Singleton Avenue and Harri hops out. His nan is there by the door, smiling.

'Harri, love,' she says, leaning over to give him a kiss. Somehow she's smaller than he remembers but there's the same scent that's peculiar to her. His mam joins them, stands there with her arms at her sides, the smile he'd expected to see strangely absent. As they enter the house, Alice points to the living room.

'There's a small box in there for you, Harri. But, before you bring it through, could you nip into the back garden for me and put the bins out? It's collection tomorrow and it'll save me a job. That's a love. And take your time, dear. There's no rush.'

Harri knows he's being dismissed. As he makes his way out through the back door, he catches snippets of the conversation.

'. . . should have . . .'

'. . . hardly in a position to . . .'

'It was . . .'

'I told you . . . eight . . . but . . .'

'. . . meeting tomorrow night . . . Harri's . . .'

'Catrin . . . forgive me . . .'

He drags both the green and black bins to the front. He sees an old lady across the street with a nest of grey hair and gardening gloves. She spots him, smiles and waves.

Back inside, Harri allows himself time to reacquaint himself with his grandparents' home. The way everything has stayed almost exactly the same throughout his life makes the place feel like a museum or a time capsule – he could be eleven years old again, diving into the box of Lego, competing with Rhys to make the most impressive contraption. He's not sure whether it's a comfort: the way the space is so static. Perhaps that was what retirement did to people: made them accept constancy, to be content with the way things were, vote Conservative, drink tea all day, do a morning of gardening, an afternoon of cards. Receive visits from children and grandchildren who lived in other parts of the country, or the world. It was different in Iraq. He'd seen whole generations and in-laws all living under one roof in a way that had reminded him of the Buckets in *Charlie and the Chocolate Factory*. But the slow grind of the war had unbalanced extended families and upset their old traditions – hunger, violence, illness, poverty had forced those in work to make appalling decisions every single day: should I feed my daughter or my mother, my son or my father? The Qur'an mandated care of parents but even religious values were hard to maintain in the face of endless war, insurgency and ethnic cleansing. They were equally easy to ignore when better offers came along: Harri knew of translators who'd taken one-way tickets to the United States, leaving behind their entire families; comparative safety, liberty and the pursuit of happiness were sometimes too difficult to resist. Not that Harri judged them. Still, there were those like the farmer who stayed put, who looked after old and young alike, who paid respects to his parents each day. He remembers the man smiling at his mother, a sign of the unbreakable bond between them. 'There she is,' he'd said. 'Heaven still sits beneath her feet.'

'Harri, love, are you coming?' His nan's voice echoes through from the kitchen.

Reverie broken, Harri picks up the box that's resting on the seat of the sofa. It's quite a weight. 'I thought you said it was a small box?'

'Well. Everything's relative, isn't it? Even size. That's what I used to tell David Timpson, anyway.' She winks theatrically.

'David Timpson?' says Harri's mam.

'Long before I met your father,' says Nan. And then, cutting through Catrin's quizzical look: 'If you open the top one first, you can take the rest home for later.'

Harri lifts the wrapped gift and gives it a shake. It rattles. 'I can guess,' he says.

He tears open the paper, studies the lid, laughs.

'Mum,' says Catrin, 'I'm not sure that's appropriate.'

'Well, I thought it was a good idea. Help him learn the geography of the place.'

Harri puts the puzzle down, revealing a large map of Iraq. One thousand pieces. 'I love it,' he says, pulling at the cellophane.

'Rhys would have enjoyed this,' says Nan.

'He's at Molly's,' explains Catrin.

'Ah, the love interest, is it? And what about you, Harri? Girlfriend? Boyfriend?'

'Mum,' say Catrin.

'What? There's nothing wrong with asking, for heaven's sake. He doesn't have to answer, does he? I'm sure he's been trained in all that. Besides, I'm not the one who minds. Blair's done some good in that, at least.'

Harri picks up another piece of the puzzle. 'Not much time for it out there,' he says.

'I read somewhere,' says Nan, inspecting an edge piece, 'that all the men sleep with younger boys. That it's perfectly acceptable. Must be a funny place to live, stoned to death for sleeping with a woman out of wedlock, applauded for taking advantage of a young man who's hardly seen a woman's face outside his home.'

Harri gives his nan a long look. 'I'm not sure I'd describe it as funny,' he says.

As the three of them work on the puzzle at the kitchen table, Harri listens to his mother and Nan debate a boundary-wall dispute. He wonders if they can see the irony but decides against a lecture. Soon the outside edges of the puzzle are done and there's just the large gap in the middle to fill. He wishes everything could be so finite and certain but people and their lives were just a jumble of unmatched pieces; it was impossible to see the whole.

'What do you think of the wedding?'

It takes a moment for Harri to realize the question is directed at him.

'The wedding?'

'Charles and Camilla,' says his nan. 'In the spring.'

'Hardly unexpected,' says Harri, 'once they'd got Diana out the way.'

'You really think they bumped her off?'

'Sure,' says Harri, amused by the old woman's scandalized expression.

His nan smiles. 'It's good to have a difference of opinion, I suppose.'

The map-making is resumed, with the names of towns and cities, rivers and mountains, filled in. Outside the light begins to dim. His mam hands him the last piece. 'Will you do the honours, Harri?' she says.

Harri takes it from her, looks at the remining gap and gently fills it in.

'We ought to be getting back,' says Catrin.

'Before you head off,' says his nan, 'I thought it would be nice to get a few photos of you. Would that be all right, Harri?'

Of course, he thinks. He'd been warned about it. At some point the cameras always come out. People wouldn't say it, probably wouldn't even acknowledge it to themselves, but it was deep down inside of them: the thought that this could be the last time they saw him. They wanted to be able to remember him, to look back on something, to be able to say there he was, there was our son, brother, father, just before . . . just before he . . .

'Smile!' says his mam, raising the camera to her eye, peering through the small aperture.

Harri puts an arm around his nan. He smiles wide, holds it in place, counts the seconds before the flash.

∼

For the last four nights, Harri has dreamt about being shot. He doesn't consider himself superstitious but when he wakes in the morning it takes a while to shake the feeling there's something lodged in the back of his neck. Today he rises earlier than the others, pulls on jeans and a sweater, decides he wants the comfort of a gun in his hand.

Downstairs, he lets Flint out to take a piss on the tree in the yard and then retrieves his father's rifle from the locked cabinet, glad the bailiffs hadn't taken the guns.

A long time ago when he was a boy and he'd made his first kill with this rifle, his father had picked up the rabbit, dipped his fingers into the red and smeared two lines of blood on his cheeks. Now, some ten years later, he doesn't need his father's approval or permission. In fact, he doesn't need anyone's.

He carefully skirts his way to the lake, scanning the water in the dim light before perching down next to a large bush that hides his form. Camouflaged, he lies there and waits, rifle at the ready, eyes alert to the shadows cast from above. Harri is used to waiting. In Iraq they are tasked with 'tactical patience', which still includes the use of HMGs, GMGs and 105mms when the situation warrants it. These don't quite flatten a building; they just make it inhospitable to hostiles. And anyone else who might have called it home.

There's a shift in the air and the shades of things and Harri's target comes into view, its mighty wings folding up like the pages of an old book. Holding his breath, Harri looks through the scope. The heron's long legs fork towards the water like lightning. He feels the resistance of the spring in the trigger and then it yields and the harsh sound snaps through the air.

Strike!

It's a clean shot and the heron goes down. Harri makes to stand but the sudden movement sends blood rushing to his head; dizzy, world spinning, he finds himself back in time and there's shouting and his body is bruised and the –

'Fucking thing's jammed!' Harri shouts, staring at his rifle like he might squeeze the life from it. He needs to keep his cool, trust all those years of training.

To his left Williams-17 is lying on the floor, while one of the others drags him back and begins to rip open his shirt. There's a lot of fucking blood but the lad's still conscious, cracking jokes about finally being able to go home and get laid.

Parry-09 is trying to get the Bowman to work but it's not picking up signal.

Heavy fire is hitting them from both sides.

'Fuck,' says Harri, peering about through the smoke. He needs to check his slates; make a Nine Line report.

Up ahead, the Viking is being licked by flames. Harri reaches for Parry's weapon as the other lad continues to request help, his heavy accent bellowing deep and urgent. His men are waiting on his word but he needs to know if there's an air asset before they move. He grabs a grenade and lobs it over the Hesco barrier. All is noise and movement and smoke.

Their current location was too fucking hot. Shots rat-a-tat-tat. Harri returns fire. 'Tawake!' he shouts. 'What's the tracker saying?'

The enormous man hurries over, head low, trying to avoid

the shrapnel coming at him from all sides. 'Closing in!' he shouts back.

Someone's calling to him – it's Parry, thumbs-up.

Harri dashes across two slabs of stone, grabs the Bowman, listens. Something whistles past his head.

He gives his report to the deep, measured voice on the other end. He waits for the response, praying, blood thundering in his ears.

'Roger that,' he says, relief a flood.

They're getting out of here.

'Tawake – you, Jones and the other two get Williams on a stretcher! Parry, keep the radio open. Top cover's on its way.'

And that's when he sees her. The little girl standing in the middle of the whole fucking hell-hole, by some miracle still alive. Covered in debris and dust, crying and bleeding. But still standing, still breathing. How the fuck that's possible he doesn't know. He could save her. Perhaps he should save her. But she was the one who'd walked out in front of the vehicle. She was the one who'd brought them to a stop. Perhaps he shouldn't blame her. But he fucking did. And right now he had his own men to look after; men he loved as brothers. And one of them was bleeding out. He could save her. Should save her. But he wasn't going to. The people here were always speaking of their fucking God – if God wills this; if God wills that – let Him save her if He fucking wanted to. In-fucking-shallah!

To their right a building shudders, teeters, begins to collapse.

There's a rumble in the air. Help on its way.

'Right, you fucking half-breeds! Get on your –'

Feet. He's on his feet. Harri's back in the here and now. The sky is brightening, the hills rise and fall, the water on the lake shimmers, is disturbed by nothing but a small greying object, like a deflated football, floating on the surface.

Harri takes a long drag of the cold air. His heart is hammering a thousand beats a minute and his hands are shaking but he doesn't drop the rifle.

Fuck, he thinks. *Fuck.*

He waits for the dregs of the inner sights and sounds to dissipate, and he cocks the rifle, leans it against the bush. He strips off his trousers and socks, makes his way around the edge of the lake and retrieves the body, his feet and toes mired in the mud. The water is perishingly cold but he grinds his teeth. It helps to anchor his body, his thoughts. He reaches for the bird. He knows they're protected but there was no one up here to witness what he'd done. The RSPB could go fuck themselves; he's done far worse.

He detours via the toolshed and then heads to the woods, bird in one hand, spade in the other. He'll bury it deep. No one will know. Flint follows, the old dog oblivious to the laws of men.

The ground is soft from the recent rain and Harri's spade plunges into the soil. He'll need a hole at least four feet deep to stop the scavengers. In Iraq he'd seen what happens when bodies weren't properly dealt with. It was a country now littered with mass graves, the violence of war hidden from view. Harri knows that some of those bodies will have been mutilated beyond recognition; intelligence has to be gathered and sometimes the getting of that knowledge was a cruel thing. There was already an investigation into military brutality at Majar al Kabir, with several dead insurgents photographed with lacerations from sharp objects, gouged eyes and mutilated genitalia.

It was sick. And it was war.

Harri lays the bird down in the pit and begins to shovel the earth back into the hole. And just like that the evidence is covered up.

$\sim$

'People forget what it was like,' says his da, staring at his pint. Harri sits opposite, leaning over his own glass, studying a dog-eared beer mat while the old man talks. 'It was a hell of a thing, you know. It started early 2001. I remember hearing the news and hoping it wouldn't spread because if something like that breaks out it's the end of the line. A disease travelling through air and water . . . there's no stopping it.

'You could say we got lucky, up here in the north of the country, but it was like living on the edge of some terrible abyss and every day seeing those images of burning animals. I had friends further south, good, strong men I'd known for years, breaking down, saying it was just too much for them to see their entire flocks being slaughtered and burned. Over a million animals were killed. Can you imagine such a number?'

Harri puts a finger in his ear and scratches around. 'I remember the pictures on the telly and the footpaths closing, the election being moved, all that shoe-washing. You and Mam arguing a lot.'

'It was a hell of a thing,' says John again, lost in his thoughts. 'You'd get a visit from a vet, and the moment they set foot on your land you'd be wondering if they'd brought it with them because, for all the measures they took, you could never be a hundred per cent sure.

'And then there was that big fuck-up at Epynt. You'll have seen it – the vast funeral pyre where they burned, what, thirty, forty thousand carcasses? They then buried maybe half of them right there in the ground. Can you imagine that? Not long after, they had to be dug up because the infected bodily fluids were leaking into the water table. I mean, how's that for effective crisis management?'

'And that's when you started?' asks Harri. He'd never known his father talk so much.

'I always did a little, you know. On the Grand National, that sort of thing. But then it became more regular. And not just the horses. The machines, too. It was a way of losing myself. I felt guilty that we'd got away with it, that our farm had escaped the worst of it. But there were all these people I knew, everything taken away from them – and what had they ever done but work, day in, day out?

'I've told you before about the outbreak of 1967, haven't I? It nearly killed your taid. All the markets closed, the farms were locked down, and I still remember the God-awful smell of disinfectant in the air. It wasn't on the same scale as the one a few years back, mind, but it was still enough to cripple whole farms, whole communities. Worse than Thatcher.

'I sometimes worry about what it's done to you and Rhys. I still do. Seeing animals killed like that. Hundreds, thousands at a time. You were both used to the cycles of the farm but not that. I sometimes think that's why you must've joined the Army. To get away from it all.'

'That's not it,' says Harri. He gives his father a gentle smile. 'You'll be all right, Da.'

The two of them look out of the window. Outside it is cold and dark and the stars are gathering above. Car lights shine on the road. A group of teenagers hang by the swings in a park, passing a bottle back and forth, the cigarettes like fireflies in the air. Harri imagines the smoke rising higher and higher, disappearing from view.

'Shall we go?' he asks.

Over an hour later, and they are parked opposite an ugly, red-brick building. Harri watches his father remove a penknife from his pocket and pull out the short blade. Holding out his right hand, his father begins to scrape out the dirt from under his nails, starting with his little finger. He works methodically, scraping, checking, scraping, just like he does for his sheep. His nails are long and thick and need cutting.

'You want me to come in with you?' asks Harri.

John shakes his head, turns his hand over, flexes his fingers. Harri knows his father takes a certain pride in the calluses, the scrapes and scars. Hands that have worked.

Harri studies the large, brick building that sits beneath the shade of an evergreen. It's a Salvation Army centre with an adjoining church. The place feels uncomfortably functional, like a hospital. The building overlooks a narrow park where a group of young boys are kicking around a football beneath the light of a dozen lamp posts. Surrounding the centre and the green space are a number of detached council houses with cars parked out front.

'They'll be expecting you,' says Harri.

His father nods.

'Da, you've got to face this. I'll be here when you get back.'

His father says nothing and they sit there, watching the night. A flash of headlights, and a truck sweeps into the car park at the other end. When the lights go off, a man steps out and slams the door. He's dressed in a coat and a cap. Harri watches as the man stands in the middle of the space and then begins to approach them. Harri lowers his window.

'Harri?' says the man.

'That's me,' he replies, recognizing the voice from the phone call he'd made some days ago. 'You must be Greg. This is my da, John.'

'Nice to meet you,' says Greg. 'First time's always the hardest. I'll be inside but feel free to join when you're ready. Others should be here soon enough.'

They watch Greg as he walks away. Just as he promised, others begin to arrive. Harri's surprised by how many there are. There's an old man who walks bent over a stick; a young woman with a shock of hair that reaches her waist; an enormous man who pauses and pants every few yards. More and more arrive; there are – ten, eleven, twelve.

'See?' says Harri.

Still, his father hasn't made a move.

'I've not told you about the wheelbarrow incident, have I?' says Harri.

His father shakes his head. 'No,' he says.

'This was in my second week out there. We were patrolling in an area not far from base camp – it was a residential area, usually free of drama. But on this particular day, someone started to make trouble for us. And perhaps because we were fresh in the field, some of the guys got excited. Hot under the collar, quick with the trigger. That kind of thing. The next moment, the whole fucking place erupted around us. It felt like every building ahead was swarming with hostiles. We were forced to make a tactical retreat. I called it in, gave the coordinates, had the place flattened from above.'

'Serves the bastards right.'

'The next day,' continues Harri, 'there was a man at our gates, demanding to speak to one of the officers. He wouldn't leave until he had and his voice was raised. And because I was on duty and because I'd not slept much, I walked right out of those gates thinking I'd be able to de-escalate, diffuse whatever it was that was causing him to stand there raving. Sounds sensible, right?'

Harri's father nods. 'Sure,' he says.

'Wrong,' says Harri. 'It's an old trick – lure those of rank beyond their safety zones and then fill them with holes. Job done.'

'Jesus, Harri,' says his da.

'That's not what happened, clearly. Instead, he stood there with his wheelbarrow as he explained, first on his feet and then on his knees, that the bombs we'd dropped had killed his parents, his wives and his children. All of them. Their remains were there, in the wheelbarrow. He lifted the cloth and there they were, a tangle of limbs. He said he was the only one who'd been out that morning, attending to his cattle as the bombs fell on his home. There was no one else, he said. No one.'

'Harri,' says his father.

'What I'm trying to say, Da, is that we all have our own shit going on and that, in the great scheme of things, this isn't so bad. You've still got your family. And all I'm asking is that you go in there. That you accept some help.'

'Christ, Harri.'

'I'm laying it on thick, I know. But we've been sitting here for almost half an hour. The meeting will be over by the time you've made up your mind. So here it is. The shove. Don't be a coward, Da. Get out there.'

His father's eyes are on the wild sky and he breathes deeply.

'Okay, Harri,' he says. He opens the door and slips out as the cold air rushes in. 'I love you, son,' he says. And, before Harri can reply, his old man has shut the door and is walking away, towards the hall. He doesn't look back. He doesn't see his son watching, eyes brimming, catching the moon as the first flakes of snow begin to fall.

~

In the morning, his father raps on his door and asks if Harri might lend him a hand, for the snow has fallen fast and thick throughout the night. It's Saturday so Rhys is also drafted in. Catrin has made them a hearty breakfast of eggs and toast and beans. She's light on her feet, tells them there's soup in the fridge for lunch, that she's going to be out for most of the day.

'Again?' says John.

'Organ practice,' she says.

Rhys raises an eyebrow but says nothing.

The three of them work hard, moving the sheep, checking numbers, tags and feet. Harri likes the steady rhythm and routine of it all, watching his da apply years of generational knowledge in a single intuitive glance. His father casts his eyes at the flock, points, says there's something wrong with that one there and Harri or Rhys go and look things over and sure as day there's something to bother at.

His da had left school at fourteen but – like most farmers Harri knows – the old man has his own kind of smarts. Some of the lads in the company were farming stock and Harri reckons there's something in that: they were fellas used to the daily labour, things not going to plan, the blood and shit and fucking weather that is never right and causes no end of drama. His da doesn't stop talking about it today, complaining about the lack of light and the rain and the snow. But there's an energy in the old man, like he's been given a shot of something strong that keeps him abuzz.

When his da had returned from the meeting, Harri had switched on the engine and the wipers had cleared the dusting of flakes and everything was made visible. 'Fucking snow,' his father had said, and Harri had laughed because it was so typical of the old man. They'd not spoken much on the way home but his father had told him it wasn't what he'd expected, that the people weren't what he'd expected. Greg was a good man. Had offered to support him through the months.

'You'll go back, then?' Harri had asked.

Over lunch, Rhys asks about the meeting and their father nods. 'It was good,' he says, raising a piece of dry bread to his lips, the end dipped in the steaming leek and potato soup. That's all that's said but Rhys seems satisfied.

His brother is muted through most of the day. Harri's been briefed about Rhys starting to act out at school and, although he'd told his mam that she ought not to worry – that Rhys was sixteen and trouble came knocking at such a troubled, troubling age – he decides he'll have a quiet word when they're some place private. Harri knows there are some things you can't say to your parents and, while he may have seen enough in recent months to hollow out his sympathies, he feels bound to Rhys; protective of him. He would do anything for his brother.

Dusk arrives as it always does up in the mountain: like the sudden pulling down of a blind. His mother gets back flushed with the cold, a little dishevelled; Rhys goes off to see Molly and John has settled into a recording of *The Apprentice*, his talcum-powdered feet resting on a stool, eyes drooping from the day's labour, Flint snoring beside him.

Harri tells them he's heading out for a drink.

As he makes his way to the pub, Harri shivers in the cold and feels the tight press of his heart beneath all the clothing. He sees the lights of the pub up ahead and feels relief at the certainty of a drink. It was one of the things the lads most missed on tour. To be able to go out on the pisser was an integral part of Army life; abstinence wasn't an option.

Inside, the watering hole is just as it's always been, with its smoke, patterned carpet, bar billiards, a fire burning hot. There's a girl behind the bar he half recognizes. As he approaches, he spots Simon at the far end nursing a drink and looking lonesome. Harri feels a ripple of something like fear. So much for a fucking drama-free night, he thinks.

'Harri Williams?' It's the barmaid, the corners of her mouth atwitch, questioning. 'What're you doing here? And what can I get you?'

It clicks. 'Becky-fucking-Evans?' he says, happy at the distraction. 'How about that. Been a while, hasn't it? Pint of the lager, please.'

'You're back, then, are you? For good, is it?'

'Two weeks R&R,' he says. He glances behind him but Simon's still lost in thought.

'Bit of rest and recovery must help. Bit of this, too,' she says, sliding over the frothing pint.

'Recuperation,' he corrects. 'Ta.'

'Tab?'

'Please.' He takes a sip, sees her watching. 'So, you're what . . . back from university, is it?' It's a lame opener but his mind is elsewhere and he can see she wants to ask questions he doesn't have the time or will to answer.

'Finished last summer,' she says.

He takes another pull, half listening to Becky's monologue. It sounds too rehearsed, like she's repeated the spiel a dozen times.

'That's grand,' he says, raising his beer and taking a third slug.

Harri can sense Simon watching him, that he's in his sights. He feels the need to take cover and approaches Joe Jenkins, a middle-aged car mechanic who's spent every evening of the last eight years in the pub after a scrappy marriage and scrappier divorce. These days it's said he's more interested in his drink than his wife and daughters.

Joe's known as Mr Fix-It – so as long as you can pay in cash, booze or drugs, he'll almost always get your car to pass its MOT.

'Joe?' says Harri.

Joe looks up, peers through the cloud of his cigarette.

'Harri, lad. Heard you were hereabouts.'

'Got a spare?' he asks.

'Take a seat.'

Harri looks over at Simon. Jeans and jumper. That serious look he's always had.

'Take a seat while I roll.'

Harri sits. The other man nods in approval, then calls out above the general din, 'Becky, love, two more pints of the same, please.'

'There's no need for –'

'You know my father was in the Army?'

'I didn't,' replies Harri, realizing too late that the man's well into his drink.

Joe nods. 'He was a bit of a cunt if I'm honest. He was in Ireland in the early seventies. It fucked with his head and it fucked with us. But the bastard knew a fair thing about vehicles. Could strip and build like no one.'

The pints arrive and Becky gives him a look that offers an exit.

'This one's on me,' says Joe. He looks at the cigarette in his hand, nods with satisfaction and hands it over. As Joe digs into his pocket for a lighter, Harri casts a surreptitious look behind him and meets Simon's gaze. He feels the heat on his cheek, hears the crackle of burning wood.

'The funny thing is, even though it made him screwy, it's also what kept him together. He'd have been behind bars if it wasn't for the Paras.'

'Plenty of the guys have been in and out,' says Harri, shifting in his chair.

'Some things never change. He used to say it was the only place where he really knew who he was and what he was supposed to be doing.'

'Gives a lot of people purpose,' replies Harri. He's unable to sit still. He looks at the cigarette lighter. It's shaped like a small screwdriver; the flame leaps from the end.

'Does that for you?' asks Joe.

'In a way,' he says. He risks another glance back. Simon's on his feet, draining the last of his glass. Harri finishes his first pint and swiftly takes a few inches off the second. He glances at Becky, who smiles, rolls her eyes.

'You think we turn into our fathers?' asks Joe.

'I'd like to think we have a choice,' says Harri, his left leg bouncing up and down, toes and ankle like a spring against the floor.

'Your da owes me, you know.'

'Christ,' says Harri. 'How much?'

'There you are. That's exactly the face your da would pull. There's no fucking escape, is what I reckon.'

'How much?' he repeats.

Joe waves him away.

'Tell me.' Harri takes a drag of the cigarette, enjoys the rush to the head. He needs it. And he needs to find Simon, who's no longer at the table; the only trace of him is the lonely pint glass.

'About forty,' says Joe. 'Don't worry about it. Your da's always been good to me.'

Harri removes fifty quid from his wallet. 'I'm going to leave this here,' he says, placing the notes under an empty pint glass. 'You can take it or leave it,' he says.

'I said I didn't want it.'

'Your choice,' replies Harri. 'We've all got one.'

Joe looks at him and then down at the cash on the table. He reaches over.

'Would you excuse me for a bit?' asks Harri.

'Come find me later,' says Joe. 'For something stronger.'

'Count on it. Thanks for the beer and cig.'

'Thanks for your service,' says Joe. They say cheers and toast and then Harri's off. He chugs most of his pint, stubs out his cigarette, then chases after Simon, who's disappeared through the back door and is probably long gone. Harri curses his cowardice as he hurries outside, the light spilling from the windows and a garden lamp that spools liquid yellow. Moths and other small, winged creatures swim in circles around it. Harri peers into the wider darkness. He's dimly conscious of the rain. His eyes adjust and slowly he becomes aware of a denser shape at the back of the car park, the sudden flare of a cigarette end. Harri moves warily towards it.

'Si,' he says.

Simon is almost shaking and Harri can hear the strained control in his voice. 'I was in there,' he says, 'and you just ignored me. You walked in and you just ignored me.'

'I'm sorry –'

'You've been avoiding me on the farm –'

'I've only been home a short while and –'

'You've barely replied to any of my messages –'

'Listen –'

'You listen, Harri. You fucking listen for once.'

'I needed time –'

'Time? We might not get any –'

'Stop,' says Harri, taking a step closer. 'Just stop for a second.' He feels the intense pull of things. All his adult life he's felt it. And he's tried to run from it, to purge it. Kill it. But it won't stay down.

He takes the smallest of steps closer to Simon, the space between them knuckle-thin. They are both damp from the rain and there are droplets of water in Simon's hair. They are shrouded in the darkness, the patter of falling clouds.

'Harri,' says Simon, throwing his cigarette to the floor.

The night is cold. Their bodies are warm and close.

They have known each other for years, known this for years. A thousand guarded glances. And now, at last, there is this.

Harri puts a hand on Simon's chest. No more running. He lets the pint glass fall, hears it hit the floor. He reaches for Simon.

They stumble back into the darkness, the taste of smoke and rain and desire, the final unfolding of hearts wrapped so long in silence.

∽

'Looks quiet,' says Harri as they pull up into the fishery.

'It's February,' snorts Rhys.

'Point taken.'

They park the car and grab their kit. At the lodge, Harri hands over their licences to a portly middle-aged man with a thick moustache and glasses. The man introduces himself as Steve and asks them to fill in a disclaimer form and runs through the rules: barbless hooks, size eight max and singles only. No dapping, no littering and no static Booby fishing. Trout should be returned to the water unless their well-being is clearly in doubt – in which case they should be dispatched and returned to the lodge.

The man slides his glasses up towards his brows and sniffs, the hairs at the end of his nose quivering. 'Any questions?'

'None,' says Harri, paying the day's fee and passing over the forms.

'Enjoy your time,' replies Steve.

The brothers head up to Top Pool first, which has the greatest depth at 18 feet, but it's also the most exposed and Harri can feel the cold soak through him. The water reflects the sky, which is a mottled white-and-grey marble, and the land beneath them is clogged with water from the melted snow. A smattering of trees on the west bank offers scant protection and Harri heads towards it, Rhys trailing behind.

He'd prefer to be making his way among the Snowdonia Mountains to the high, natural lakes; those managed by the Cambrian Anglers were some of the best – the water was cold and clear, and the rock marks the sky with sharp lines that entertain the eye. When he was younger, Harri had enjoyed trekking up the stony pathways, where the old, abandoned quarries and their history would linger; ancient spaces where you'd find stone chapels and derelict houses; places the miners would come to pray before spending the Saturday casting out the lines. Hard men with hard lives: the mines were hidden under the Earth's skin, and men worked in them beneath the mountains; men who'd refer to the deep, dark caverns as slaughterhouses because so many of them died down there in the pitch black, their lungs filled with slate.

He thinks about Simon, the way he must labour each day. His touch, gentle as moonlight.

'Over there?' suggests Rhys.

Harri nods and they settle down and ready their tackle: rods, lines, flies and nets.

Rhys casts out and Harri watches the light and wind and the way the water moves. He waits and watches, observes the rise here and there, scans the edges of the lake. At one end, there's a slight peninsula and the breeze sends the water running in a lane, and Harri has the feeling he should make his way there, where the food is likely to be channelled and the trout will rise to feed. But there's no rush. Rhys has settled in. For a moment or two he watches his brother slowly reel in the line and then he casts his own. Although the water is deeper here than at the other pools, it's also teeming with trout: rainbows, browns, blues, goldens and tigers.

'Got a bite,' says Rhys. Harri looks over and sees his brother's rod begin to bend.

'That was quick.'

'It's a fighter,' says Rhys, who gives some line before guiding the fish back. 'Few pounds, I'd guess.'

Harri brings in his own line and picks up the net to help his brother. He can see it, silver in the lake, bright, wavering fins angling through the water; a lovely-looking fish it is, bright and bold. Harri quickly discards his gloves and dips his hands beneath the water, gasping at the freeze.

He'd only once made the mistake of handling a trout with dry hands; it was one of the few times his father had really cuffed him.

Bringing the net under, Harri quickly and carefully lifts the living thing up and out, grabbing it just above the tail behind the fins, avoiding the fragile gills. With an expert twist, Harri removes the hook from its mouth. Its eyes stare, gills and mouth gawping, body writhing left and right. He places the trout gently down into the bucket as Rhys comes over to look.

'Not a bad first strike,' he says.

They stand, looking at it for some time.

'What's this trouble at school about, then?' asks Harri.

Rhys wipes his nose with his sleeve. He looks back at the fish. 'There's been rumours.'

'Rumours?'

'About you.'

Harri thinks of Simon and feels the tilt of the world on its axis. 'I see. Do you want to talk about it?'

'No,' says Rhys.

'Is there anything else you want to tell me?' asks Harri.

'Is that why you left?' Rhys is staring at him hard, his brows heavy over his eyes.

'That's some of it,' replies Harri.

'I wouldn't have cared,' says Rhys. 'I don't. You didn't have to leave.'

'I'm sorry,' says Harri, knowing something of what it's like to feel alone.

'The war's bollocks, you know,' says Rhys. The words come out with a sting.

'War is always bollocks,' says Harri. He doesn't wish to dig into the politics. He just wants to check his brother is okay and to spend what time they have together beneath the sky like they used to as kids.

Rhys looks down at the trout, captive in the bucket: its silvery-green sides and the strikingly beautiful reddish-pink, slightly iridescent line running along its length. 'You want to put it back?' asks Harri.

Rhys lowers the bucket into the murky, disturbed water and the fish swims off, tail flapping with impatience and pride.

They continue like that for some time, the light and the water changing. A few times they move up and down the bank to where the water is shallower. The pool is shaped like a heart.

Insects dance on the water and in the air. They reapply repellent to their wrists, ankles and necks. Harri watches the water, feels that out here time could stop. Clouds pass overhead; the sun briefly carves its way out.

No single cast is the same: water, air, light, man, line, fly and fish are in perpetual flux and sometimes the subtlest of changes leads to pressure on the line, a sudden rush and a spark of pure, innocent excitement.

At midday, they share the sandwiches made by their mam in the early hours. They sit, watch the trout rise, share observations about the water and the weather. It is comfortable. At length they fall back into silence. Harri takes a swig of coffee from the flask. It's still hot. He hands it to Rhys. His brother sips once, twice, and then smacks his lips.

'Fucking gnats,' he says.

'You want some more spray?' asks Harri.

'No, I'm good. Thanks.'

They look out at the water. On the whole Harri has always preferred to fish alone. But he's enjoying this, being out here with his brother, noting the differences between the trout hiding beneath the surface.

'You ever read those books Da gave us?' asks Rhys.

'Books?'

'A stack of them. On fishing. Sheep. Dogs. Horses.'

'Taid's books? The old ones? Hardbacks?'

'That's them.'

'No,' says Harri. 'Did you?'

'No,' replies Rhys.

'You think Da ever read them?' says Harri.

Rhys smiles, shakes his head. 'He ever tell you the story about his uncle Cai?'

'What's that?' asks Harri.

Rhys takes another swig of the coffee. 'Well, the story goes that Uncle Cai used to go to church on a Sunday and sit behind these ladies with their big hats. And when the vicar got everyone to bend their heads to say a prayer or two, Uncle Cai would take out his nail clippers and have at the hats in front . . . He never told you that one?'

'No bells ringing,' says Harri.

'He'd cut away feathers and bows and all sorts. Later, he'd make flies out of all the bits and bobs. Became quite a thing, so it goes. Course, the ladies got to knowing but they didn't mind. They'd add decorations just for Cai and then boast about it – compete over who had the best hat, like they were responsible for bringing the fish home for tea.'

'Not a bad story, that,' says Harri, rubbing his hands together, fingers and palms still cold.

'I guess you've got used to a warmer climate,' says Rhys, handing over the flask.

'I guess.'

Rhys leans forward in his chair and looks up at the sky, turns to his brother. 'Harri,' he says, his voice suddenly as quiet as the listening fish in the dark pool before them. 'Have you ever . . . you know . . .'

They're both aware it's not a question you should ask. That it's one of the worst things you can say to someone who's been in combat. But it's the one question everyone wants to ask. Most people are too frightened to, because some answers change things in a way that can't be undone, their words make the world spin too fast, and the image of loved ones becomes blurred.

Harri looks at his hands, the sky, the water.

Once the sun has climbed, they try Farm Pool, where the fish gather at the margins of the lake towards the treeline. Later in the day, they make a final effort at Home Pool. This lake proves weedy in parts and it's the shallowest of the three pools they try. Despite losing some flies, they both enjoy some top-of-the-water action and, thanks to the abundance of feed near the foliage, they net several blue trout in quick succession.

As they're packing up their equipment, Rhys pauses, puts a hand on Harri's shoulder. 'I miss you,' he says.

'I'm still here,' replies Harri with the shadow of a smile.

'You know what I mean,' says Rhys.

~

Harri finds it impossible to sleep and no amount of counting sheep over fences does the trick. His stomach feels like a milk churn and at some time around four in the morning he heads to the bathroom, turning on the landing light as he goes. He vomits in the toilet and wipes away splattered muck from the side of the bowl before flushing the whole lot away. It's nerves. He tries to be stoical but it's hard.

He'll be leaving home in just over twenty-four hours. He's not ready.

On his way back to his bedroom, he pauses at the bookcase on the landing and makes a cursory search before finding what he's looking for: Taid's old books. He'd forgotten all about these until Rhys had reminded him. He pulls a couple from the shelf and takes them to bed. Switching on his table light, he opens the first, a Stud Book from the International Sheep Dog Society dating back to 1958. It reads like a phone book and he soon sets it aside, reaching instead for a slim fishing guide by a man called John Henry Cliffe, which is all about angling in North Wales. To Harri's delight, every page is covered in careful, concise marginalia. He recognizes his father's tight scrawl but there's also a neat cursive – Taid's perhaps? He turns to the contents and the glossary, searching for familiar place names. He soon finds what he's looking for: a couple of lakes in the Snowdonia Mountains his father had taken him to as a young boy. He turns to the relevant section and deciphers the brief notes. In cursive: *Too exposed but pit-deep & plentiful.* And his father's cramped reply: *Still cold but no fish: four hours . . . nothing!*

Harri settles in, eyes roving across the pages, the years, wanting to make his own contribution, to continue the strange, silent conversation between the generations.

After almost an hour, he finds himself restless and heads downstairs, doing his best not to wake the others.

Flint is in the kitchen looking guilty and Harri soon discovers the cause: a puddle of urine in the hall. 'Christ,' he says, soaking up the mess with newspaper before getting on his hands and knees to wash the stone floor, squeezing out the cloth into a bucket of warm water.

As he scrubs the tiles, he finds dry pine needles from old Christmas trees. He looks around the room. The hall feels too wide and empty without his mother's piano.

Flint wanders through, tail and head hanging low. As much as he loves the old dog, Harri wonders if his da is right – the dog should be sent to a better place. But what can he say? He looks at the emptiness of the hall, feels the painful never-ending quiet of a place that had once been filled with music. He looks at Flint, the dog's mournful eyes. No, he thinks, his mam has lost enough.

In the kitchen, Harri turns on the radio, volume set low. Two hosts are talking about Prince Charles and Camilla's wedding, which is set for 9 April, not long before Harri comes home after his tour. It was a strange word to use, that. Tour. Like they were walking around the fucking Eiffel Tower. As he waits for the kettle to boil, he hears footsteps on the stairs.

Meanwhile, a royal correspondent speculates the wedding will cost upwards of four million pounds.

'Christ alive,' says Harri. He makes two cups of tea and

wanders back through the house, where he finds his mam in the laundry room.

'Can't sleep?' asks Harri.

Catrin nods, smiles. 'You and me both.'

'I made you a cuppa.' He places one of the mugs on the side, next to a pile of folded shirts.

'Thanks, love,' his mam says, her back bent, sorting his clothes into lights and darks.

'You don't need to do that, you know,' he says. 'I can manage well enough.'

'I like doing it,' she says, pulling at the arm of a fleece.

'No one *likes* doing laundry,' says Harri. He walks over to her. 'Mam?'

She ignores him and begins to shovel the whites and beiges into the drum. 'You won't understand it until you've children of your own,' she says. 'It's a chore, but . . . it's done with love. Especially these days, when I don't get to see you. I like to think of you wearing the clothes I've washed and folded. That you'll think of me, even if it's just for a moment. I know it's stupid but that's just how it is.' The drum is full. There is no more shovelling she can do. She shuts the door, stares at the settings.

'Mam?' says Harri. He can see something is wrong.

'I was trying to be helpful,' she says, turning the dial.

'You are helpful,' he says.

She rises but does not meet his look. 'I saw them.'

Why, wonders Harri, will no one look him in the eye? Is he really so changed, so difficult to speak to?

'Them?' he says.

'The letters,' she replies. There's only one door to the room and Harri is blocking the exit. The washing machine begins to spin and the sound of thrashing water fills the small space.

The letters? thinks Harri. And then it sinks in: of course, the letters.

He takes his mother in his arms. 'You shouldn't have seen them,' he says. There are four – one for Simon, one for his nan, one for Rhys and one for his parents. He hadn't sealed the envelopes; it would have seemed too final to do that. 'Did you read them?'

'Just the one,' she whispers.

He knows the contents of those letters, has agonized over every single sentence. They were the kind of letters you could send only once. When it came to his parents, he'd decided to get the most painful, obvious truth dealt with as quickly as possible.

Dear Mam and Da

If you're reading this, then I'm afraid things haven't gone as planned and, as you'll know by now, I won't be coming home.

There is the scent of fabric conditioner in the air. The machine hums, as it removes the dirt and dust and blemishes of days past, ready for the days ahead.

March

Iraq Body Count: 905

502. Referring to negotiations on the formation of the ITG [Iraqi Transitional Government], Mr Blair commented to President Bush on 1 March that: 'We needed a stable outcome.'

– *The Report of the Iraq Inquiry*, Volume VII, Section 9.3

II

On the train, Catrin feels listless. She flicks through a book of poems by Hedd Wyn but finds the glory of war and general patriotism oppressive.

Where, she wonders, is the poetry for her son? Who will remember that he, too, is out there, serving? Risking everything. Perhaps no poetry could tell her everything she needed to know about the war they were waging. Last week she'd come upon a blog called *Salam Pax* and, reading through the entries, she'd realized how very little she understood. Here was someone who listened to Snow Patrol, drank the occasional beer, talked about art and free speech, satirized both the Americans and his own leaders, who wandered the streets of his city with a video recorder, trying to avoid having stones – or worse – thrown at him. Is that who they were fighting for? Or was it the people throwing the stones?

She doesn't know. All she really knows is that she misses her boy.

Catrin looks around the carriage, counts each piece of large luggage that marks an escape. Just above her there is someone's yellow North Face bag, its straps swinging with the motion of the train. There are a fair few mountaineering shops in Snowdonia with bags like that, each upwards of a hundred pounds. Catrin's often amazed at what people will pay for specialist gear and how quickly people see themselves as specialists. Years ago, she'd gone with John to the Game Fair in East Anglia and he would compete in the clay-pigeon trials; he'd always complain about the contenders with guns worth more than a decent second-hand Land Rover who, in his words, couldn't shoot for shit. And yet she'd seen how he'd get talking to the owners, take a look at what they had, the engraved side-by-sides and the distinctive over-and-unders. She'd seen the gleam of envy in his eyes. They'd taken the boys to the fair just the once, after Rhys had turned eight and was old enough not to make a nuisance of himself. They'd gone with Tim and his family, pitching tents, wine and grub heaped in the boot along with some of the dogs. The four of them had slept next to one another in musty sleeping bags. Rhys had spent most of the night sneezing and Catrin hadn't got much shut-eye with the noise and the hard ground and the tossing and turning, but she remembers the feeling of serenity at having her family so close, sheltering together. She can't think why they'd never gone back.

Looking about her, she picks out a man who's about Harri's age and she indulges in a daydream, imagining his life now, not on the battlefield or on the farm but in one of the nearby cities or London itself. He'd be a trainee lawyer or something equally safe and stable, something with opportunity, something that would make people take him seriously. He'd have a long-term girlfriend with nice parents and together they'd be looking at getting on the housing ladder and discussing kids while debating the pros and cons of private school. Catrin would grow old and visit them and make comments about the price of things in the city and they'd roll their eyes at her but laugh to let her know that it was all good-natured.

The fields of Wales roll by and Catrin watches as they pass a large woodland area. Not far from the farm, there's one of the oldest yews in the world, one of several in the country whose roots and small rings at the centre of the trunk stretch back three, four, even five thousand years. Long ago such a tree would have been a tribal centre, a place of council, the inauguration of kings. Their history was written in the natural world but it was so easy to overlook; people often failed to see what was right in front of them.

Her mind conjures up a picture of Harri walking back from the lake, rifle in one hand, heron swinging from the other, its long, limp body hanging like a sack of potatoes, its feet brushing the hard ground. She'd seen him from the bedroom window, broad-shouldered and brooding. It upset her, seeing the bird like that, Harri like that, but she hadn't raised it with him, fearful of what it might lead to.

Her boy has changed – there is no doubt about that. What, she wonders, have they done to him? And what more was that awful place going to do?

The train pulls into Chester and Catrin changes platform and waits for the transfer, distracted. She watches two pigeons walking along a wall, their heads bobbing. The larger of the two has its feathers puffed up and seems to be stalking the smaller bird, its short beak bearing down. Catrin shivers in the cold.

She wonders if John will be out repairing the other section of the drystone wall by himself; perhaps he'll have asked Simon for help. Since they'd cut down on the hands, John'd had to put in more hours, calling in favours when necessary. She pictures her husband bending his back against the sun, sorting through the stones, putting the copings, wallheads and throughstones into separate piles. She's still angry at him and worried that if she opens her mouth something dreadful might emerge, words that she couldn't blot out. They'd made a truce while Harri was home but it hadn't lasted.

And John suspects, knows even. She could see his hurt and rage and, despite it all, his tenderness. This morning, he'd taken her hand and asked her not to go, his words falling with a heaviness that weighed upon her and she felt wretched, because the way he looked at her told her that he knew, and despite everything it wasn't possible to brush aside more than twenty years together, no matter how strong the winds blew.

I wish you'd stay, he'd said.

The train is packed and Catrin's glad when it reaches London at exactly 5:37. She makes her way through the station towards the barriers, where people bunch together, impatience stamped on their features. Once she's through, Catrin checks her pockets for her Oyster Card and her mobile and looks for signs to the Underground. All around her people are either static – their faces turned to the information board with its changing times and places – or dashing about, dodging between the bystanders. Everyone seems so sure of what they're doing and where they're going and even though Catrin's been here before – has checked and checked again the directions – all the noise, movement and light leave her flustered. At last, she spots a sign for the Tube and begins making her way to it, ashamed and frustrated in equal measure at being so quickly disorientated and overwhelmed. She knows the differences between hawthorn and blackthorn; can pluck a chicken and skin a rabbit; is able to flip sheep and jump hedges on horseback – but in this place of glass, steel and concrete she's at a loss.

Catrin takes the escalator deep down until she can hear the rumble of the approaching trains. She enters a busy carriage filled with men and women and children who could be from anywhere in the world. The sliding doors close with a hiss. A young man with a dark beard, wearing a thobe, a cap on his head and sandals on his feet, locks eyes with her and immediately stands.

'Please,' he says with a perfect smile, gesturing for her to sit.

'Thank you,' she says, quickly sitting, her eyes moving to the feet of the other passengers, wondering what this young, polite man would say if he could sense the spike of momentary fear and loathing – and then shame – that had filled her heart.

She looks at the wiry hairs on his feet, between the leather of his shoes, the same kind of sandals that Harri used to wear when he was out with the shearers, working the farms, competing with the groups of professional New Zealanders who came over in the spring and summer. She pictures him, legs out, forearms sweating, hand gripping the clippers, the lemonade and cake waiting for them on a bale nearby while the flies buzzed about his head. Yes, a different world from here, where sandal rests beside the loafer, high heel, brogue and trainer.

As the carriage chugs through the stations, Catrin people-watches. She begins to settle, to feel again the appeal of the city, the way a person could get lost in the bustle, anonymous among the crowds. But she's being fanciful. Who knows what things are like for the underbelly of this city? There was no such thing as living the dream. There was just dreaming and living and the heart-breaking space between that some called hope.

With the arrival of her stop, Catrin exits, tapping out, keeping her bag close. She's done her best all day not to think too much about her appearance, to enjoy the journey without worrying if she's wearing clothes that are too formal or too informal, if she'll embarrass Matt, herself.

Holborn is overwhelming on a Friday evening. Everything is noise and sound: hooting, shouting, blaring and beaming. Commuters and early revellers brush past her, hustling to their own destinations. There is nothing still about the city, nothing calm. Her overnight bag feels heavy and cumbersome and she begins to feel hot and sweaty and, worse, lost.

Mercifully, she finds a map near an intersection and her heart sinks. It's a ten-minute walk. She ought to have gone to Chancery Lane. A ten-minute walk was nothing on the farm, but here, amid the din of the tightly packed street and squeeze of people, it feels like an Olympian task.

She trudges on, regretting the slight heel on her shoes. As she weaves her way between the rivers of people, she looks up at the darkening sky and begs the clouds to hold. Along a single street, she passes more shops and banks and bars. The restaurants are as diverse as the people on the streets: there's a Chinese, a Mexican, an Indian and even an Ethiopian. Catrin is certain there must be every cuisine, every taste, in the world. She passes by two men standing in a doorway, smoking; they're wearing leather jackets and have piercings and the distance between them is vanishing. Catrin walks on, taking several turns, keeping an eye on the narrow black-on-white street signs, worrying that she's got herself lost until, to her relief, she finds herself at a street leading to Gray's Inn Road.

A few minutes later, Catrin reaches the Sunny Art Centre. The name sounds naff but the building itself, with its wide glass windows and walls decked with canvases, is impressive. A young woman, dressed in a dark pencil skirt and looking like she's fresh out of school, stands at the entrance, holding a clipboard. She turns and smiles as Catrin approaches.

'Hello there.' A smart, RP voice. 'May I take a name, please?'

'Catrin Williams,' she replies, gripping her bag, strangely anxious to be here at last, in a place so unfamiliar and to be seeing Matt so soon.

The girl facing her is wearing so much makeup Catrin wonders whether it peels off at night. Perhaps the young woman is hiding a smattering of acne. Catrin has only ever gone for a bit of darkening around the eyes, a deepening of the lips.

The young woman smiles at her awkwardly. 'I'm sorry,' she says. 'Could you spell that for me?'

Surely she doesn't need to spell Williams? 'Charlie. Alpha. Tango. Romeo. India. November. I'm a friend of Matt,' says Catrin, the word *friend* sitting strangely on her tongue. But they'd agreed it was for the best. Still, she would have liked some resistance from Matt when they'd discussed it, even if it was performative. Perhaps he could have teased her. Called her his mistress, his *amour*. Sometimes he'd slip too readily into practicality; it brought too much of the outside world into their private one.

'Would you please wait a moment?' says the young girl.

Catrin worries at the clasp of her bag. It was an art exhibition, for heaven's sake. Not a bloody royal pageant. And where was he? Matt, her *friend*?

The girl continues to stare at her list of names and then, as if a telepathic message had been sent her way, she smiles and ushers Catrin through.

At last! Catrin feels the ache in her heels but also the rising excitement at seeing Matt, here, in his domain. She's surprised to sense something else, too – pride, perhaps. And ownership. As if a carnal part of her has claimed him – all that he is and all that he does and the fierceness of it causes an aching, ravenous desire. She wants to find him, to take him away from all these people, to hold him close, to possess him and be possessed by him.

A young man with dark stubble takes her coat and case and this small act helps to quell the flames, cool the fire. But the hunger's still there, waiting. Where is he? Impatiently, she scans the display board. The exhibition is called *Travels and Tales through Vietnam*, which Catrin had never liked but she'd not had the heart to tell Matt. She ought to have done, though – it sounded like a Victorian board game.

There's a crowd of people gathered in the reception room, chic in their designer clothes, holding sparkling flutes, chattering as if they've known each other all their lives. Perhaps they have. A waiter offers her a glass of champagne. She takes a large sip and searches for Matt. Where is he? She doesn't know a soul here and to be left alone like this, like a last-minute extra on a film set, further cools the lick of her desire. She stands, island-like, wondering if this was a mistake.

And then – Matt! She sees him appear on the other side of a doorway and all doubt is cast aside. He's wearing a collared pink shirt with the sleeves rolled up, blue chinos and brown suede brogues – the kind of look she'd never have imagined him in all those years ago when they used to run around the tarmac of their old school. She admires the way he's pulled himself up and, although she's wants to run to him, like the girl she once was, she holds herself still and watches him standing there, the centre of it all. How could she not feel that draw, the magnetism of his charm and his success, and the life that went with it? All that might have been, all that could be.

He's nodding and smiling and shaking hands but his eyes are roving, hunting. She knows why and the knowing is ecstasy. When at last she is caught, it's as if all the world is dulled and diminished and it's just the two of them blazing hot.

'Catrin?' he says, pulling someone along with him. Kiss-kiss. The press of his hands on her body! Even over her dress she can feel his heat, the promise of it.

'Please meet my assistant, Miss Birdie Prusheck.' A woman appears at his side, young and beautiful. For a dreadful moment Catrin has the urge to claw out her eyes.

'Pleased to meet you,' says Catrin, offering a hand.

'Catrin's one of my oldest and dearest friends. We grew up together in the small country, avoiding the tyranny of parents and the boredom of suburbia.'

'A pleasure,' says Birdie. Catrin feels herself being weighed. There's a hint of a knowing smile at the corner of Birdie's lips that Catrin can't quite untangle but it unsettles her.

Birdie makes her excuses and Catrin watches the young woman flutter among the other guests, smiling, touching shoulders here, tilting a head there, sparrow-like. Catrin can't help notice the way Matt's eyes also linger on his assistant, her lips, her plumage. Again, Catrin feels the power of her sex and the need to claim what's hers.

'Let me introduce you to some friends,' says Matt. He guides her by the arm and she feels herself surrendering to his insistent touch. As they walk between the small gatherings, she notes a few turning heads. She wonders what people are thinking and saying, and delight and desire twine inside her.

'You got here all right, then?' asks Matt.

'Not a hitch,' replies Catrin, regaining her composure. 'Though I got off at Holborn rather than Chancery Lane. But the rain held off.' It's been a while since they last saw one another but is that really the best she can do? The journey? The weather?

'Glad to hear it,' he says, and then he stops and leans close. 'I'll be stealing a kiss soon. And when this is over,' he whispers, his lips deliciously close, 'I'm going to fuck you all night long.'

Before she can respond, he steers her towards four people talking over their flutes.

'Gentle people,' says Matt with a flash of teeth, 'this is my old friend Catrin Williams. She's helped me with work I was doing at the Mawddach Residency. I've got to do the rounds, so perhaps you lot of reprobates can take her under your collective wing?'

'Delighted to,' says a rotund gentleman in a velvet smoking jacket. Matt gives her hand a quick squeeze and then moves off, leaving her stranded.

'Name's Paul, by the way.'

Introductions are made all round. There's Steven, in a dark pinstriped suit, and an old, stick-thin lady called Celia, who gives off a strong matriarchal air and reminds Catrin of her own mother. Last in the list is a woman in her thirties who offers a hand and the name Iona and has the look of a lioness.

'So you're an old pal?' asks Paul.

'She's either that, or the next flavour of the month,' says Iona with an ugly laugh.

'I beg your pardon?' says Catrin, not quite sure if she's heard correctly. The champagne is already going to her head.

'Don't mind Iona,' says Celia. 'She always becomes rather dull after a glass of wine. Iona, sweetheart, why don't you make yourself useful and find some of those delightful canapés the nice man was taking round?'

Iona clicks her tongue and stalks off without a word.

'I apologize for my niece's behaviour. I'm certain she's been trying to get into Matt's bed for weeks, the poor girl. She's very modern. Far too eager and willing, if you ask me – not that she has. I've told her that if she only read some Sidney, she'd know the chase was half the fun. Wouldn't you agree?'

Catrin sips her wine, wondering what the old bat is talking about.

'That said, Matt's never been too fussy – I've heard he'll sleep with anything on two legs: men, women and everything in between. I suppose Iona finds it rather difficult not to feel left out. Matt was the same at school, no doubt?'

Catrin nods dumbly, trying to process the verbal torrent. *Flavour of the month? Men, women and everything in between?*

'He was very popular,' says Catrin.

'I do so love your accent,' says Celia, smiling at her like she's just bestowed an indulgence from the Pope.

Paul, standing opposite Catrin, rolls his eyes. 'You can see where Iona gets her charm,' he says.

'Please,' says Celia, 'I was being sincere. It makes a nice change. Everyone at these events speaks like they're doing a documentary for the BBC with a poker up their posterior.'

'Posterior?' chimes Steven with a laugh.

'Irony, Steven. Believe it or not, I do possess *some*

self-awareness.' She turns to Catrin and smiles. 'I'm sorry, you must find us terribly dull.'

'Speak for yourself, you old hag!' says Steven.

There's more light laughter but Catrin's lips feel like stone.

'So Matt's on the loose in North Wales,' says Paul. 'Has anyone alerted the authorities?' Slight titters. A waiter walks over and tops up their champagne glasses.

'Is that Chopin?' asks Celia, cocking her head. 'Who knew Matt had taste in music.'

Catrin smiles. None of them know what she knows: that it's a sign from Matt. He's not by her side but he's thinking of her.

'Nocturne No. 8,' says Steven.

'Someone save us,' says Paul, placing a hand on Steven's shoulder. 'What next? A discussion of *Ulysses*? Or Soviet Montage? You don't want to get these two started, Catrin, or you'll end up dreaming of ways to kill yourself.'

'Remind me why we're still together?' Steven asks.

'Because I'm a sucker for charitable cases?'

The sound of clinking glass interrupts their playfulness and voices hush. Catrin realizes the place has been filling up steadily – there must be a good sixty or seventy people gathered.

'My friends, thank you for joining me this evening,' begins Matt. 'I'm delighted to welcome you here. You've been invited because you've all got deep pockets, or at least you did the last time I saw you. If that's changed, then my condolences. The exit is that way.'

There's some polite laughter and a cheer.

'The trick,' whispers Paul, having sidled closer to Catrin, so only she can hear, 'is to get everyone tiddly enough to lighten purses and wallets.'

Catrin nods and takes another sip of champagne. She's feeling quite *tiddly* herself.

'Vietnam,' continues Matt, 'is a country steeped in history, tragedy and hope.'

'Not his best line,' says Paul. 'Bit on the nose.'

'Some of the images you'll see are of an upsetting nature, depicting as they do the ravages of first-, second- and even third-generation mutilation caused by the use of Agent Orange.'

'He's always liked to have a political angle,' whispers Paul.

'Ten per cent of tonight's proceeds and all donations will go direct to the Vietnamese Association for Victims of Agent Orange – the VAVA. A further ten per cent will go to the victims of the tsunami that struck last year. Please be generous. While you're gathered here, I'd also like to thank my assistant, Birdie, my agent, Paul Roland, and the good people of Sunny Art Centre.'

Catrin turns to Paul, who smiles. 'I know. Birdie. What were her parents thinking?'

'So please grab another drink, walk around at your own leisure, mix and mingle and, if any of the work piques your interest, do speak to Birdie or Paul. We have the place until ten thirty so enjoy yourselves and thanks again!'

A round of applause follows and Catrin catches Celia rolling her eyes before explaining, 'I've seen and heard it all before. Tugging on the heart strings. But he needs to sell his work as much as any other person, I suppose. Just ask Paul.'

'You've known him a long time, then?' asks Catrin.

'We were neighbours about fifteen years ago.' Catrin's about to ask more but Matt is suddenly at her arm. 'I've come to rescue you from the jaws of Celia Pinnock, QC. She's not done too much damage, I hope?'

'Just a little,' says Catrin. The words come out flatter than she intends and Catrin feels her face flush.

'I see,' says Matt and exchanges a look with Celia.

'I think that's my cue. I'd best find out where Iona has got to;

the girl's been gone far too long – probably got herself stuck in the lavatory or some such nonsense. And, Catrin, please don't think me an old prune. It's been a pleasure to meet you, if only briefly. You'll come and say goodbye before the evening's out, won't you?'

Catrin can hardly refuse, and, with that, the old lady is off, walking majestically across the floor.

'She's an absolute bloodsucker, that one,' says Matt. 'But we're very close. I hope she's not left you feeling too drained?'

'No,' replies Catrin. She wonders what Matt's not been telling her but she can't ask here. Steven has also disappeared but Paul's still hovering.

'Well,' says Matt, 'you've met my agent. I hope *he's* behaved himself at least.'

'When do I not?' says Paul.

'He's agreed to give you a guided tour of your own this evening, while I make the most of tonight by loosening purse strings. Paul knows more about these paintings than I do, so you're in safe hands, until I return. And I *will* be back, you can count on it.' He gives her a wicked smile.

'Shall we?' says Paul, offering his arm.

He takes her into the first room, which is dominated by four large portraits of members of the hill tribes of the Sapa highlands. One of the wall panels offers details about the subjects' ethnicities – Black H'mong, Giay and Red Dzao – and their way of life. The paintings themselves are a few yards in width, with a focus on the bright patterns of the traditional dress, the lines of paint capturing the movement and easy grace of the men and women. The backgrounds are done in broad brushstrokes of green to capture a sense of the rice terraces.

'These,' Paul says, 'were painted while he was actually in Vietnam; he had them shipped back by air. Here you can see that the long, fluid movement of the paint gives the impression that the paintings were done at great speed – but, in fact, each stroke, each angle, has been meticulously considered, sketched out beforehand. It's like a dinner party: the only way for the whole event to seem effortless is to prepare and prepare again and then, once you have done all you can, run with whatever happens.'

Catrin admires the four images and tries to imagine Matt at his easel, mixing paint, filling the canvas with colour. She'd once asked if he'd like to paint her. Matt had laughed. Without clothes? he'd said. They'd been up at the residency, tangled in sheets. She'd thrown off the duvet and arranged herself into a dramatic pose. Like this? she'd said.

'Which do you like the most?' asks Paul, his question dragging her back to the present.

Catrin regards the four paintings, looking from one to the other, and then points.

'That's my favourite, too,' says Paul with a delighted smile. His eyes are small but they twinkle in the light and Catrin finds herself warming to this eccentric character with his good humour.

They move to the next room and Catrin's surprised to find a wall covered in what look like the scribblings of a child on creamy A4 paper. After the earlier room with its large canvases and colour, these dark charcoal scrawls are disappointing. Rhys had done better work in nursery.

The wall panel reveals the pieces were done 'on location', which doesn't mean much to Catrin. What does it matter where an artwork is done? It was either good or bad. And these, thinks Catrin, are very much the latter. She stands in front of one circular scrawl done in Hội An and tries to make out the shapes. Was that the canal? An umbrella? Or someone on their bicycle wearing one of those cone hats?

Paul leans forward so his chin is almost resting on her

shoulder. 'This is the money-spinner,' he whispers. 'He can just bash these out yet people love them. Signed, unique and small enough to hang – or hide – anywhere in the house. You see those red stickers next to them? Those show someone has bought one. We always put out a few stickers to begin with; it gives a sense of urgency. No one likes to be the first.'

'And these schemes are where you come in?'

'Schemes?' Paul laughs. 'Absolutely. The invitation list is also important. You want the kind of people who like others to know they've been invited to a private art exhibition; people with deep pockets who can snap up an original from an up-and-coming.'

'Is Matt up-and-coming?' Catrin's surprised.

'It's what almost everyone's called, no matter how long they've been in the game – until they've actually upped, that is. I have artists in their graves who are still up-and-coming.'

As they walk along the gallery wall, Catrin catches snippets of conversation; men and women talking about equities, bathroom refurbishments, the war.

'What do you think?' asks Paul. 'A favourite?'

She stands and contemplates.

'How much are they?' she asks.

'Two and a half,' says Paul.

Catrin feels her surprise in the whites of her eyes. She pauses, scans the collection, then looks back to the drawing done in Hội An, with its circles and vague shapes. 'That one,' she says, pointing.

Paul walks over, pulls out a small packet of red stickers and puts one next to the frame.

Panic flares in Catrin. 'I can't . . . I didn't . . . No pockets,' she says, 'let alone deep ones.'

'Now there's a scandal,' replies Paul. 'But don't worry, I won't be sending you an invoice. This was Matt's idea. He said you'd been a help in recent months, and he wanted to surprise you with this.'

Catrin looks from Paul to the picture. No one has done anything like this for her in a long time. To think that Matt had been planning this, thinking of her.

'Personally,' he says, lowering his voice to a conspiratorial whisper, 'I think they're dull as ditch-water but you mustn't ever tell Matt that. He's rather proud of his little sketches – largely because they sell, which, he thinks, proves his vision and talent. Poppycock, of course. It's all advertising and curation. Same with books, music, film, business. Here, would you like another?'

Paul holds out a fresh glass of champagne from a passing waiter. Catrin takes a sip and her mouth sparkles.

The two of them drift on and Catrin begins to feel as if she's floating like the bubbles in her glass. And then she sees Matt talking to Celia and she finds her soles back on the ground. Before she can even attempt clumsy lip-reading, she's pulled along by Paul, who seems to be taking his role as tour guide with a delighted zeal, as if sharing trade secrets is something he's been longing to do for years.

In the third room, the work returns to oil on canvas and the subject is traditional crafts and vocations, much of it inspired by the artist Tô Ngọc Vân.

'More fluff,' says Paul, his voice low, nodding at the wall panel. 'Useful padding. Some might say essential – it helps the critics validate their expensive education; they'll pick up on a reference like that and deep dive. They're mainly advertising their own expertise but also, helpfully for us, the art.'

'You don't –'

'Paint a flattering picture, so to speak? It's best to approach these things with eyes wide open. Or maybe I've just gone a bit long in the tooth? Tell me, how old do you think I am?'

'Fifty-five?' says Catrin.

'Sixty-six,' replies Paul, glee written across his features.

'Never,' says Catrin.

'Never married, more like. Does wonders for the hairline and skin.' He points towards the images on the wall. 'How about these?'

Catrin studies twelve paintings of various sizes and walks towards the picture on the far left. A woman is sitting at a potter's wheel, one hand dipped in a bucket of water, the palm of her other hand pressed against the side of the spinning clay, which sits in the middle of the wheel. Her thumb is pressed into the centre, widening the cavity of the grey-coloured clay. She is turned slightly away from the viewer and, on her right, two young boys watch, each holding an unfired clay animal. Their clothes are covered in dust and their carefree joy is perfectly captured. Behind them, tables and benches are strewn with glazed and unglazed vases, plates and bowls, plain or painted.

Catrin remembers the time she and John had taken the boys to the Corris Craft Centre south of Snowdonia – Harri must have been ten or eleven – and they'd spent the day exploring the mines and making small bowls in a room that looked much like the one in the painting. Harri had got his Superman shirt covered in clay, despite the aprons they were made to put on, and the instructor – an older woman – had taken a shine to Rhys and had made him a small Welsh Dragon, which he'd painted the day afterwards. She wonders what has happened to it. So many things get lost over the years.

'This one?' says Paul, coming to stand next to her.

'It reminds me of my boys,' says Catrin.

'Are they back at home?' asks Paul.

'Rhys, my youngest, should be. Though who knows these days; he's sixteen and acts the total teenager.'

'I wish him a speedy recovery from said affliction,' says Paul.

'And Harri, my oldest,' continues Catrin, 'recently returned to Iraq.'

'That must be difficult,' says Paul.

'It is,' admits Catrin. The thought of her boys is like a cold press on her skin. To speak their names, while she's here, is a betrayal. 'Do you have children?'

Paul smiles and shakes his head, his eyes heavy. 'My one great sadness,' he says. 'But I have Steven. And he is my one great comfort.'

'I'm sorry,' says Catrin, surprised by the strength of her feeling.

'You're kind,' he says. He pulls out his phone, glances at the screen. 'I'm so sorry, there's something I need to see to. Will you be all right for a moment?'

Alone, Catrin seeks refuge in the final room. It's lighter and more spacious, with six images of a utopian Vietnam, inspired by some of the country's visionaries. She wishes Matt would find her again. This, she thinks, is his real life, one in which she'd be a competing distraction, one among a number of – what was the word? – *flavours*.

She stands before the last painting, which shows a family around a table, sharing a meal, a joke. She remains in front of this picture for a long time, regarding each face, the way the four of them sit together. She raises her glass to her lips, tastes nothing but air. She feels light-headed and wonders what Harri is up to. He wouldn't believe that she was here, among these people. And she wouldn't want him to know it.

Unbidden, unexpected, Catrin has a moment of clarity that pierces the fog: she's going to call things off with Matt. Not today – she wouldn't do that to him on his big night – but later this month, perhaps. He was intending to head back to Wales in a week or two and she'd do it then. She can already picture the moment. They would be somewhere private on the Orme or at the far end of the pier, the wind blowing in their hair. There'd be the hint of tears in her eyes and he'd cling to her but nod in a way that told her he understood. They'd share a last, final kiss and promise to remain friends. They'd send each other Christmas cards each year and the occasional text, tinged with a tenderness and nostalgia for what they'd shared.

'There you are!' The sudden noise startles Catrin. It's Celia. 'I've been looking all over for you. I see you've been abandoned by both Paul and Matt. That's men for you.'

Daydream dispelled, Catrin regards the other woman with tired detachment. 'What do you want?' The question escapes before Catrin can pull it back but the older woman hardly seems to notice.

'Nothing but your delightful company,' says Celia. She has the same relaxed confidence as Matt; Catrin wonders if it's something they're born with or whether it's underpinned by money or power. What was it that made people so comfortable in their own skin? Too tired to care, she peers down at her feet, which are still aching, despite the champagne. She wishes she'd eaten more canapés.

'Oh dear,' says Celia, looking over Catrin's shoulder. 'Here comes trouble.'

Catrin turns to see a wide-hipped woman with a thick cascade of dark hair barging her way through the entrance, her mouth a thin line.

'That's Claire,' Celia informs her. 'Matt's wife. Poor woman.'

A terrible, twisting urge to hide grips Catrin as questions and observations rise like a flood: *Why's she here? What's she doing? She looks frumpy. Tired. Angry. Hadn't Matt said they'd parted amicably? Had something happened? Does she know Catrin's here? Did Matt invite her? Would he have done that? To her? To them?*

'You know all about it, I suppose?' says Celia. 'Matt hasn't exactly treated her too well. He's followed a long line of painters ruled by their penis. The last straw came when he was caught sleeping with a student of his. It was quite the embarrassment. Claire had always turned a blind eye before but this attracted rather too much attention and was something she couldn't ignore. I feel for her – and their children.'

Unable to tear her eyes away, Catrin watches Claire, who looks so small and angry and sad as she marches through the crowd of turning faces. And for a moment, between the shock and fear, she feels a strange sense of connection, like she understands this ill-treated mother-of-two. Celia was right: it was what men did. They betrayed you. Sooner or later someone else caught their eye and they chased them without looking back. And who was left behind? Who was forced to deal with the consequences? Men made love and war but they made so little time for anything else. Women were forced – yes, *forced* – to fill in the times and spaces in between. It made her sick and full of fury. How dare they do this to her! To them!

Catrin watches Matt's wife stride forwards as if she's about to do battle and then, as she reaches one of the large canvases, she pulls out a knife. In one swift movement, before anyone can stop her, she slashes at the picture several times. There are gasps, more people turning, some of them taking steps back, others running forward.

'How very Mary Richardson,' says Celia. She shakes her head as if she's seen it all before and perhaps, being a QC, she has. Catrin looks at the scene and feels the shock of violence but also a warmth, as if she's been bathed in something indulgent. It is, she realizes, the heat of vengeance.

Yes, she thinks. *Yes.*

Other thoughts surface. In another life, she might have been friends with Claire. Instead, Catrin may well be contributing to the breakdown of this woman's marriage, the rupturing of her family. And, in the meantime, what is Catrin doing to her own? And for what? A man who told half-truths? Who couldn't keep his trousers up? Who slept with men and women and everything in between?

'I have to get back,' says Catrin, turning with half an apology to Celia. 'I have to get home.'

Celia holds her gaze, takes in all that Catrin is, the fullness of her femininity – to really see her for the first time that evening. 'So he got to you, too, did he?'

Catrin looks away, ashamed and bitter.

'He's a damn good artist but he's no saint. But then,' says Celia, finishing her sentence just before Catrin is beyond hearing, 'we're all guilty of something.'

10 March 2005

Dear Mam, Da, Rhys

How are you all doing? What an amazing two weeks of R&R. Thank you. I'm already missing the place, you lot and the general quiet. You wouldn't believe the noise you can be battered with here. Sometimes it's just one barrage after another.

Honestly, those two weeks were just perfect.

The weather has been getting even hotter here, so those cold showers are now easier, though I still sweat like a pig in a blanket when I'm out on patrol. Last week we got into a firefight and it was a bit of a hell-hole but we got out of there in the end. No injuries.

We got lucky with the arrival of the Yanks. You should have seen it: there was a gunner sitting there with his balls hanging out, everything swinging around in the heat, shouting that it was fine to have his legs blown off, so long as he still had all his bits.

Whatever's said about right and wrong, I'm glad we're on their side. Even at the risk of friendly fire, which can sometimes be a bit too friendly, they pack the biggest punch.

I've got to go. Know that I'm well enough and I love you all.

I'll be back in a few weeks, the lambs will be out on the hills and the skies will be clear blue. It'll be a bright new world.

All my love,
Harri x x

507. In conversation with President Bush on 8 March, Mr Blair said that the US and UK should not seek to influence the selection of the new Government, but that they should try to 'shape' how it would address certain issues, such as Iraqiisation.[*]

– *The Report of the Iraq Inquiry*, Volume VII, Section 9.3

[*] Letter Quarrey to Siddiq, 8 March 2005, 'Prime Minister's VTC with President Bush, 8 March'.

12

Mid-March arrives with a dry spell; the greens of the mountains have lost their gloss; the ewes regard one another with disinterest as they graze the ground, which remains soft but no longer sinks beneath the weight of their feet. The trees have shaken off the diamond rain and the lake near the farmhouse lies quiet, reflecting the clear sky. In the nearby woodland, the eyes of a stoat shine in the gloom of a tree cavity and she sniffs the still air, protective of these woods that she has claimed and doubly protective of the small lives inside her.

John, whose whole life has revolved around the weather, makes the most of the interlude and, having checked on the fell sheep, now gives his time to the drains and gutters. Later he will check the fences, the hedges and the walls. Presently, he stands on the upper rung of a ladder, several feet above the ground, gloved hands scooping out the leaves and sludge of the gutter. It smells of soft rot and he dumps the dark, soggy mess into a bucket that sits on the slate roof of the farmhouse. Once the bucket is full, he climbs down, careful to keep the ladder steady against the wall. It's tiring work, going up and down, shifting the ladder across every yard or so, but his leg is holding up and he feels the old satisfaction of resisting the green tides of the wild, the roots and tendrils, the spurs and spores. It's an endless tug of war and one that no man can win – and there's a comfort in that, he thinks.

The bucket is full and John makes his slow descent before tipping the dark contents into the barrow and moving the legs of the ladder along. He catches his breath, peers through the kitchen window and sees Rhys staring at a textbook. Poor lad should be outside on a day like this but Catrin has been coming down like an iron rod of late; after the headmaster, Mr Fairhurst, agreed she could teach some of her pupils at the school, Rhys making trouble is an embarrassment. The boy was being an idiot, and John had told him as much. He didn't mind some rough and tumble – he'd had his own share of it over the years – but there was a time, a place and a cause. You don't throw fists because of a few throwaway words. Still, it was clear the lad wasn't suited to school and John's been arguing with Catrin over whether or not Rhys should be allowed to leave once he's done his exams. John's all for it, knows what it's like to be stuck in a room, bored and restless. But Catrin's pushing for another two more years, at least.

More concerning, thinks John, are all the goings-on with Molly. John's okay with a girl and a boy learning one thing and another and he'd slipped the lad a condom and laughingly told him not to be so sheepish.

All he wants is for the lad to be safe – mistakes were easy to make and he knows the younger lot are freer and looser than things past; knows, too, that Catrin's fears have wormed their way inside his skull.

Dear Catrin, his Catrin . . .

The afternoon she'd left for London, part of him thought she might never come back. But there she was, home that very evening, looking exhausted, her eyes glistening. She must have pegged it to make the last train to Llandudno.

Relieved to see her again but confused by her sudden re-appearance, he'd pressed for an explanation but she'd not said a word, just gone straight to bed.

She's been acting strangely ever since but at least she is here. It must mean something, that. He's not asked any further questions and she's not volunteered anything, so it hangs between them, neither wanting to speak of it, because who knows what might happen if they do? Over the last few days, they've found a degree of balance, built on the foundations of the farm's needs – Catrin buried in the paperwork, John out here cleaning and clearing and getting ready for the lambs. He's even insulated the water pipes in the kennel. But the questions inside his head haven't stopped; they turn and tumble like a threshing machine, keep him awake at night, morph his fingers into a rock-hard fist. Because it's not just the trip to London: there are other dots that, when you join them up, create a picture he can't bear to look at for the simple reason he still loves Catrin. He loves her, he loves her, he loves her.

And what can he do? What can he do but get on?

That's what Harri had said. Get on, Da. Face it. And John is. Thirty-three days straight, not a break in the chain, not a single flutter on the horses or the slots. But it was hard and harder still with a wife who . . . a wife he feels he's losing. Lost, even.

And he cannot let go of his anger.

John finishes scooping out the muck from the gutter, the old rotting leaves from the last year. Clean gutters to mark the arrival of spring. Once he's done here, he'll take one of the stable brushes and give the roof a gentle clean, scraping off the debris and the moss that has started to grow on the shell of his home. Yesterday he'd seen a blackbird up here, using its beak to rip up the dark moss, searching for an easy meal beneath the soft green, its sharp eye and yellow beak framed by the paper-white sky. For no reason that John could see, the bird had released a sudden song and he'd stood there listening, an audience of one, and he'd thought, yes, that was it; that's why the struggle was worth the fight. Moments like these.

John finds Catrin scrolling through the computer. Flint struggles to his feet and walks over, sniffing at his legs.

'Hello, old thing,' he says. The dog's tail beats lazily from side to side.

'I think,' says Catrin, glancing in his direction without a smile, 'we might be eligible for some of the old grants that have been rolled into the Single Payment Scheme. Might even get something via the Higher Level Stewardship.'

'How much?' asks John, wondering if the next thirty years will be like this: efficient and transactional.

'Forty pounds per hectare, for livestock removal –'

'Right.'

'Shame we don't have any water meadows,' says Catrin. 'Three fifty.'

John lets out a long whistle. 'I'd turn the whole damn place into a water meadow for that.'

'The creation of woodland inside LFA is two hundred. Outside is three fifteen.'

'LFA?'

'Less favourable land.'

'All land's good land.'

'Spoken like your father. It's a five-year scheme, so you're looking at, what, fifteen hundred plus, per hectare.'

'Worth a gander. That's some work and upfront cost, though.'

'There's the usual, too. Management for hedgerows, hedge banks, ditches and some notes here on fencing.'

'Fair bit of that needs seeing to; I'll need to rope Rhys in, mind.'

'Did you see his mocks?'

'Mocks socks,' replies John.

Catrin's face scrunches up in irritation.

'The lad'll be fine,' he says.

Catrin flicks through to another webpage. Flint wanders over and nestles at her feet.

'Oh,' says Catrin.

239

John rubs at his stubble. 'Oh?'

'I've been reading the wrong page,' she says. 'Should have been looking at Woodlands for Wales.'

'Oh,' says John.

Catrin looks at him. She shakes her head. She gives a small smile, her lip quivers and then, without warning, she bursts into tears.

'Catrin,' he says, taking a step towards her, uncertain on his feet, unsure of what he should do or say. His wife was not one for tears. And, unfurling like bracken fronds in sudden light, he feels his fears and doubts stretch wide. *Is this it?* he thinks. Is she going to tell him she's had enough? That she can't take any more of the shit-shovelling? That she's going to leave him?

'Oh,' says Catrin, wiping her eyes, shaking her head, as if she's as surprised by this sudden outpouring as he is. 'Oh. Oh. Oh.' She smiles and sniffs, the tears disappearing as quickly as they'd come.

John takes her hand, as full of fear as he has ever been. *Please no*, he thinks.

'It's the hormones,' she says. 'They're raging.'

Relief saturates every sense. 'Hormones?' he echoes.

'You've not noticed? The sweating, the flushing, the restless nights?'

'Well,' he replies, unsure what he should say, still too drained by the release of tension, the loosening of the screws of his heart.

'My menopause,' says Catrin.

'Oh,' says John, awkward now with the word uttered out loud.

'Oh?' says Catrin with a snort.

'Oh,' says John. They both start to laugh, the two of them together, Catrin still holding his hand.

Catrin shakes her head in wonder, laughter still in her voice and a few fresh tears in her eyes. 'Oh,' she says. 'Men.'

And this word, with its sly vowel that flirts and flits between *a* and *e* kills the music in John's throat. He still holds her hand but it's he who now feels the flush of heat, the world atumble, the terrible, burning restlessness.

Men.

~

John knows where every coin in this car is; it's like he can scent copper and silver and gold. He can picture pounds and pence slipping from pockets, sliding between cushions, rolling under beds, tables and cupboards. There are adverts on the TV, the radio and in the papers; the shops promote the lottery and scratch cards with huge sums promising dreams come true. And how he aches to itch! Wherever he looks and wherever he goes, the reminder is insistent, the struggle endless.

The GA meetings are a help. Over a month, he's done. And tomorrow it will be one day more and so on until he's buried in the ground.

But, God, it's hard. When he closes his eyes, he sees spinning numbers, hears the charge of hooves on racecourse turf and he pictures the big win – a win so big it'll prove him right and let him put his debts and doubts to sleep. No more begging and borrowing and no more lying.

He drags himself out of the car, knowing he's got to walk past temptation, knowing the way his feet will feel the insistent pull, the magnetism of the bookies.

He walks quickly, head down, thinks of the farm, his wife, his sons. He approaches the Win365. He holds his breath. Keeps his feet moving. One foot and then another. He stops. He looks at the posters in the display window. He puts a hand on the door.

And he's inside. This pit of vipers. This circle of hell.

And then there's a hand on his shoulder. He turns. It's Greg.

'I saw you enter,' says the other man. 'Come on. Neither of us wants to be here.'

And as simple as that he's outside again. The two keep walking, saying nothing until they get to the restaurant. He's not been here since last year, when he kicked up that fake fuss over the undercooked chicken, and he's not sure if the waiter recognizes him. If he does, the young man gives no indication.

'I have a reservation,' says John. They're taken to a table and seated opposite one another. Greg's a small man with greying hair and a round face, dressed in a slightly crumpled suit. He works as a surveyor. Not the sort of man John would ever imagine being friends with but they'd struck up a certain camaraderie since the first GA.

'You just saved me,' says John, once they're settled.

'You might have saved yourself.'

'Thanks,' says John. He's not so convinced. Why did everything have to be so hard?

'How d'you become a millionaire by gambling?' asks Greg. John shrugs.

'Start with billions,' replies Greg, smiling.

They order beers, starter and main each, and some poppadoms.

'What do you call two cows going all in on the final hand?' asks Greg as the dips arrive.

John pulls at his lip as the waiter brings the beers.

'High steaks.'

'Good one,' says John. He takes a sip of his beer, the foam lingering on his upper lip.

'To progress,' says Greg, raising his glass. He then leans forward conspiratorially. 'And there's more good news: Parliament are set to pass a new Gambling Act next month. I've not looked into the details but I've heard it'll impact on those f-ing fixed-odds terminals.'

'And I'll say cheers to that,' replies John.

Bowls are placed on the table. The rice steams.

'Nice place, this,' says Greg. The waiter smiles and leaves them to it.

'Last time I was here,' says John, 'I claimed the meat wasn't cooked and refused to pay.'

'The meat wasn't cooked?'

'It was. But I was in a bad place. Wanted to spread the misery. Went straight to that bookies afterwards.'

'I see,' says Greg, easing back into his chair. 'So this is both confession and atonement?'

'Something like that,' says John.

The conversation drifts to members of the GA and one of the new attendees, who recently admitted to suicidal thoughts.

'You been there?' asks Greg. 'God knows I have.'

John nods and when his lips part the words spill out. He tells Greg about the piano. How his wife hadn't spoken to him for days, turning as cold as winter, only thawing when their boy Harri had come home. How she'd been forced to cancel on her students, keeping on just a few after Harri had spoken to Mr Fairhurst at the school; how the ghost of the piano haunted the hall, his wife saying she could hear its notes at night calling to her; how she had beat her arms against his chest, asking him what else were they going to lose, what else were they going to lose?

Greg listens in silence and brings his palms together and threads his fingers. He doesn't pull a face or whistle through his teeth like he's watching a drama on TV. He simply sits there and listens, and for that simple act of kindness John is grateful.

'I don't know what's going on,' says John. 'She went to London. Was supposed to stay the night but she came back that evening. Must have got the last train to Crewe and then switched to Llandudno Junction. Her lips were sealed tight.'

'She didn't say anything?'

'Just that it was a mistake to go.'

'And that's it?'

'That's it. She didn't seem happy, though.'

'Well,' says Greg, 'you know I'm not one to give relationship advice, but I don't think anger's the answer.'

'But that's the problem,' says John. 'All I want to do is blow his fucking brains out.'

'I suppose that's an option,' says Greg. 'Although we'd miss your sunny disposition at the meetings if you got yourself locked up.'

John smiles and downs his dregs. 'I'm a miserable bastard, aren't I?'

'What are you going to do, then?' asks Greg.

John folds the napkin. He looks to his left and signals for the bill. He pulls out his wallet. 'I'm going to find out the truth,' he says.

The bill arrives and the waiter stands with the card machine. 'Was everything to your satisfaction?' he asks.

'Yes, thank you,' says John. 'I've been telling my friend here that this is the best restaurant in town.'

'Thank you, sir.'

John leaves a ten per cent tip.

'And when you find the truth?' asks Greg, pausing at the door.

'I don't know,' says John.

Outside, it is dark and the clear skies of the day have folded over and the rain falls once again.

'I'll see you later on this week at the meeting?'

'I'll be there,' says John.

'Unless you've been arrested,' says Greg.

'There is that,' says John.

He folds the collar of his coat around his neck.

John drives quickly along the narrow lanes, his eyes on the road, alert to other vehicle lights, but all is quiet. He could be the last man on Earth. His mind is on Catrin, joining the dots. It made no sense. There she was, being the rock, the force, knitting him back together, helping him solidify himself, helping him to get his roots back into the ground. Being mother and wife.

But at the same time . . . there was the invitation from Matt. All those times she had disappeared to see friends in town. There was the trip to London. John's thoughts flit back and forth and sometimes his lips open as if he might address the night air. He can't understand it. How could she do that to them? How could she sleep in two beds and pretend things were no different in the waking world?

John knows he's open to accusations of hypocrisy, that for years he had his own double life, but his secrecy was built on guilt and desperation, propped up by an addiction he couldn't control. Surely it was different?

He's so lost in thought and feeling that he doesn't see the two eyes shining bright against the darkness. Doesn't see them until it's too late. He applies the brakes, the wheels sliding along the rain-covered road, his heart leaping, his car ploughing forward, the front slamming into the body of something heavy, a shape in the darkness, a life. It'll be a damn ewe, sure as the moon is in the sky. Two months from birthing and all. These thoughts fork through John's mind at the same time as his own weight strains against the belt, the airbag's pop is like the sound of a gun, and his head whips forward before jerking back, hitting the headrest. His whole body feels as if it's vibrating and his breath comes out in great ragged heaves.

The bag slowly deflates and John pulls at the handle of the door and fresh air streams in, along with the smell of burning rubber from the tyres. There is pain across his chest where the belt has strapped him down and his neck feels strained but otherwise he is fine. He takes in some slow lungfuls of air, puts on the hazards, unbuckles his belt and reaches for the torch in the back pocket of the seat. Outside, unsteady on his feet, he heads towards the mangled shape at the side of the road. He sees the legs of the thing kicking out, the wheeze of pain. 'Well, fuck,' he says. He'd hoped it would have been killed on impact but those legs are too desperate to be the final movements of a dead beast, nerve endings and electric signals shooting through limbs.

John shines the light around him. By law he should call the police and they, in turn, would call the vet. It was a lot of paperwork, a lot of money and a lot of pain. He knows there's no gun in the car but he's got his hunting knife with him. Hell, he'd use a rock if he had to. He walks back to the vehicle, pausing mid-step. He should think it through. There is, after all, the liability of the thing to take into account. He walks over to the Land Rover, studies the front. A few dents but it's a solid thing. Cost a few bob to fix but it'll run well enough and Joe Jenkins will see him right. Some cash in hand would help. He goes back to the ewe, which gives a feeble kick as he checks the tag on the ear, notes the markings on its back. It's one of Alwyn's. The animal's eyes are sad. John wonders if it knows it's dying. Walking back to the car for a second time, John feels himself to be off-kilter and he sits. Tapping the number into his phone, he brings it to his ear, listening to the ring. 'Pick up, you bastard. Pick up.'

On the eighth ring, the receiver is lifted. 'Hello?'

'Alwyn. It's John.'

'John, it's late to be calling, man. What is it?'

'I'm on Pennant Road,' replies John. 'One of your sheep was out and I was coming along too quick and didn't see her. I'm sorry, Alwyn, she's in a bad way. I'm past the B-road, about a hundred yards on from the garden supplier.'

'Shit a ton of bricks. Are you okay, John?' They're both aware that, in the eyes of the law, Alwyn is at fault. That he is responsible for his livestock and any undue harm they may cause to members of the public. They also know that there's no way in hell John should have hit the ewe; being a man of the place, a shepherd himself, he should be well-versed in the risks of the road. Anyone who's lived here longer than a few seasons knows well enough to drive at half the speed of the signs, to keep his eyes alert.

'I'm fine. Fine.'

'The sheep?'

'Not in a good way.'

'Still alive?'

'For now.'

'Shitting bricks. And the car?'

'Dented but nothing major.'

'Have you called it in?'

'Thought I'd ring you first, see if you were about.'

'Can you bring the girl in, John?'

'That's what I was thinking.'

'Need me to come down?'

'You'd be twenty?'

'Twenty, twenty-five.'

'I'll wait here.'

'Okay, then, John. I'm glad you called and you're all right. You've done me a favour. Hold tight now.'

He's glad. He had no desire to cut through the neck, watch the animal bleed out while its life drained, its heart and lungs working to their last. He'd have done it if he had to but this is better. Christ, it's better.

It starts to rain and John steps back out of the vehicle, pulling his hat on over his eyes, reaches for his long trench coat in the back and strides over to the animal, still on the ground. He folds the tails of the coat under him and sits down next to the ewe. The small stones and scrub are uncomfortable but he ignores the way they dig.

247

'I'm sorry, old girl. I don't know what you were doing out here all alone, away from the rest of your pals. But I'm sorry. You should have been a mammy. Maybe that's what you're thinking now but here you are, hit by the dimwit sitting next to you, who should have known better.' John shakes his head at the rain that is pooling in the creases of his wax jacket. The ewe is still rasping, its body heaving up and down. The road flashes dark and then yellow as the hazard lights of the car blink on and off. Apart from the wind and the rain and the wheeze of the animal beside him, the world seems still.

For the second time that day, he wonders what it would be like to be the very last man on Earth. Would he still tend to the livestock? Would he get up in the mornings, shower, shave, look himself in the mirror?

John does not leave the dying animal's side and he is soaked through by the time Alwyn arrives, a horse box behind the car.

'I should have seen it,' says John, as his friend walks over, gun in his hand.

'Damn creature shouldn't have been on the road. Must be a breach somewhere. Main thing is you're still standing on your own two legs.'

John watches as Alwyn leans over, checks the ewe, gives a growl of anger, frustration, sadness. He aims the gun and fires. The terrible wheezing stops. 'Will you help me put her in the box?'

They each take two legs and carry her round the back of Alwyn's car. He opens the door of the box and then they swing her in. It is still raining and now Alwyn is dripping, too. He nods at John. 'I'll see you right about the car. Just let me know what the repairs are, won't you?'

'I'll do that.'

'And, look, I appreciate you giving me the call.'

'I should have seen it.'

'Look at this weather,' says Alwyn, gesturing at the wall of rain dropping from the night sky. 'Anyone could have missed it.'

The men shake hands and return to their cars.

Back at home, the place is quiet and dark. Catrin will be in bed and Rhys should be, although they've both noticed he's started staying up later and later, a beam of light often escaping under the door of his bedroom. He remembers doing the same when he was younger. He wanders through into the living room and switches on the TV and puts his feet up. Flint pads by and collapses next to him and then begins to snore. John tries to shake the sound of the wheezing ewe from his mind, the pitter-patter of the rain. He should shower or have a bath. He flicks through the channels, one after the other, settling on an old Western on Freeview. Unable to sit still, he reaches for the book of poetry that's on the coffee table. Catrin's always liked reading. She's folded over a few of the pages, underscored some of the lines. It's too obscure and abstract for him. He knows there's something to it but why not just tell it as it is? Tonight, he'd hit a stray ewe. It had struggled for breath until Alwyn had killed it. There it was. Dead. No need to say more than that.

John turns over the pages, then puts the book down. He'd never had options like Catrin. He'd not gone to university. It was always the farm or the farm. But she'd made the choice, hadn't she? Stuck with it, with him.

He knew the boys were the glue, more than anything else, and that was okay. That was the way of things. Their two boys. The one upstairs, a boy aching to be a man.

The other, far away, beyond their tender touch; a man aching to be the boy he once was.

525. In the last week of March, the US and UK Governments were encouraging the Iraqi parties to conclude negotiations to form a new Government.[*]

526. Sir Nigel Sheinwald told Mr Hadley that the UK was increasingly frustrated with the stalemate and concerned about its consequences.[†]

– *The Report of the Iraq Inquiry*, Volume VII, Section 9.3

[*] Letter Sheinwald to Adams, 23 March 2005, 'Conversation with National Security Adviser, 23 March 2005'.
[†] Letter Quarrey to Siddiq, 1 April 2005, 'Nigel Sheinwald's Phone Call with Steve Hadley, 31 March'.

13

Over the last few weeks, Matt has not stopped reaching out to her. He's emailed, texted and left voicemails. He's apologized, tried to explain himself, told her how much she means to him. And because her resistance has been ground down, because she wants an explanation, because she wants to vent, because the past months cannot be swept away in a single evening, and because there are still glowing embers, she has finally agreed to meet him.

Wanting some time to settle her thoughts, Catrin takes a detour to Llandudno Pier. She has over an hour until she has to see Matt and wanders slowly along the wooden runway, pausing now and then to peer at the small, wind-battered stalls on either side. One of them offers a wide array of ornate shells. Dreamcatchers dangle from hooks, swing in the breeze. The other night she'd dreamt about both Matt and John, the two of them caressing her body; she'd woken up in sweats and in the cold wakefulness of the early hours she'd felt ashamed and vulnerable, as if she had somehow betrayed herself.

Catrin fondles the shells, wondering if there's anything in the old wives' tales of shells capturing the sound of the sea, and more besides. She recalls a folk tale about a woman who was told that if she buried her dead husband inside a huge clam shell, he would be reborn three days later. The widow does exactly this and, when she prises open the lips of the clam, there is a baby inside, smiling up at her. The wife raises the child, who grows into the same man as her husband. But, being the child's mother, she can never love him in the way she had. Tormented by her conflicting desires, she goes mad and takes her own life, stepping off the edge of a steep cliff and plunging into the sea.

As she's pondering this disturbing tale, Catrin's confronted by an old woman who looks as if she's just stepped out of the story itself. Her grey hair is held in a bun, and shells and bangles wrap around her wrinkled wrists and neck.

'Everything all right, pet?' she asks, her voice husky, bright blue eyes uncomfortably piercing.

'Yes, thanks,' says Catrin. 'I was just looking.'

'Those are ten pounds each. Not so much for a good night's sleep, I can tell you.'

'They're lovely.'

'They'll capture those dark dreams, keep them locked away.'

'I sleep well enough,' says Catrin. 'It's my husband's snoring that's the problem.'

'We all have nightmares, pet,' replies the old woman, smiling wide enough for Catrin to see the glint of a silver crown catching the light.

Catrin moves on, leans over the rail and looks down at the sea below as it laps at the cast-iron supports that hold up the pier. She closes her eyes, listens to the murmur of the water, the steady rhythm of the waves, the breath of air that whispers its way along the long stretches of blue, sends the water curling in on itself, rising and falling, rising and falling.

What is Matt going to say? And what is she going to say to him? Will she see him with his magnetic smile, find herself drawn to him again, want to touch him, want him to touch her?

Walking further along, Catrin comes to the Pavilion, which is filled with blinking, beeping arcades. She wanders in, eyeing the machines with their carefully balanced coins. They seem so tantalizing, stacked like little skyscrapers on the edge, looking as if they'll tumble at the slightest nudge. But she'd played enough with the boys when they were young to know it was an illusion, that the machine could swallow whole bags of coins and that the dazzling, sparkling wealth would always be out of reach. Resting on top of the coins are a few extra prizes – nail-art stickers, badges, wax crayons, key rings and sweets. Just enough to tempt children, to hook their attention. They catch them young.

In the darkened space inside, she sees a young man dropping coin after coin into the slot. It's impossible not to think of John. She feels the urge to go over, to shake the young man and tell him to give it up, to tell him it's not a path anyone wants to follow, that he'll hurt himself and those he loves.

She wanders over to the end of the pier and looks out towards the horizon. She remembers coming here with the boys and seeing bottlenose dolphins. A large crowd had gathered, cameras filming as they rose out of the water, bodies arcing back down to disappear beneath the sea. The boys had been so excited. She could still picture the way Rhys, bless him, had stood there with his mouth open at the magic before them, his excitement contagious. She misses the emotional simplicity of those early childhood years, the way anger or joy was plainly written on faces and pointed to more obvious causes: a missed nap, a new toy, a kiss on the forehead. These days it was so much harder to know what her sons were thinking and feeling; and, no matter how much she might press Rhys, who worried her more and more, he resisted her efforts. And, when he did try to explain himself, it was often in monosyllables that left her as confused as before. When she'd sat him down and asked about the scuffles at school, he'd just looked sullen and said it wouldn't happen again. And, while there have been no further incidents, she remains concerned. Perhaps John was right. Would Rhys be better out of school, working the land with his father? For reasons she cannot fully grasp, the thought fills her with a terrible sadness. It feels like she's giving in.

She searches the sea as if it might offer up an answer, a miracle, but there is nothing save the endless turning of waves.

Her feet take her back down the pier and soon Catrin finds herself on Mostyn Street. She spies Billy Lal's Bargain Centre next to a KFC and, feeling nostalgic, decides to indulge herself. Billy Lal, an old favourite of tourists to Llandudno that has been here longer than the Poundland and the Poundstretcher, both of which must have arrived seven or eight years ago. She used to bring the boys at Christmas time, give them a fiver each and let them go wild, choosing cheap plastic tat that they could wrap up and put under the Christmas tree.

Inside, there's a low hum from the lighting above. Two aisles are filled with a dizzying number of items from China: plastic dinosaurs, yo-yos, stationery, toiletries, homeware, clothes, knick-knacks. One basket contains a collection of pocket Bibles, no larger than a thick matchbox, with the proud title of *World's Smallest Bible*. Catrin reaches for one, opens the rice-paper-thin pages, finds the writing too tiny to read without glasses.

Her phone vibrates; it's a text from Matt letting her know he's reached the Orme.

It takes her several minutes of marching at double time to get to the tramway, where she finds a pale-faced man with droopy eyelids slouched behind the ticket desk.

'One way or return?' he asks.

'Return,' she says breathlessly, her body hot.

The man hands over a ticket and a leaflet that tells of the tram's history: over a hundred years old and the only funicular on public roads. It would have been quite the engineering feat at the turn of the last century. She steps into the tram's carriage, which is proudly named St Tudno after the patron saint of the place. A few older men and women alight, although it's not a busy ride, with it being mid-week, early afternoon. Catrin wonders how many couples, over the decades, have spent their afternoons and mornings riding up the side of Llandudno's very own little mountain, a mile-long journey up the back of the Sea Monster. And how many of those journeys have ended in proposals, break-ups, divorce? Open spaces were always easier for such things, as if the air and the ground were able to soak up some of the laughter and tears.

The tram begins its ascent and, sitting with her back to the mountainside, Catrin's able to look over the whole town, the beach and the pier stretching into the dark-blue sea, where the tide is far out, the sky grey above it. Hard to think the tsunami was just three months ago, that all the way around the world people are still trying to rebuild their lives.

She sees a line of donkeys trotting along the sand and remembers Harri and Rhys sitting on the worn saddles. Twenty pence per ride in those days.

Catrin sees past and present, the one overlapping the other.

But what of the future?

And what Catrin does not see, because she is making haste, because her thoughts are atumble, because he is well-hidden while he waits for the next tram, is that she is being followed, that she is being watched, that there is a man who sees her, past and present.

But what, he is wondering, of the future?

~

There's a short walk to the Rest and be Thankful, the squat, pebbledashed café where Matt will be waiting. Outside, up here, where she feels above the world, it's warmer than Catrin had expected and the views, as always, are impossibly beautiful. Ahead of her, a troop of pensioners stands on a viewing platform, the men holding cameras and binoculars, no doubt hoping to scout the rarities of the place – the silver-studded butterfly, the Kashmir goats. Catrin passes them along the trail and one of the men turns to her, smiles, his eyes lingering too long.

If it wasn't for the modern fireplace in the centre of the café – with flames that lick against the sides, the logs giving a pleasant background crackle – the café would feel faded and soulless. The wooden floors, expansive windows for viewing and the cheap uncomfortable chairs give the whole room the impression of transition. Matt is already seated. There's a white plastic bag at his feet.

Catrin walks over and he rises from his chair. He's about to reach out to her but hesitates, arms hanging awkwardly at his sides.

'Catrin,' he says.

'Hi,' she says.

'Can I get you something to drink?' he asks.

'No, thanks.' She doesn't feel like sitting but Matt is already back in the chair. There are bags under his eyes but other than that he looks the same. Even his shirt seems well-ironed and she's not sure why but this disappoints her. She perches on the skeletal frame of the seat.

'I suppose I should explain,' begins Matt.

'You slept with one of your students,' says Catrin. 'You lied about your divorce. And you're known to be a serial womanizer who has had – and is having – multiple affairs. What's there to explain?'

Matt begins to roll up one of the sleeves on his shirt. 'I don't know what those . . . what they told you but it's not as simple as that. You can't possibly believe it is?'

'The facts are there,' says Catrin, her own words setting alight her anger.

'Relationships aren't mathematical formulas. There are contexts. Besides, let's not pretend you're an innocent victim here.'

'I never said I was,' says Catrin, her brows furrowing, heart skipping a beat. 'But you lied to me.'

'I've never lied to you, Cat,' says Matt, leaning forward, his look as serious as she's ever seen. 'Sure, I've not told you every detail of my marriage and I've never told you about all the relationships I've had but holding back a few private matters is not the same as lying. You can't sit there and tell me you've not held things back about John, that the two of you don't have issues you prefer not to talk about.'

'Celia said you slept with everything and anything that moved.'

Matt shakes his head and leans forward. 'Celia likes to stir the pot. She was probably just having some sport.'

'It's not true, then?'

'Claire and I had an understanding. Things were dry in that department – for both of us – for a long time. So, yes, I suppose you could say I took advantage of that, a fair bit more than she did, which didn't help things. But I'm hardly the devil-made-flesh here. It's always been between adults.'

'The student –'

'Mature student. Thirty-four, for God's sake.'

Catrin closes her eyes. This wasn't going the way she'd anticipated. 'You told me you loved me.'

'I do,' says Matt. 'It's as simple as that.'

'Nothing's that simple.'

'Some things are.'

'But you've been sleeping with other women?' says Catrin, almost hoping it's true because it would make things so much easier.

'While we've been seeing each other? No,' he says. 'No, no, no.' He's shaking his head and she can see the twitch of his mouth as if he's about to smile, as if there's something funny in how wrong she's been about him.

Catrin looks away. She needs time to think over what she's heard but there is no time, there is only the now, the moment – how can she think or say anything sensible when there is no time to think? – and Matt is already speaking to her, reaching across the table to hold her hand and she is letting him, and she is relenting, her body responding as she knew it would and she feels as if there is no defence against this, but he's speaking, Matt is speaking and what is he saying? He's saying –

'For all I knew I was your bit on the side.'

Catrin pulls her hand away. 'Don't say that.'

'The facts are there,' replies Matt, a little cruelly.

Catrin buries her face in her hands. It wasn't supposed to happen like this.

'I always knew this would end,' he says. 'Even though I love you. And I think you love me, even if you never admit it. Because it's not enough. You were never going to leave your home, your family. You might have daydreamt about it. I did. I've thought about convincing you that your boys are old enough to look after themselves, that you deserve to see the world, that you deserve so much more. But I always knew you'd pull away. Back when we were young, you might have come with me. But you pulled away then, too. And now – after so many years?

'You know, when I saw Claire that night, slashing at the canvas, that was some of what went through my mind. I didn't care about the painting. All I could see were the missteps she and I had made, all the things that had led to that terrible moment. It was so far off what could have been. Because I loved her and, believe it or not, I still love her and I love our kids and I think, had things been different, had we taken a different approach, been more understanding of one another, then we might still be together. But that's not how things work and it's easy to look back and see how things might have been. And it's easier still to lose things, to let things fall apart.'

Catrin closes her eyes and feels his hand in hers again.

'Do you want to get some air?' he asks.

They walk hand in hand for the final time and, as they walk, Catrin half expects Matt to beg her to see him again, or to make a suggestion about going somewhere more private. And, if he had, if that had been his agenda all along, she would have lost all faith in him. But he doesn't. They walk like old lovers, in silence. When at last they reach the far end of the Orme, that wild ancient rock that peers out towards the sea, they pause, hands still together.

'This is for you, by the way.' He passes her the small plastic bag. She pulls out a framed picture, takes a moment to recognize it as the charcoal sketch from his exhibition – the same one Paul had put the small red sticker next to.

'I can't accept this,' she says.

'Please,' he says, pushing it back towards her.

Catrin puts the gift back in the bag and looks up at Matt.

'I suppose this is it,' he says.

'I suppose it is,' says Catrin, thinking how like her daydream this was – and wasn't – turning out to be. That she really does – and doesn't – want to let go of his hand. That she does – and doesn't – want to say goodbye.

She leans towards him. He looks at her and they kiss – a long, final parting.

'I'm going to go now,' she says.

He smiles. 'Goodbye, Cat.'

It's a hard thing, to turn away from someone you love; to leave them to their own thoughts and solitude. But that is what Catrin does, following the trail back towards the tram that will take her down the mountain, back to an old life, the one she has chosen.

And, because she is wrapped up in her own sadness, she does not notice the man in the café, sitting next to the window,

binoculars raised to his eyes, watching. She doesn't know that
John remains there, watching Matt, who is, himself, releasing
his hurt and shame to the wind. And sometime later, when she
is driving back to the farm, she doesn't know that John follows
Matt back down the path, that when Matt reaches his car John
jumps into the passenger seat next to him and presses the barrels of a shotgun into Matt's side.

She doesn't know that back at the farm there lies the sawn-
off end of this shotgun hidden beneath an old tarpaulin in the
toolshed, and that last week John had spent half an hour cutting
through the metal with a diamond-edged saw and then carefully
filing the barrels until the ends were smooth as pearl.

She doesn't know that Matt turns white and almost shits himself there and then, that for the first time in his life he genuinely
thinks he's going to die. She doesn't know that John, by contrast,
feels calm and in control, while he weighs forgiveness against
vengeance.

She doesn't know how John digs the barrel of the gun deeper
into Matt's side till the other man winces and how this gives
John a flush of satisfaction. She doesn't know how the first thing
he says to Matt is: 'You've been fucking my wife, haven't you?'

And she doesn't know that Rhys is being sent to the headmaster's office for landing a fist on another boy.

She doesn't know that Harri is staring at civilian bodies lining
the road as gunfire rattles ahead and shrapnel, fire and smoke
torrent around him. She doesn't know that he is biting his lip
and praying that he'll survive, that he'll be able to see his family
and his home again among the dark-green mountains.

And how could she know this? She is in her car, driving home,
relief swelling inside her because it is over, because soon she
will be heading to the school to teach little Sophie with her
button nose. And after she's finished her lesson with Sophie,
she will pick up Rhys, who is a going through a bumpy patch

but is a good lad when it comes down to it. And she feels happier still because there is hope for John and because Harri will be home in a month, her boy with his plans and his goodness. And Catrin thinks how lucky she is, when she considers all the terrible things going on in the world, all the people who are sick, dispossessed, alone. Yes, she is lucky. And as she drives on along the winding lanes towards the school, the same winding lanes on which John had hit that ewe the other week, poor thing, her mind turns to the hyacinth flowers that are beginning to appear at the front of the house and how much she enjoys their sudden burst of colour and sweet, drowsy scent.

April

Iraq Body Count: 1,145

531. The JIC reported that the week of the Iraqi elections had seen more than 1,000 recorded attacks by insurgents, one of the highest weekly totals since the invasion.

539. In a meeting with Sir Nigel Sheinwald on 13 April, Mr Paul Wolfowitz, US Deputy Secretary of Defense, warned that there was a danger of losing the momentum generated by the January elections.* In his view, 'Iraq was going in the right direction, but not fast enough'. Sir Nigel agreed.

– *The Report of the Iraq Inquiry*, Volume VII, Section 9.3

* Letter Phillipson to Adams, 16 April 2005, 'Nigel Sheinwald's Meetings in Washington, 13 April: Middle East Issues'.

3 April 2005

Dear Mam, Da and Rhys

Good news: the prodigal son is due home in under thirty days.

I'm going to sleep for a week. We've been on stag rotation for five days straight and I feel like one of the walking dead. You should see the bags under my eyes; it's like someone's taken a sharpie to my face. I hardly know what day it is. Can't sleep though because we're only about a hundred yards from the firing points and there's fair drama going on.

It's hot, too.

How are you? Write to me.

They say the last bit's the hardest. You long for home with it being right there in front of you. I can almost smell the horse manure and sheep shit.

I'm ready for fresh clothes, a beer, a walkabout. To be away from this oven-hot sun and the sound of guns.

I'll try and write again soon.

I love you,
Harri x x

14

The stink of blood and shit is all around. John joins Rhys and Simon, the three of them checking over the yearlings. The animals have been penned in, as the weather's taken a turn for the worse. The more inexperienced ewes may need help and, while they expect to lose a dozen or so, they always try to keep the number of dead to a minimum.

Rhys is on his hands and knees beside one of the ladies, who is panting in pain. The soon-to-be-mother bleats, her eyes wild. John watches on as his boy places a hand on the back of the beast and tells her to be calm and brave and then he picks up the clear plastic bottle and squeezes thick lubricant on to his hands, rubs them together and spreads it along his forearms, grimacing at the cold.

'Don't be shy,' says John. 'You can't use too much. Isn't that right, Simon?'

Rhys glances at Simon and, before he can control himself, his face splits with laughter.

Simon stares at his feet, head shaking, struggling to contain a smile.

'Da,' says Rhys, shaking his head.

John knows he's missing something but he doesn't care. He's happy to be outside in this, his favourite time of the year.

Rhys carefully pushes his fingers, his hand and then his arm into the ewe, his eyes focused through the feeling of his fingers, which are tentatively reaching for the lamb's head. The ewe bleats, its legs begin to thrash and John holds them still. Rhys pushes his arm in further, reaching for the feet that he knows are just beyond his grasp. And then suddenly he has them and holds them firmly, pulling gently, trying to put an end to the whole messy affair.

'Easy,' says John.

'The bastard's not coming out.'

'Twine?' asks John.

The boy nods and John reaches for the orange cord that's tied around one of the nearby posts. He quickly unknots it and passes it over. Rhys slowly removes his hand from the ewe, whose breath comes out in great ragged huffs; he makes a loop with the twine before going back in. It's easier this time with the animal stretched and lubricated. Rhys is able to reach the lamb and with some care he ties the twine around the lamb's two feet.

'Come on, you stubborn little shit,' whispers Rhys. 'Out you come.' Gently, he pulls on the twine and slowly, and then with a sudden expulsion, the lamb slops out.

John removes the twine and places the bleating, newborn lamb before its mother, who looks down at her little miracle of life, recognizes it and begins to lick at the slime, establishing the bond between mother and offspring.

'Well done, lad,' says John. 'Just the one?'

'So it looks.'

'You did a good job there.'

'Should have seen the one yesterday with the umbilical around its neck.'

John wipes his hands on a rag and passes it to Rhys, who is looking at his sticky arms with bemusement. Simon has moved on, eyes and hands on the ewes, his experience showing in each touch.

'I'm sure Harri's going to be upset knowing all the things he's missing right now,' says Rhys, cleaning his hands.

'No doubt,' says John.

'You think he's going to be okay?'

'Course,' says John. Harri's letter had arrived a few days ago. They'd already sent off a reply, including some photos of the farm. It was impossible not to count down the days. John walks around the enclosure, towards the two lambs that have been abandoned by their mothers. They are huddled together beneath the heat lamp, looking lost and lonely and as helpless as they are. One is standard stock, looks as plain as most of them are, but the other has unusual markings on his feet and Rhys has named him Toes, even though John is always telling the boy he shouldn't be naming them, that it didn't do any good when it came to taking them to the slaughter. A farmer had to keep a certain distance, had to accept he was in the business of feeding the nation, of breeding and raising animals that were going to be killed.

'Hello, Toes,' John says, breaking his own rule. The lambs watch him and bleat. He had done his best the other day, rubbing the mother's scent into his new fleece, placing it under her nose, but the spark never lit. John had his eye on her now, as he was sure the ewe had done the same the year before and a ewe that wouldn't mother was no good on a farm and that was that.

He reaches down a hand, his fingers on the soft wool of the lamb called Toes. There was a good chance they'd lose a lamb or two and, if that happened, John would be able to skin the carcass and create a false coat; he'd then place it over one of the abandoned lambs in the hope it might trick the mother into taking them on. It was never a certainty but you did what you could. For now, they'll have to hand-feed them from bottles and keep them warm beneath the lamps.

John looks over at Rhys, who has his keen eyes on the other sheep, scanning ewes and lambs alike. He's a natural farmer. The right temperament. Not too sentimental but tender enough to care. Practical. Better than Harri, in some ways, but then Harri always had something of the dreamer in him. Perhaps if the

269

two of them can work together, side by side, they'll make a success of it. John would like that. Rhys with his dependability and strength. Harri with his vision. Give them a bit of time and maybe they'll have families of their own and John can take it easy, watch his sons grow, live into old age and be a grizzly old taid in the way his own father was never able to be, robbed as he was by that falling machine.

'Can you finish up here?' asks John.

'Sure,' says Rhys, hardly looking up.

'Course you can,' says John. 'I'm going to take the dogs out and then later, if you want, we can get on the quad and check the other ewes?'

'Got it,' says Rhys.

There was always a risk that ewes could get separated or stuck in badger sets or similar. Sometimes they would trip or roll, find themselves off their feet and on their sides, unable to stand, a hopeless, desperate situation that would mean death for both the ewe and the unborn lamb.

'I'll see you later, okay?' says John.

Rhys gives the thumbs-up.

In the kennel the dogs stand and stretch and whine. On one side, just above the freezer where the frozen rabbits are kept, he's got the large whiteboard that Harri had attached to the wall. He takes the marker pen from the side and draws another x in one of the small squares. It's one of the many ways he's learning to strengthen his resistance against the itch. This chain-building, avoiding the racing papers, blocking the numbers of Mike and the others with their tips and temptations, not going into town alone unless he has a specific destination and reason, the weekly meetings, getting on his knees at night and asking for guidance from God or whatever sodding being had the crazy idea to build the lonely universe – all these things help. Every day he fears something will happen to spiral him off and sometimes he hears the voice that tells him it's all for shit but then he goes for a walk, he calls Greg or one of the other members and they talk him down and he forgives himself and, in these simple acts, he finds strength.

Forgiveness, he thinks, remembering those tense moments with Matt, the whole twisted afternoon. The way he'd followed Catrin. Jumped into the car just as Matthew was about to start the engine. How he'd pressed the two barrels of the gun against the side of the man who'd been sleeping with his wife.

~

'It's over,' Matt had said, looking down at the barrel and blinking.

'Over?' snapped John, his heart thundering. 'I saw the two of you up there. Over? You were *over* each other like a fucking rash.'

'I don't know what you want me to say, John.'

'Nothing. I don't want you to say anything at all. I don't want you to write to her, to call her or to text her. I don't want you to come within a hundred miles of this place.'

'Okay,' Matt said. His voice had been calm, unwavering, although he hadn't stopped glancing down at the gun in John's hands, at its solidity, its dark metal and darker intent.

John had expected more than this. He'd expected fear, guilt, denial. Anger, even. Something more than the sad acknowledgement, the strange, tired passivity.

'I don't want you to even *think* about her,' John said.

'I can't do that,' said Matt.

There it was, John had thought. There was the resistance. He'd dug the barrel of the gun into Matt's ribs and was gratified to see a wince of pain. All he had to do was to squeeze the trigger and the insides of the car would be plastered with red, bloody paint. Artist turned art. 'You can and you *will*.'

'I love her,' said Matt.

'Don't say that.'

'And you love her.'

'Of course I fucking love her.'

'Then you should be able to understand. It's not something you can turn on or off. There's no tap.'

'But you didn't have to sleep with her,' said John. He felt his anger and his resolve beginning to dissipate. The gun was heavy in his hands.

'I'm sorry, John. I don't know what else there is to say. Really, I'm sorry.'

'Fuck!' said John.

He'd wanted to pull the trigger.

Instead, he had checked the safety of the shotgun, put it back into the duffel bag and zipped it up. It sat on his knee, heavy and cold. He had felt Matthew breathe out, noticed the slight tremble of his hands. He'd been gratified to know the man was scared after all.

'There have been a couple of times over the last few years when I've thought about ending it,' John had said. 'It wouldn't be difficult, you know, not up on the farm.'

'I think we've all been there,' replied Matt. 'When my wife took the girls, when I thought I might not see them again.'

'And then you took my wife from me.'

'It wasn't like that,' said Matt. 'It was never vindictive, never meant to harm.'

'But it did,' John had replied. 'It has.'

The two men had sat in silence. Outside, two gulls circled above. The time on the car's dashboard blinked. At John's feet there was an empty packet of salt-and-vinegar crisps. John heard Matthew breathing in and out and he'd been put in mind of the ewe on the road and how it had been lying there in the rain, its life leaking out of it.

'What are you going to do now?' asked John. Matt might have gone to the police. He could have given his statement, have had John locked up.

'I'm going to drive home,' said Matt. 'And I'm going to see my daughters.'

John had nodded. He'd thought about Catrin. His sons. 'I'm glad I didn't pull the trigger,' he'd said.

'Yeah,' said Matt, and he'd slowly wiped his sweating hands on his knees. He had then looked down at the bag on John's lap. 'Me, too.'

'I'd like to forgive you. But I'm not sure I can,' said John. And then: 'You'll stay away from my wife.'

'Okay,' said Matt. 'Okay.'

'Fuck,' said John. He'd opened the door and the cold wind cleared the humid, sweat-scented air. He stepped out of the car, shut the door with a thud and walked away, as if the two of them had done nothing more than discuss the weather, the way a heart can speed up, or slow down, or break apart.

John lets the dogs out and they walk over to the woods, the trees a motley of greens, their leaves out for the spring. Flint staggers far behind them, the old dog taking his time, sniffing at length at each tree and scent that catches his attention, as if he knows it might be his last. John studies the trees as he walks, notes their growth and shape, the way they stretch for the light. Last week they'd staked out another few hectares to make the place even larger. With the grants on offer from the EU, it's a good opportunity to guarantee some income over the next few years. He's also been thinking about Harri's proposal – to purchase some of the land and create a fat camp. A fitness retreat, Harri had called it. John didn't much like the idea of having strangers rambling all over the place but Harri had assured him it wouldn't be like that. There wouldn't be crowds of people littering, leaving gates open, spooking the livestock.

John walks through the trees, listening to the birdsong and looking out for mushrooms, the names of which he'd learnt at school, identifying them by their colours, markings, length and breadth of hat.

He watches the dogs catch the scent of some small nocturnal creature and his mind drifts back to his sheep. They've not had any major issues so far, save those two under the heat lamp. On the whole, the ewes knew what they were doing and he was able to ride around, checking and tallying. Sometimes there's a minor problem or two and he has to get down off the bike and help out, lube, twine and rags at the ready.

In a few months, the lads from New Zealand will be over, teams of shearers working the farms, stripping the sheep from their thick coats, giving them a bit of air to breathe with the sun and the warmer weather. The wool would be bagged up and sent off for little more than pennies. They'd be down by the farmhouse, sweating it out, cracking jokes.

When he was fifteen, Harri had got together some of the local fellas his age and they'd done a fair job of it but most of them were too young to compete with the guys from New Zealand, who'd had years of training and the stamina and the muscle to get through a whole flock in a day. John had been proud, though. He'd enjoyed seeing his boy take the initiative, making something of himself even at that young age. And then, that same summer, Harri had told them he wanted to join the Army. That he'd worked it all out. That he was going to try for a scholarship. John hadn't been able to get his head around it. Harri had explained that he wanted space, time, money, independence.

'You want to travel?' John had said. 'Go travel: see the world for a few years. There are all kinds of jobs you can do but for God's sake don't join the bloody Army. I'll stump you for the flights there and back, wherever you want to go. But don't do this, Harri. You go off to Australia, New Zealand, America, I know you're coming back. But you never know with the Army. They'll train you up and spit you out and what then?'

The boy had insisted. He'd beaten his war drum over and over. And Catrin had gone along with it and they'd made a deal. If he got the scholarship, they'd go along with it. And what had Harri done? Gone and bloody done it.

John looks about him, at the dogs and the trees, his land, and the red sky that is beginning to soften into oranges becoming yellows, blues and greys. 'No trouble today,' he says, and taps his head. 'Touch wood.'

His phone rings. It's Catrin's mother, Alice. He's been thinking all this time about forgiveness and redemption. New beginnings.

'I've got it,' she says.

John smiles. 'You're a star, you are.'

'When are you coming?'

'A week or two, if you can wait? Once we're further along with the lambing.'

'You can't come sooner?' says Alice. 'It's taking up a lot of space.'

'I'll do what I can,' says John.

'And the money?'

'By the end of the week.'

'I don't believe in miracles. But perhaps this will convert me.'

John smiles. 'I'll see you soon, Alice. And thank you. I'm grateful.'

'As you should be,' she says, and John has the image of Alice sitting at the telephone, chewing the end of a pencil.

As he heads back to the farm, he calls Tim and is pleased to hear the joy in his old friend's voice. Yes, of course, Tim says, come over any time this evening. Once the light has faded.

~

It's dark when John knocks on the front door, his fist coming down three times against the wood. He waits, listening to the sound of dogs howling, to steps approaching, the turning of a key, the raising of a bar.

Light floods from the house and there Tim stands, his silhouette bright against the night air.

'John,' he says. 'Welcome.'

It's a large, well-furnished house. John knows Catrin has always been envious of the space, the style, saddled as she was with a home that was already made up, had the stamp of generations on it.

They walk into a living room with heavy, dark-wood furniture. It's not to his taste but, as he sinks into the armchair, he must admit there's a solidity and quality that's reassuring.

'It's been a long time,' says Tim, passing him a whisky, the insides of the crystal glass giving a pleasurable clink. 'It almost feels like you've been avoiding me.'

John nods. 'Some truth to that.'

'Word has it that you're a changed man.'

'Recovering,' says John. He takes a sip, enjoys the burn of the whisky.

'I'm glad to hear it. We've missed you; the quality of the bar billiards at the Black Sheep hasn't been the same without your keen eye.'

John appreciates the compliment.

'You've always had my back, Tim.'

'That's right.'

'Last year, you made an offer,' says John. Adding: 'To my wife.'

Tim swirls his glass. 'I remember.'

'If it still stands, I'd like to take it up.'

Tim whistles through his teeth when he hears how much money John wants but he doesn't say no, just refills his glass, pours another inch into John's own. 'That's quite the sum,' he says. 'And quite the gesture.'

'I've had our bordering fields valued. There's a fair few hectares of ripe pasture,' says John.

Tim rubs the stubble on his chin. 'Will you give me a moment?' He disappears and then returns with a map, which he unfolds and places on the coffee table between them, his movements swift and eager. 'You're suggesting this section here?' he says, tapping the paper.

John leans over, uneasy at Tim's sudden enthusiasm, a ripple of doubt running through him.

'Something like that,' says John, intentionally vague, worried he's going to promise too much, too soon. Tim was, after all, a farmer. And farmers would always take advantage of a bargain. John looks at his old friend, weighing up his decision. It was one thing to sell land to his son; it was another matter to be offering it to someone outside the family. And yet.

'I think,' says Tim, 'I'll only need this bit.' He traces his hands around several of the low-lying pastures.

'Need?' says John, puzzled, peering at the map; the area Tim has traced is much smaller than what he'd initially suggested. This would be no bargain.

'You see these contour lines,' says Tim, 'and the water here and here? If I can combine these, I should be able to rewild.'

'The fuck is that?' says John.

'Rewilding,' says Tim, laughing at his friend's expression. 'Biodiversity, John.'

'I'm no clearer. Not sheep, then?'

'No, not sheep.'

'Those are fine fields for grazing, they are,' says John.

'And it's a fine place for so much more than that,' says Tim, waving his hand at a stack of books on a table behind him. 'We've got to look to the future, John.'

'When the hell did you learn to read?'

'I've been thinking on it some time.'

'You sound like Harri,' replies John, finishing his drink. 'It's the present I'm worried about now. Tomorrow's John can look after tomorrow. One day at a time does me just fine.'

'We all have our ways of getting from day to day. And this,' says Tim, 'will take years.'

'I'll not be able to purchase this land back?' says John. 'It's a one-off, is it?'

'It is,' says Tim. 'As I said, what I have in mind will take a long time. Decades, maybe. But, look, it's a small piece of land, John. I'm not trying to steal your boys' inheritance. If anything, I'll be doing them a favour in the long run, you can trust me on that. You could call me a convert.'

'Well, we've all had our conversions of late,' replies John. There's no doubt it's a good price for the land. A hell of a good price. His friend was doing him a favour.

'There's something else,' says Tim.

'What next? Rockets to the moon?'

'I'll leave those to Silicon Valley,' says Tim.

'A good Welsh valley is that?' says John. 'Or a new bath sealant?'

Tim smiles. It's been a long time since he's heard John like this.

'Well?' says John.

'Harri stopped over when he was last here.'

'He did?'

'Talked about some of the ideas he has for the farm. He's on to something there, John. There's plenty of folks looking to escape the towns and cities for a week, hoping to lose a bit of urban weight. And we've already got our fair share of veterans – with more to come – who will help them with it. It's a sound idea.'

'It's hot air at this stage,' says John. 'Long three years yet. The Army has its dues.'

'Nonetheless. Worth listening to,' says Tim, folding up the map. 'In the meantime, I'll have someone draft up the contract of sale. When do you need the money?'

'End of the week,' says John.

'That'll be a challenge but I'll see what we can do.' The two men stand and, as Tim walks him to the door, he asks after John's family.

'Well enough,' says John. 'Harri's home in a few weeks, as you'll know. Rhys is having a bit of trouble at school but he's been a big help with the lambing. We're thinking he might join us full time after the summer.'

'And Catrin?' asks Tim.

John pauses before he answers, turning on the step of the house. 'She's counting down the days,' he says, and pauses again on the threshold as if he's about to say more, as if he's about to confess that he'd almost pulled the trigger, that he's spent agonizing days waiting for the police to turn up at his door, that he'd buried the shotgun and the sawn-off barrel in the dead of night, that he's still suspicious of his wife when she's on her phone or when she goes out, that he watches her intently, that he's still trying to forgive her, that he's not yet forgiven himself. He almost tells his old friend that he still feels the ache and itch of money and the thrill of odds and that Red 23 haunts his dreams and in those nightmares he sees his son's bloody hands.

But John says none of this to his old friend because he's still a proud man and because there's hope in his heart that maybe these things will continue to change and improve, that maybe there are times it's better not to speak, that truths do not need to be uttered but can be allowed to lie still, that when words have the ability to bring walls and cities down, maybe silence is the answer, silence is peace.

'I'll be seeing you, Tim,' he says.

He walks to his car. He drives home and the dogs howl in the yard. They howl and howl until he yells at them to settle down.

17 April 2005

Dear Mum, Da, Rhys

It's been a rough few weeks and I'm ready to get back home. I'm feeling something sick and tired. I just hope I make it. We've had some bad news in the last few days and it's hit morale pretty hard.

I'm not sure if it's being reported and if you've seen it but there have been issues with the air bridge and some of the guys out here haven't been able to get back. There doesn't really seem to be a solution. The transport's old as fuck and basically any kind of delay causes complications. I still hope to be back in the UK by the end of the month but it's not a certainty.

We should be flying to Cyprus soon for a few days out of theatre to destress – what they call 'decompression' – which makes us sound like inflatable lifeboats. Ironic, really, that we're the ones who need rescuing.

Mum, Da, I think it's fair you know that it's not going to be easy for me when I get back. Not for any of us. But we'll make it through. I promise.

I love you all and I'll see you soon.

Your son,
Harri x x

540. The JIC assessed the impact of Iraq on the threat from global Islamic terrorism on 13 April.[*]

Its Key Judgements included:

I. The conflict in Iraq has exacerbated the threat from international terrorism and will continue to have an impact in the long term. It has confirmed the belief of extremists that Islam is under attack and needs to be defended using force. It has reinforced the determination of terrorists who were already committed to attacking the West and motivated others who were not.

II. The Iraq conflict has resulted in an increase in co-operation between terrorist networks . . .

III. Some jihadists who leave Iraq will play leading roles in recruiting and organising terrorist networks . . . It is inevitable that some will come to the UK.

– *The Report of the Iraq Inquiry*, Volume VII, Section 9.3

[*] JIC Assessment, 13 April 2005, 'International Terrorism: Impact of Iraq'.

15

Catrin drops the can of beans and runs to Flint, who has slipped on his old legs, his body shaking, tongue hanging out, his limbs contorting with the seizure. He's had a few of these in the last six weeks and Catrin knows it's a sign she needs to make a decision soon, but how can she make a decision like that, even when it's made out of love?

With some effort she tries to shunt the kitchen table aside so he doesn't knock against it. The table is weighed down with coffee mugs and notebooks, Rhys's homework and animal log-books; it's heavy and everything clatters and vibrates as she pushes, the four legs scraping against the yellow tiles of the floor. Flint continues to writhe.

Grabbing some of the free local newspapers that are stacked up to one side, she carefully slides them under her boy, the paper scrunching and ripping, but eventually she gets it in place, knowing that he might defecate or urinate, his body no longer his own. It is a terrible thing to witness. She hopes his bowels don't give way because he's a clean dog and because they are due to have lunch in half an hour and she knows the smell of shit will linger.

The front of the newspaper displays a picture of two shop-fronts with racist graffiti sprayed over the walls and windows. Flint is still shaking and she can see the sweat that is beginning to form under his legs where the skin is pink.

'All right, I'm here, I'm here,' she says. She gently places a light hand on his side so he's aware he's not alone but is careful to keep away from his muzzle; she knows the jaws can snap involuntarily. His hair falls away as she strokes him, the old winter coat shedding in the warmer months. Every few days she has to sweep up the black hair that gathers in the corner of the room. She has been sweeping up after her boy for years and soon there will come a day when he's not here and she'll still be finding his hair when she hoovers, in the living room, or in the hall, or at the back of the car. And she'll have to hoover it up because you can't live in a house or keep a car in a state; you can't let particles of skin, old dead dust motes, settle on everything, linger there, never to be disturbed – even if they were once part of something living, someone breathing whom you'd burn the world for. You had to wash bedsheets. You had to drink water. You had to make dinner. Your organs knew this: your lungs inflated and deflated, your heart pumped, your liver and your intestines, your kidneys and your brain continued to perform; no matter what went on in the world, they worked on, industrious to the end. Live, said the heart. Live, live, live.

'Easy, boy,' she says. 'Easy. I still remember you as a puppy, don't I? Small, fat thing stumbling about like you'd had a drink too many.'

The shaking subsides and Flint rolls over. He licks his paw, looks up at her, his nose still shining.

Catrin's eyes are hot.

Flint looks at her and she sees and feels the full weight of time, as if it's a physical thing, a force like gravity, all those hours they've been walking together, all those times he's sat with her, been her shadow, her companion, part of her days and nights, never judging, always loving, no matter what, because he is part of the pack, part of the family, and even wolves, even wolves with their wild natures, will care for their old, look after their injured and mourn the dead. And how much more will she feel, with half a million words to reach for, to show the way she aches and to mourn the passing of this connection, which is the oldest and closest of all connections between man and animal? She looks at Flint and feels all of this and she wonders if it's time, because she will not see him suffer. John hasn't mentioned anything, knows the choice is hers, that it can be no one else who calls it.

'You're all right, aren't you, boy-o? You're all right, cariad, love?' As if he understands, Flint gives her hand a lick. 'Jesus, you'll be the end of me, you will.' She gets to her feet and walks over to the fridge and opens the door – its artificial light pools out. The cold and the smell of preserved meat gives her a strange sense of floating, as if she's stepped from one time into another. She takes out the packet of cheap ham, knowing that Flint is watching her, and as she takes a few pink slices and holds them out to him he stretches forward, teeth, tongue and jaw at the ready, as greedy as ever. 'You stay there, for a bit, won't you?' she says, resting her hand on his side. His tail beats upon the floor.

Once she's certain Flint is okay, that his appetite is still there, Catrin returns to the beans and she places the opener on the side of the can, tightens the two wheels around the rim and begins to turn the handle. Every few moments she looks behind to check on her boy, to be sure that his eyes remain open, that his body is taking in the air. His tongue is out and he's panting but, yes, he's still with her and she tries to focus on the task at hand, takes a deep breath and relaxes her shoulders. But it's hard to concentrate on a tin of beans when her mind and heart are filling up and there seems to be no more room for anything at all, even this simple, stupid task, these beans in their orange sauce and the bread that needs toasting and the cheese that needs grating, all these tasks that she needs to do and she can't; she can't just press 'pause', even for a moment, put everything on hold, even though she needs to take a moment, let things settle; but, no, her heart is still beating and her lungs are still inflating, deflating, and she is the rock, hasn't she been the rock on which others can pause, rest, find comfort? So she keeps twist-ing, Catrin Williams, wife, lover, mother, daughter. That's it, put the beans in the pan, put the bread in the toaster, go through the motions, get through the day and don't think about Matt, who hasn't called or messaged since they parted; don't think about Mum, who's started to struggle with the stairs; don't think about John, who's being too kind; don't think about Rhys, who's been told to take a few days away from school; and don't think about Harri. Don't think about the fact it's only four days until he comes home and, no, don't think of the letter, that awful letter that arrived yesterday, the letter she's not shown anyone else; no, just count down the days, the hours, the minutes. Four days and he'll be home. Four days, four days, four days, how is she going to get through those four days? And all these men, all these bloody men, running around in her head, with their bloody wars and agendas and opinions taking up her time and her attention, all these bloody men, how dare they do this to her, lean on her, treat her like an island, come visiting, resting, recuperating, demanding and cajoling, and then off they go, all of them going, going, going. How dare they?

'Mam?'

Catrin turns, sees Rhys in the doorway and she feels herself letting go and it is a difficult thing to speak but she manages to issue her commands, tells Rhys to make lunch, it's not so diffi-cult, toast and beans and cheese, he can manage that, can't he? All she needs is some air and, yes, she's fine, she's fine, everything is fine, would he just get on and please sort out lunch this once, would he, please?

~

The air is mild and the smell of recent rain is rising from the grass and the new leaves on the trees. She wonders how many times she has walked along the small dirt path, trees on either side and she wonders where thoughts and feelings go to when they have been spent. The path begins to climb and Catrin catches her breath, leaning against a tree, using a stick to scrape the mud from underneath the soles of her walking boots. She continues her journey, peering up at the branches, saying the names of the trees she recognizes. She would like to be sitting at her piano now, a pen in hand, working on her song. Her song. Her son. Strange how they seem to have linked themselves. It's been in the making for six months; all this time the incomplete melody has been sitting at the back of her mind. She's tried to work on the composition at the school but it's not her piano, her space, her home.

Again the mud begins to stick to her boots, her feet getting heavier with each step, and again she dislodges clumps of dead leaves and dirt. The edge of her scarf is moist with the dewiness of her breath. A burst of startling, blue sky filters through the treetops. She can hear a pair of songbirds performing for one another. There's a cool wind that filters its way through the weave of her clothing. Further up ahead, there is a treehouse that John made for the boys when they were younger. She walks over to it, noting the way the wood has become stained, mossy with rot and mould. She shakes the ladder, testing its strength, puts a foot on the first step, rests her full weight on it. Things hold. The ladder reaches some four yards above the ground, up to the small house. She grips the sides of the steps with both hands and gives a firm shake. It wobbles but feels firmer than expected. Another boot, another step. Stupid, really, to be doing this, alone, without a phone and no one knowing where she is. She could fall, break a leg, a rib – bone piercing lung. But no: another step. When had it been built? The summer of '93? John had spent weeks making it. His father had been alive back then and had instructed things from the ground, passing up nails and wood and rope. While the men had worked, the boys had been running around, gathering long branches, making their own den on the ground, which they called the Cave, a lair that was said to lead to a deep underground place, where monsters beneath the earth would gather, only to be defeated by the might and courage of Harri and Rhys. She wished that's all they had to deal with now – monsters of the mind, imaginary beasts that could be banished with the wave of a wand or a jab of a stick.

Nearing the top, Catrin looks down and she wonders how she ever allowed them to play out here, unsupervised, when there were a hundred different ways they might have hurt themselves. At last she pulls herself up on to the platform, gasping at the effort.

Peering over the lip of the floor, she sweeps aside a layer of leaves, watching as earwigs and other crawling insects scuttle away, retreating to the dark. The wood beneath is warped but she's made it up and now all she wants to do is sit here and rest, to sink back into the past. She keeps to the corner of the rectangular shelter, knowing that the floor is likely to be better supported at the edges. The whole structure seems to wobble beneath her weight and Catrin feels the rhythms of her heart leap. She takes off her hat and scarf and looks about, wondering if the boys have fond memories of their childhood and if those moments of joy offer foundations secure enough to weather whatever storms come their way. She has given so much of her life to them, has placed so many limits on her own freedom in order to widen theirs. She knows what her mother would say: the role of a parent is one of sacrifice and, if that's not what Catrin had wanted, she oughtn't to have had children. And yet.

She pulls out the folded letter from her pocket and reads it again.

I just hope I make it.

Catrin feels as if the news is spiralling around her, ever closer. Within a few days of twenty American soldiers being killed in Baghdad, Jalal Talabani was elected as President of Iraq. Three days later, Pope John Paul II was buried and it seemed half the world was in mourning. Fast-forward twenty-four hours and thousands of Iraqis would attend an anti-American protest in Firdos Square, while UK citizens celebrated the wedding of Prince Charles and Camilla.

While soldiers and civilians died, the newspapers filled their pages with pictures of the beaming couple. Charles, dressed in a black morning coat, grey waistcoat, pinstriped trousers, blue shirt with a white collar and a polka-dot tie. Camilla in a silk chiffon dress with Swiss-made appliqué-woven discs and an oyster silk basket-weave coat. Suede shoes, wide-brimmed hat with ivory lace and feather, and calf-leather purse. The whole look had taken over a month to make. After the ceremony, Camilla had changed into another outfit for the blessing – a mixture of pale blue and gold with subtle detailing.

Catrin had flicked through the pages of the magazines while she sat in the hairdresser's, the young girl Kirsty cooing over how beautiful the whole thing was. Catrin had sat there listening and reading while her greying hair was pulled back by the plastic teeth of the comb. She'd spent the whole day avoiding the news, not because of the royals and their wedding but because it was the same day as the Grand National and John had asked her to stay with him. It was one of the most televised sporting dates in the year, played on every screen in the country, and he couldn't watch it, he said. He couldn't afford to think about it. They had spent the day riding the horses, reins in hand, feet in stirrups, just like they had done when they were younger, covering miles of undulating fields beneath the wide sky – and, for the first time in a long time, Catrin felt close to

John. She'd been surprised to find herself happy riding beside him. Perhaps there was hope.

They'd ridden high up the hills and then unsaddled, left the horses to graze, walked up towards the summit. They'd held hands in the evening and watched the sunset as the sky bloomed red and orange. The two of them seemed to glow in the sunset. John had sat there and apologized for the way he'd behaved, said that he'd not been himself for years and that he hoped she would, in time, forgive him. They'd sat in silence for a while and then he'd turned to her and asked if she'd spoken to Matthew recently. She'd said no, that he was back in London. John had nodded and looked at her and his eyes had been so serious as he asked if she would ever see him again. Catrin knew what John was asking and she'd felt her throat tighten up and she'd shaken her head, not trusting herself to speak. John had squeezed her hand and then said he would never mention it again but that he was glad. He was glad, he said, because he loved her, that he couldn't imagine his life without her.

The sky's red bloom had continued to wax and at length John put an arm around her. They'd talked about the past: when they'd first met, the death of John's parents and Catrin's father, her miscarriage, the changes they'd made after moving to the farm, the birth of their sons. They'd talked about the present: John's weekly meetings and his new friendship with Greg, Catrin's piano lessons and her new pupils, and Rhys and the fact it was probably the right thing for him to leave school in June. They'd spoken, too, of Harri and his plans.

They had said little of the future, undecipherable as it was. Instead, they had kissed – properly – for the first time in a long time. And in that tender touch was all they had needed to say of things to come, of their hopes, their fears.

Later, when all was quiet in the farmhouse, when all the animals had been tended to and darkness had fallen, they had made quiet, tender love. And in the small hours of the morning, when Catrin was still awake as her body went through its changes, she thought that maybe she could be happy. And as the sun surfaced, she thought about the scientists in California who'd recently found a way to measure the smallest mass ever, a cluster of xenon atoms, billionths of a trillionth of a gram, a startling seven zeptograms, and she'd wondered what else they would learn to measure in the future. She'd wondered if they'd ever learn to weigh love.

Catrin opens her eyes, breathes in the smell of the rippling wood.

She unfolds the page and reads Harri's letter again, slowly, because each word is his.

I love you all and I'll see you soon.

As she folds it up and puts it back in the pocket of her jeans, a bird lands on the side of the shelter and begins to sing: a robin, puffing up its red chest, dancing along the wood. Catrin is cold and the damp leaves beneath her are beginning to soak into her trousers and her mind is already spinning towards tomorrow but there is this, the present, the song. The bird sings away, oblivious of its spectator, until she shifts a leg; it gives a startled flutter and flies away, tweeting in surprise.

Catrin begins her slow descent from the ladder, one wobbly step at a time. She loses her footing on the penultimate rung, slipping, her heel snapping through the final bit of supporting wood and landing painfully at an angle on the hard earth. Wincing, she wiggles her toes, makes a circular motion with her ankle and leans gently on the ball of her foot. Nothing broken.

It's later than she expected when she gets home. She checks on the horses, noting that the front door of the stable needs sanding down and repainting, some of the mortar between the bricks needs repointing and the ivy needs trimming. The two horses watch her. A head stretches over the stable door and Catrin rubs its nose, reaches for the packet of polo mints in her pocket, puts one flat on her hand, feels the tongue against her skin. She'll have to muck out the place tomorrow or the day after and repack the straw. They'll bag up the manure and have it sent to a company that uses it as fertilizer – it doesn't bring in much but it helps to get rid of the stuff, which is the main thing. It's the same for the wool. Nowadays, half the battle is dealing with all the waste the farm produces. That, and making ends meet. Harri's right: if the farm is going to sustain itself, they need to look at alternatives. But give it time.

She's about to head to the chicken coop, when there's the sound of a car horn and a white van hurtles up into the yard. John is in the driver's seat and – stranger still – her mother is sitting there next to him, her mouth a thin pencil line.

A door slams and Catrin turns to see Rhys bursting out of the house, grinning. There's a smudge of bean sauce on the left corner of his lips and her stomach groans but she can eat later. For now, there is the strangeness of her mother and husband sitting side by side in a white van.

'What's going on?' she says.

John gets out, winks at her, hurries round to the other side to help Alice from the seat.

'Mum?' says Catrin, walking over. The dogs in the kennel are going berserk. Flint staggers out of the house, his nose sniffing the air.

'I don't understand,' says Catrin. 'Will someone please tell me what's going on?'

'Well, that was a pig of a journey,' says Alice. 'Hello, Daughter.'

'Mum?' says Catrin, hugging her mother. 'What are you doing here? In this?'

'Yes, I never imagined riding in a white van either, dear. But needs must.'

'Needs?'

'Come, we've got something to show you.'

As they make their way to the back of the van, another car pulls up into the yard.

Catrin raises a puzzled eye at John.

'They're here to help,' he says. 'You'll see. Come.'

Catrin stands behind the rear of the van as John opens the doors. At first she doesn't know what she's looking at, but then, as she makes out the different parts, her heart misses a beat.

Surely not?

It wasn't possible.

She looks at John. He nods, smiling.

Catrin takes a step forward, places a hand against the wood as if she's feeling for a pulse.

She turns again to John, and this time she cannot help the tears that gather.

'It's a piano,' she says, her statement ordinary, the reality extraordinary.

'It's not just *a* piano,' says John.

'It's *your* piano,' says Alice.

Catrin covers her face with her hands. 'How?' she says.

'Really, Catrin. I may have grown up with the abacus but I know how to work my way around a computer. All I had to do was to find the listing and pull one or two strings.'

'One or two strings,' says Rhys. 'That's a good one.'

'*Really*, dear,' says Alice, giving the lad a withering look.

'You got it back,' says Catrin, her voice raw.

'Don't look at me,' says Alice. 'It was John's idea. I just helped with the detective work.'

'But how?' asks Catrin. She looks back at the van, its loved contents.

'I'll explain later,' says John. 'For now, maybe we can let these fellas get going?'

John directs the two men as they set to work and Catrin watches every step as if she's seeing things in reverse. The men work quickly and quietly. The piano begins to take shape and the hall breathes again, as if it knows that the piano has been missing all this time and it was just waiting for the instrument's return. The men are about to leave when Catrin's mother walks over and lifts something from her handbag.

'Dad's tuning lever,' says Catrin, smiling, taking the old tool in her hands. She'll need to call a piano tuner later in the week, but for now, with time and patience, she'll be able to do a rudimentary job.

Once the two men depart, Catrin inspects the piano and begins the long process of tuning the keys, letting her fingers dance. She feels childlike, as if she's discovering music for the first time. Her mother sits on the piano stool, offers some advice as she works. There are over two hundred strings and Catrin labours with her tuning lever, mutes, checks each note against the chromatic tuner, starting first with middle C and tuning the octaves, adjusting the pins, tightening once the sound is just right and checking her progress with each major third interval. There is nothing more satisfying than listening to everything vibrate symphonically.

Hours pass but Catrin has no awareness of the time. Rhys brings her tea and toast and an old box of mint chocolates. The sun falls and still Catrin works, her hands, knees, legs and back beginning to ache. John appears at various intervals smelling of livestock.

At long last, when it is well past dinner time, Catrin is done. She plays some scales and smiles appreciatively and turns to find her mother, John and Rhys watching.

'You've no idea what this means to me,' she says.

'I do,' says John. 'I do.'

'Are you going to play for us, then?' asks Alice.

Catrin looks at the keys, contemplates. 'Give me a moment,' she says, disappearing. She returns with a sheath of papers.

'Is that what I think it is?' asks Alice.

'It's not finished,' says Catrin. 'But yes.' She takes a seat, rests her fingers against the black and white keys, which are cool and full of promise.

Catrin scans the sheets of music. She doesn't really need to look at them. She's worked so long on the composition that it seems to live inside her, just as the song had lived in the robin. She tidies up the sheaths of paper, cranes her neck to see the three of them there, watching. Rhys gives her a double thumbs-up. She smiles.

And begins.

Her body sways as she plays and it's like her fingers have their own lives, like they were made to do nothing else, and as she plays her soul is filled with something almost heavenly and she loses awareness of all that is around her – there is just the music and all her movement bends towards it; all her thoughts, all her feelings, shape the song and are shaped by it.

She plays and her audience of three is enraptured, caught by the beauty of the song and the beauty of its player: daughter, wife, mother.

So enchanted are they that they do not hear the other sound, a different kind of pitch and rhythm, less music and more alarm, a call to action.

It is the phone.

And as the piano sings the phone rings, it rings, and it rings, and it rings.

And then it falls silent.

And still the music plays, the notes rising and falling.

The call comes through a second time and its discordant pitch punctuates the melodies of the piano. And John – who has never thought his wife so beautiful, who has never loved her so much – hears the intrusion but dismisses the irritating, insistent sound. Nothing can spoil this.

And, as the phone reaches its final note, Rhys, too, hears the highly pitched call, like a siren. It seems to weave its way between the notes, a different colour to the black and white keys his mother plays. But he refuses to be drawn in, caught as he is in his mam's spell.

And Alice, who has the sharpest ear of all, despite her age, also hears the phone but she is well-practised at ignoring things she deems ugly; and how easy it is when her daughter is here, playing like this, as Alice always knew she could, like a dream, a miracle – and her own composition no less!

And so the sound of the phone dies down while the music of the piano goes on. Catrin's body sways with the music, her hands following the long threads of sound she has woven these long, cold months. As she nears the final lines, she has a sense of the ending but it remains unwritten and she cannot conjure up the final sounds; they elude her, hiding from sight. The music ends, expectant, taut.

Catrin is rewarded with applause. She smiles. She feels loved.

But whoever is on the other end of that call to arms, whatever it is they have to say, it must be important. Because the phone rings a third time. This, it seems to say, is the conclusion. These are your final notes. Here is the ending.

And Catrin, who is still basking in the echo of approval, glides through into the kitchen and takes the call, her ear to the receiver, waiting for whoever is on the other side to relay whatever urgent message they have to share.

And, as she listens to a man's voice, a man she has never heard before, telling her something she cannot bear to hear, something terrible happens to her smile. It's as if all the muscles in her face can no longer abide to be as they once were; they no longer know how to arrange themselves; they just know that nothing can be the same again.

And when Catrin returns to the hall, her legs and feet somehow navigating space, the light reaches her eyes but her mind struggles to interpret what she sees. She knows there are three people standing before her but they seem too happy to be real. Because how can anything or anyone be happy at a time like this?

She tries to form words. To ask who they are and why they are so happy yet nothing works. Or perhaps it does. Because, although she says nothing, not a word passes her twisted lips, they see that everything has gone askew, that whatever reality there is has somehow shifted.

Yes, she is saying something. She can hear the weight of the words.

Words – which begin all things, even endings – find their way.

'It's Harri,' she says, her voice the final sound, the end of all music. 'It's our boy.'

2016

June

Iraq Body Count
2003–2016: 188,770[*]

---

[*] Figures based on current information. The IBC continues to update its
numbers according to further evidence.

[. . .]

3. The consequences of the invasion and of the conflict within Iraq which followed are still being felt in Iraq and the wider Middle East, as well as in the UK. It left families bereaved and many individuals wounded, mentally as well as physically. After harsh deprivation under Saddam Hussein's regime, the Iraqi people suffered further years of violence.

4. The decision to use force – a very serious decision for any government to take – provoked profound controversy in relation to Iraq and became even more controversial when it was subsequently found that Iraq's programmes to develop and produce chemical, biological and nuclear weapons had been dismantled. It continues to shape debates on national security policy and the circumstances in which to intervene.

5. Although the Coalition had achieved the removal of a brutal regime which had defied the United Nations and which was seen as a threat to peace and security, it failed to achieve the goals it had set for a new Iraq. Faced with serious disorder in Iraq, aggravated by sectarian differences, the US and UK struggled to contain the situation. The lack of security impeded political, social and economic reconstruction.

338. When the UK sought a further Security Council resolution in March 2003, the majority of the Council's members were not persuaded that the inspections process, and the diplomatic

efforts surrounding it, had reached the end of the road. They did not agree that the time had come to terminate inspections and resort to force. The UK went to war without the explicit authorisation which it had sought from the Security Council.

339. At the time of the Parliamentary vote of 18 March, diplomatic options had not been exhausted. The point had not been reached where military action was the last resort.

— *The Report of the Iraq Inquiry*, Executive Summary

16

Simon breathes in the air of the surrounding farms, fills himself up with the endlessness of the land. In the distance he can see the pub where he and Harri had met in the dead of night all those years ago; the memory of it is so potent it brings him to a stop. He looks at the trees, the fresh green of the leaves. He remembers Harri, how he'd approached, electric in the dark. Touch awakening to touch.

In the yard he finds Catrin standing with her arms crossed, looking down at John, who's on his back, peering up at the vintage MG he'd purchased last month, on the condition it would be ready for Rhys's wedding.

'Bore da,' says Simon.

Catrin smiles and shakes her head. 'I told him this was a bad idea.'

'It'll be ready,' says John, reaching for a spanner.

Simon crouches down and looks at the rusting underside. He can smell the oil and the grease and John's sweat. He used to resent John's stubborn, blunt masculinity; it had taken him years to learn there was a tenderness in the man. He'll never forget when his mother had died and John had held him close. *You'll always be family to us, Simon*, he'd said. And Simon had felt comforted and accepted, strange though it was for such a thing to follow such sadness. Afterwards, John had spoken about his own parents, how it was a hard thing to be in the world without a mother and father. To lose the people you love.

'Three weeks,' says Simon, passing John a different spanner and then getting to his feet. 'Plenty of time.'

Catrin scowls and kicks at the soles of John's shoe. 'You're an old goat.'

'You know what they say about old goats,' says John.

Catrin gives his foot another kick. 'Come on, Simon,' she says, leading him to the farmhouse.

Inside, he's almost barrelled over by the young pup whose body shakes and twists and is all paws and tail. He crouches down and gives the little black lab a playful rub. The pup scrambles up and dashes to grab a rope toy from under the piano. The instrument is polished each week but it hasn't been played for over a decade. To sit there and play is to invite a pain that does not subside.

It goes like this:

A single misstep. The guttering click of an IED and a sudden blast of white light and heat. Harri's body flung into the air. His body landing like butcher's meat. There is bone and blood and burning. Harri groans and soon there is someone at his side, applying a tourniquet to his leg, bandages to his arms.

An agony of time passes and, when he awakes, Harri is not where he was. He is not the man he was.

'Simon?' says Catrin, pausing in the doorway of the kitchen.

Simon remembers Catrin calling him from the car, already on her way to Birmingham. It had been late. He'd been eating spaghetti bolognese and helping his mother with a parking fine. There'd been an old poinsettia on the table in front of him, its leaves glowing red.

They wash their hands and then make their way to the laundry room, where Catrin loads him up with freshly ironed sheets; it's changeover day at the guest house and they've only a few hours in which to get things ready before the new arrivals are due. Together, they stroll over to the converted barn with its large glass windows. Inside, it's decorated in muted tones and florals – greys and light browns, with the exposed wooden beams giving the feel of the outdoors. The bedroom smells musky and Catrin pulls aside the curtains and opens the windows.

As Simon begins making the bed, he finds a used condom under the mattress and discreetly disposes of it in the bathroom bin. He should be used to it after all these years of cleaning up after guests on their romantic getaways but the sticky mess of other people's sex still makes him gag.

'You'll be looking forward to Provence,' says Simon as they slip cases over the pillows. John and Catrin hadn't been back to France since their honeymoon and Simon wonders which of the two – the people or the place – will seem most changed.

'After thirty-something years of marriage? I'll say so,' she agrees. He can hear the undertow of her exhaustion. People aged but the work on the farm remained a constant. He watches as she straightens a picture in the corner by the door – a charcoal scrawl on thick, rough-edged A4 paper. Signed at the bottom. It's at odds with the rest of the decor but he knows the artist, knows there's history there. Harri'd told him his suspicions; back then, Simon had never been able to imagine Catrin as unfaithful. Over time, though, he's begun to believe in the possibility of it; had felt how a person might dream a different life from the one that was cast.

'I hope Rhys has the stamina,' says Catrin. 'Marriage comes with its ups and downs.'

'No doubt,' says Simon. He thinks of Harri. How dreams can turn.

'Did you hear about Blair?' asks Catrin, giving the room a once-over. 'He's been made a peace envoy to the Middle East.'

'I heard,' says Simon. They make their way downstairs. He clears the bins while Catrin begins an inventory of the kitchen.

'John's been fuming,' she says above the clatter of knives and forks. 'Sixty million the man's worth now.'

Simon plugs the hoover into the socket and pulls on the cord to gain some slack.

'Still reading the report?' asks Catrin.

'Slowly,' replies Simon. The Chilcott Inquiry had at last been made available to the public: published in twelve volumes containing more than two and a half million words of dry prose. It had all the facts but none of the heart.

He switches on the hoover, wishing they could, for once, let the dust settle.

∽

The North Wales Veteran Rehabilitation Centre rests about a mile from the farmhouse. Simon takes a shortcut along a footpath and encounters Rhys with a sheepdog at his heels. Theirs had not been an easy friendship but, while the years had hardened some things, they had softened others. And now, here they are, like brothers.

'Your parents are in the yard bickering over the car,' he says.

'Some things never change.'

'Ready for married life?'

'Ask me in six months,' laughs Rhys, running a hand through his hair.

'How's Molly?'

'Preparing for the big day. Glued to the spreadsheet but otherwise well,' says Rhys. 'You heading to the Centre?'

Simon nods. 'And then making the climb.'

Rhys turns his eyes to the hills and shakes his head at the rolling fells, still so sparsely populated after the winter of 2013; neither of them will forget the long days and nights digging out the sheep from twenty-foot snowdrifts, the lambs perishing by the score.

'Take it slow,' says Rhys.

The two men part ways and soon Simon reaches the Centre, with its stone walls and wide windows; visitors are always impressed by the stunning views of the surrounding hills. He scans the glinting glass, the stonework, the plant pots, flowers and WELCOME sign. Satisfied, he approaches the sliding doors and tests the stability of the metal ramp before wandering inside, where he's greeted by the background music of Tom Jones singing 'Green, Green Grass of Home'. To his left is a small waiting area with a blue velvet sofa, matching armchairs and a coffee table laden with magazines, from *Shire* and *Country Life* to *LandScape* and *Wellbeing*. Nearby there's a hot-drinks machine with recyclable cups stacked neatly on top and Simon makes himself a double-shot espresso while he continues to check the place is ready for their guests.

Built in 2007 with the help of friends, family and various grants, the Centre can accommodate up to sixteen people. It takes a holistic approach to healing, combining CBT with horticultural and animal therapy. Downstairs, there are two lecture rooms where specialists from Bangor University help to deliver the Pain Management Plan, teaching returning service personnel and those transitioning to civilian life about the nervous system, pain perception, and the interconnectedness of biology and psychology. There's also a trauma gym with specialist equipment to help veterans regain mobility, fitness and confidence. At the rear of the Centre is a communal kitchen, living area and library.

They've done so much, thinks Simon, sipping his drink. And there was still so much more they could do. He heads to the reception desk, looking up at the large framed photograph hanging on the wall behind. It shows Harri with his arm around his late nan. There's a playful, loving light in Alice's eyes as she clutches her grandson's hand.

And there, thinks Simon, is the debt they would all, in time, have to pay.

He checks the post, scanning the envelopes. There's one of particular interest that he takes with him, his heart beating a notch faster at the thought of what it might contain.

Onwards now, passing lecture rooms and the gym. He peers into each, satisfied that everything is ready for next week.

Over the years they've welcomed so many from the military: men and women who come looking for a place to heal, to learn, to feel seen. People who have suffered outside and in from the turbulence of their service.

It's quiet but on Monday they'll have twelve guests arriving and then the place will become kinetic, and Simon will be on his feet, dawn to dusk. For now, though, there is a chance to rest and reflect. To be with the people he loves.

At the back of the building, there's a garden created by staff and volunteers from Bodnant. They'd used native trees, fern and horsetail found throughout the local woodlands, while the orchids, sea campion, violets and marigolds give the place some colour. At the centre of the garden they'd included a small pond with a fountain. He listens to the gentle ripple and splash of the water as he makes his way along the cobbled path towards a rose-clad wall that shields the pond where guests can relax in privacy.

Just before the pond with its sleepy fish comes into view, Simon pauses and reminds himself of all the things that are in his control, and all those that aren't.

He takes a deep breath of the Welsh early-summer air and then continues around the corner. And there he sees it: the wheelchair.

And there, turning at his approach and reflecting his smile, is Harri.

'Ready?' says Simon.

∼

The sun is on their arms and a light breeze combs the spirited grass. Halfway up, they turn to face Carneddau, whose arrowhead peaks point towards the blue sky, not a cloud in sight. Among the wide slopes of grass and heather, wild horses roam as free and proud as the birds above – the kestrel, the buzzard and the merlin, whose magic is witnessed in the tips of its feathers, the glint of its eyes.

'How are you doing?' asks Simon.

Harri looks down at the new Triton foot and bionic leg beneath the cut of his shorts. He taps the shell twice and smiles. It isn't the same as the real thing – the blood, muscle, fat, tendons, ligaments and bone – but the team at Headley Court had done their best.

'Better than the last one.' Harri taps the leg again. 'Touch wood.'

'I asked how *you're* doing,' says Simon.

Harri laughs, reaches out and messes Simon's hair. 'I'm good,' he says.

They look back at the peaks opposite and Harri points. 'One day I'm going to climb those again.'

Simon's been among those living mountains, has followed the winding streams to their source, hauled himself up the windswept rock, spotted the Welsh poppy with its yellow petals. 'I'll come with, if you like?'

They continue their ascent, Simon watching from the corner of his eye, mindful of the new prosthetic, untested as it is.

Mindful, always, of Harri.

In time, they reach the wooden bench that rests at the top of the climb. They sit and look out at the valley. The farm where John and Catrin will be tending the livestock. Tim's land to the west, the nature reserve that joins the two.

Simon hands Harri the envelope. Harri looks at the address before cutting through the flap. He pulls out the letter. It's from the British Association for Music Therapy. Simon watches Harri, eager for a sign.

At last, Harri looks at him. He smiles. 'We've got it,' he says.

Simon takes the letter. Sure enough, they've been awarded a grant to provide music therapy at the Centre. Almost three thousand pounds. For a piano of their own, perhaps. One that Catrin might play, feet at the pedals, hands on the keys, ready to entertain, teach, heal.

The two of them stare out across the mountains spread before them, the ewes and their lambs, feel the light breeze on their cheeks, take in all the colours of the living, breathing world.

'Isn't it beautiful?' says Harri. He looks down at his prosthetic, back up to the world.

Simon takes Harri's hand. 'It's beautiful,' he says.

Acknowledgements

There are many people who gave their time, expertise and kindness to help bring this book to fruition.

First and foremost, I would like to thank my agent, Emma Leong. I am lucky to have found representation in such a discerning reader, tireless champion of new writing and someone in whom I feel complete trust. The excitement of those early emails will always be with me. My thanks also to Claire Conrad and Mairi Friesen-Escandell in the UK office, and Ian Bonaparte in the US.

My sincere thanks to my editors Helen Garnons-Williams and Ella Harold at Fig Tree. From the first telephone call back in December 2022, I knew the book was in the best pair of hands a writer could hope for. I am grateful to Donna Poppy for her eagle-eyed copyediting. Thanks, too, to Ellie Smith, Charlotte Daniels (the cover designer), and to all the team at Penguin.

Thanks to Humphrey Bucknall and Max Kuhnke for their advice on the military. To Nicola Misquita, Alexander Reut-Hobbs and David Gutman for help with all musical matters. To Chris Humpleby, who provided invaluable guidance on horse racing and the gambling industry. To Hamit Dardagan, co-founder of the Iraq Body Count, for granting permission to use the IBC statistics that his organization has so diligently recorded.

I owe much to my writing group: Victoria Finan, Quintin Forrest, Jimmy Kelly, Catherine Menon, Natasha Perskey, Stacia Saint Owens, Lauren Van Schaik and Susan Vittery. Special thanks to Katy Darby, for introducing me to the group; her

City University Writers' Workshop was insightful and inspiring and she continues to offer superb advice.

Posthumous thanks to Paul Sussman (1966–2012) and Mavis Cheek (1948–2023), whose course at Tŷ Newydd I attended when I was seventeen. Enormous thanks to Cathy Galvin, founder of The Word Factory, and to Gemma Seltzer, founder of Write and Shine.

To other writer friends with whom I've enjoyed talking shop: Christopher Allen, Melissa Fu, Mina Ikemoto Ghosh, Giselle Leeb, Sean Lusk and Helen Rye.

To my English teachers and directors of studies throughout school and university: this book would not exist without you – Tom Biddle, Mrs Cox, Mrs Harrington, Peter Hunter, John James, Robert Macfarlane, Corinna Russell and Alastair Storie. Particular thanks to Henry Hitchings, whom I am lucky to consider a friend and whose mentorship has helped me on this path.

To my friends Serge and Tom, who keep me grounded and going with equal measures of laughter and love. To Jake, for sharing a smile at the absurdity of things. To Emma and Jen, who know what it is to read *The Faerie Queene*. I will always be there for you.

Thanks to Justin and Christine, my aunt and uncle, whose farm in North Wales helped to inspire the setting for this book.

To my parents, who trusted me to find my own way. To my brother, Robin, whose love of reading inspired my own. To my dog, Wispa, for the long walks. To Luke, who read countless drafts and has listened to me wrangle with imaginary people and places as I brought them to the page. I love you all.